THE HIG...

MW00475484

Beautiful you... up under the... ther, Sir Edward Danville. His passion for piquet had brought the family to the brink of ruin.

Sylvia and her twin sister, Louise, had vowed never to follow in Sir Edward's footsteps, but now Sylvia was shocked to learn that Louise had done that—and even worse.

Sylvia had to save her sister from this fatal family folly—yet how could she when she had taken an even greater gamble of her own? She had dared to fall in love with Viscount Thomas Radcliff, a high-minded physician whose dedication and skill would never heal her heartbreak if she were unfortunate enough to lose him along with her good name. Clearly Sylvia had to beat the odds stacked high against her. . . .

IRENE SAUNDERS, a native of Yorkshire, England, spent a number of years exploring London while working for the U.S. Air Force there. A love of travel brought her to New York City, where she met her husband, Ray, then settled in Miami, Florida. She now lives in Port St. Lucie, Florida, dividing her time between writing, bookkeeping, gardening, needlepoint, and travel.

THE GAMBLER'S DAUGHTER

by
IRENE SAUNDERS

A SIGNET BOOK

NEW AMERICAN LIBRARY

A DIVISION OF PENGUIN BOOKS USA INC.

NAL BOOKS ARE AVAILABLE AT QUANTITY DISCOUNTS
WHEN USED TO PROMOTE PRODUCTS OR SERVICES.
FOR INFORMATION PLEASE WRITE TO PREMIUM MARKETING DIVISION,
NEW AMERICAN LIBRARY, 1633 BROADWAY,
NEW YORK, NEW YORK 10019.

SIGNET TRADEMARK REG. U.S. PAT. OFF. AND FOREIGN COUNTRIES
REGISTERED TRADEMARK—MARCA REGISTRADA
HECHO EN DRESDEN, TN, U.S.A.

SIGNET, SIGNET CLASSIC, MENTOR, ONYX, PLUME, MERIDIAN
and NAL BOOKS are published by New American Library, a division of
Penguin Books USA Inc., 1633 Broadway, New York, New York 10019

First Printing, January, 1990

1   2   3   4   5   6   7   8   9

PRINTED IN THE UNITED STATES OF AMERICA

1

The Church of St. Barnabas appeared warm and welcoming as shafts of sunlight glinted through the stained-glass windows onto the old oak pews. It was filled to capacity for the first time in many years with fashionably dressed ladies and gentlemen, the very pink of the *ton*, as well as many of the local people. It had been built, centuries ago, for the sole use of the Colchester family, but they had long since turned it into the village church, though the vicar had always been a frequent visitor at Colchester Castle. The voice of the present incumbent rang out loud and clear.

"Who giveth this woman to be married to this man?"

There was a distinct stirring in the congregation. David Beresford, the present Earl of Colchester and brother-in-law of the bride, on whose arm she had walked down the aisle, turned to glance toward the entrance. There was a remote chance that her papa, Sir Edward Danville, might be hastening to do his duty. Seeing no sign of the man, however, Colchester stepped toward the young couple and took Louise's hand to perform her absent father's part in the age-old ceremony.

Sylvia Danville, an exact copy of the bride save for the pale blue gown she wore, sighed heavily, for she could feel her twin's disappointment. As if it were not bad enough that their papa had paid not a sou toward the cost of their come-outs or, indeed, Louise's wedding today, he had made a fool of himself once again last evening by overindulging in Colchester's fine French brandy.

When the others had left Colchester Castle for the

church, his valet had been trying desperately to force a concoction down his master's throat that was guaranteed to take care of the obvious ill effects. This time, she decided, the potion must not have been efficacious.

She tried not to think of tonight, when she and Louise would sleep apart for the first time in their lives, for they had been closer than two peas in a pod since the day they were born. At times even their mama and papa could not tell which one was which of their black-haired, blue-eyed twins, and the two had taken advantage of this on many an occasion by pretending to be first one and then the other. But Elizabeth, their older sister, always knew, and her husband, David, who had just given the bride away, could tell from the very first time he saw them.

Of course, they had both known they could not always be so close, but until Louise had told Sylvia that she was going to accept Timothy Fotheringham, it had not occurred to her that she might be left alone like this. It sounded nonsense now, but she had somehow expected events to be simultaneous—that they would meet two young men, fall in love, have a double wedding, and perhaps even go on a wedding trip together.

Instead, Sylvia had been taken completely unawares when Louise suddenly told her she intended to marry the charming but rather irresponsible young man.

"Has he already asked you?" Sylvia had inquired, trying to hide the immediate feeling of hurt.

Louise had laughed. "No, not yet, but I know he will, and when he does, I'll pretend that I'm surprised and need time to think about it," she had said, her eyes sparkling with mischief. "You see, he's absolutely right for me, for I need someone who will let me have everything I want, and agree with everything I say, without my having to go into a decline to get my way, as Mama has always done."

Sylvia had at first been astounded, but as she thought further about it, she realized that her sister had always been the more dominant of the two of them. It had never occurred to her before, because she had always wanted the same things as Louise—until now.

Timothy Fotheringham was decidedly not the type of young man that Sylvia would have chosen for herself, however, and she wondered if her sister was having any doubts now that she had no way of turning back, for the ceremony was at an end and the immediate family were assembling in the vestry for the signing of the register.

From the body of the church a distinct murmuring could be heard, and then Sylvia sighed with relief as a slim, fair-haired gentleman appeared in the doorway. Their father had finally arrived, somewhat pale and short of breath, but immaculately attired as always.

"Didn't realize it was so late," Sir Edward blustered, looking the image of injured rectitude as he approached the young couple. "You might have waited for me, Louise, but as long as the knot has been tied good and tight, that's all that matters. Don't I have to sign somewhere?"

As the vicar placed the register in front of him, and her mother, Lady Danville, stepped forward to join her husband, Sylvia watched, feeling strangely set apart from the proceedings, as though it were a play and she was the audience.

As soon as the final signatures had been appended, the bridegroom turned to Sylvia and held out his arms. She went quickly into them to place a brief kiss on the cheek of her new brother-in-law, for during his short courtship of her twin, she had grown quite fond of him. Blond-haired and good-looking in the extreme, with an exceedingly charming manner, he was at the same time rather ineffectual and easily led. Louise would most certainly enjoy holding the reins of their household in her capable hands, but would she also like having to make every decision for them both from now on? Sylvia wondered.

"How very sisterly." The deep, gravelly voice behind her held a distinct note of sarcasm. "As I have no jealous bride to show concern, I am sure you can do much better than that for me, my dear."

Sylvia recognized the voice at once, but hesitated for a moment before turning around to face the speaker, Sir Roger Albertson, Timothy's cousin, who had stood with him at the altar. "I was not aware that any congratulations were in order for you, Sir Roger," she said coldly, holding out a gloved hand. "I must thank you, however, for your services to my new brother-in-law."

He glanced around. The bridegroom had been detained by a well-wisher, but Lady Beresford, his hostess and the twins' older sister, was staring quite pointedly in his direction. With an elaborate flourish, Sir Roger took Sylvia's hand and raised it to his lips, looking at her with a dangerous glint in his eyes. "No doubt you save your favors for more private occasions, my dear," he murmured. "I pray that a suitable opportunity will present itself."

She looked with distaste at the hand he had just released, vowing to give the gloves he had besmirched to one of the maids as soon as she took them off, but that would be some considerable time away. First they must return down the aisle to face the wedding guests armed with rice and rose petals, and then return to the castle, where a magnificent meal awaited them.

"Sir Roger was not being impertinent to you, was he?" Lady Beresford had joined her young sister as soon as she could tear herself away from an overdiscursive elderly uncle. "I am disappointed that a man of his ilk is closely related to our new brother-in-law, for I cannot like that connection at all."

"I find it difficult to understand why Timothy chose him, for Louise told me he's a bit of a loose screw and that there were other cousins he could have selected." Sylvia frowned, and added, "I'm sure that his advances to your maids are not welcomed either, Elizabeth, for I've twice seen him pulling one into a dark corner of the castle."

"Oh, dear, with so much to arrange, I'm afraid I've been a little remiss, but I'll see that Mrs. Fowler is made aware of it and sends only menservants to his chamber. I cannot recall when we last had that kind of

problem." She put a comforting arm around her young
sister's shoulders. "You're going to sadly miss Louise,
I know, so I'm arranging with our mama for you to
stay here for a few weeks, on the pretext of helping
me keep the children occupied. I trust I am not being
presumptuous."

Sylvia's face broke into a smile of genuine pleasure.
"I was hoping you'd ask me, for I don't think I could
face Danville Hall and Papa's attempts at matchmak-
ing just yet. I'll stay on here until I become a nui-
sance, I promise. That is, of course, if David does not
mind."

"Didn't you know that David only married me so
that he could have you and Louise for sisters?" Elizabeth teased.

Sylvia grinned. "Now, that's not true, I know, for
he did not meet us until the day before your wedding,
but we both adored him from the minute we saw him.
It's most unfortunate that he does not have a younger
brother just like himself," she said regretfully.

"I do believe they're finally ready to go back into
the church, so you'd best take your place beside Sir
Roger. Now, don't give him the slightest opportunity
to say anything untoward—and don't forget, you must
stand with David and me in the receiving line when
you get back to the castle. The less you are in that
man's company, the better I shall feel." As she spoke,
Elizabeth steered Sylvia toward the procession that
was forming and stood by while her sister placed a
reluctant hand on Sir Roger's arm. "When you come
out of the church, wait for me so that you may return
to the castle in our coach," she said loudly, glancing
coldly in the direction of Timothy's cousin.

Sir Roger gave her a slight, rather supercilious smile
as though to indicate that he knew what she was
about, then patted the gloved hand lightly placed on
his arm. He seemed about to make an observation,
but Elizabeth did not give him the opportunity as she
turned swiftly around and went to take her own place
next to her husband, a little further back in the line.

"You look as if you're about to do battle with

someone, my love," Colchester remarked softly. "I hope it's not going to be me, for you ladies seldom abide by the rules when you pick a fight, and I can't even hit you back in your present condition."

"Of course it's not you, David. I'd never dare to argue with you in public," she said a little too sweetly. "But as for that rake Timothy selected to stand up with him, he's likely to get the sharp edge of my tongue if he tries to lead Sylvia astray."

"Ah, yes, I should have known he was the culprit, but he'll not get the chance, my dear, so you need have no more concern," her husband assured her comfortingly. "His unsavory reputation as a gamester has preceded him, and he has already indicated his eagerness to take some of us on at cards. In view of this, my dear step-papa and I, with a little help from Tom Radcliff, have laid plans for him, from the time the young couple leave, until early tomorrow morning, when he will depart for London in Sir James and Mama's coach, a poorer if not sorrier man."

"It sounds as if you're out to fleece him, and I cannot say that I'm sorry," Elizabeth said, placing her hand upon his arm as the procession began to move. "But I do sympathize with your mama for having to bear his company on her long journey home, for Sir James will probably ride alongside for a good part of the way."

"I doubt she'll know Albertson's even there for at least the first half of it, for his head will feel much too sore for him to desire any but the quietest of conversation and, sweet though my mama is, she is more than capable of keeping a rakehell like him in his place," David assured her.

In a surprisingly short time the wedding party and all the guests had been safely transported from the church to the castle, where a sumptuous meal awaited them, toward the end of which the young couple received endless toasts. The bride then made her escape in order to dress for the journey, for their wedding trip would take them first to London and then to Paris for a lengthy stay.

* * *

"I'm so glad I'm not forced to return to Danville Hall just yet, for it won't be the same without you," Sylvia said rather wistfully as she helped her sister out of her wedding gown.

"You'll simply have to meet someone as quickly as possible and get married also," Louise told her firmly. "As soon as I saw Timothy, I knew he would be just right for me, for there is no question that with his looks I shall bear him the most handsome of children."

Sylvia appeared shocked. "You haven't already discussed that with him, have you?" she asked. "I know you're outspoken, but really, Louise . . ."

"Don't be silly. Of course we haven't talked about that. But he *is* very handsome, and now it's so near I can hardly wait until tonight to find out what it's all about." A nervous giggle belied her brave words, however, and Sylvia felt much relieved. This was more like the sister she knew so well.

"I'm sure you're every bit as nervous as I would be if it were I," she said as she finished buttoning the deep blue carriage dress Louise had chosen for the start of their journey. "Perhaps it will be his first time also."

Louise looked scornful. "What utter nonsense! There's no such thing as a man-about-town who has not had experience in such matters," she said with assurance. "Timothy's sister, Caroline, told me that young men have liaisons with girls in taverns while they're still at Eton."

"At Eton?" Sylvia looked disbelieving. "But they're only little boys when they go there."

"There are plenty of older ones to show them how to go along," Louise retorted, swirling around to see how her gown looked in the back. "I hope I don't look too provincial in this when we reach Paris."

"If you do, then Timothy will just have to go out and buy you something else," Sylvia said with a laugh. "After all, he is supposed to be one of the richest young men in London this Season."

Her sister frowned. "He was," she said meaningfully, "but Caroline also told me that after his last gaming losses he plunged so deeply into debt that his father threatened to cut him off altogether, and made him promise that he'd not gamble again for a year. He only agreed to continue his allowance because we were to be married. I'm supposed to be a sobering influence upon him."

"It's a good thing, then, that you didn't inherit Papa's propensity for gambling." Sylvia looked more than a little worried. "Do you really think you can make him change his ways?"

"Of course I can," Louise said confidently. "I'm going to start right away, for I'll not be like our mama, never knowing if there'll be a roof over our heads from one night to the next. By the time we return from Paris, he'll be completely reformed."

Louise was exaggerating, of course, for the one thing their father could not gamble away was their house, as the entailment did not permit such a thing.

There was a knock on the door and Elizabeth's head appeared around the edge. "Are you two going to talk all day? Your bridegroom is becoming most impatient to be off, Louise," she scolded lightly, her gray eyes twinkling as she glanced from one twin to the other. "Has Sylvia been suggesting you take Timothy's dreadful cousin along with you?"

Louise scowled. "No, and she'd better not, for I'm glad to get Timothy away from that man," she pronounced. "Had I met him earlier I would have most definitely talked Tim into choosing someone else to stand up with him. Unfortunately, I was not introduced to him until yesterday, when it was too late."

Elizabeth put an arm around each of her sisters' shoulders. "Now you can both stop worrying about Albertson, for David assures me he has made the most satisfactory of arrangements to keep him occupied until he leaves. Just enjoy your wedding trip, Louise, and my little ones and I will try to keep Sylvia from missing you too much."

Tearful hugs were exchanged, and then Louise walked

sedately down the stairs to where Timothy was eagerly waiting to be off. He took her arm and they hurried across the hall, turning at the front door to blow kisses to the watching guests before disappearing into the depths of the beribboned equipage. A horn sounded, and the carriage was gone from Sylvia's sight. She shivered as she felt the first pangs of loneliness and uncertainty.

"Let's pay a quick visit to the nursery and see if the children have awakened yet," Elizabeth suggested as the guests began to make their way to the ballroom, from which the sounds of an orchestra tuning up could be clearly heard. "Little John was quite chagrined that he could not stay up with the Partridges' children. He's at that impossible age, almost two, when he's not quite a little boy, nor still a baby, like Patricia."

"I thought I heard the sound of tantrums during Papa's speech," Sylvia remarked, forcing a grin. "He takes after his father in wishing to have his way, I'm sure."

"Not if one listens to David or to his dear mama, but then, Lady Moorehead would be the first to concede that she is somewhat prejudiced. I've been most fortunate in having such a delightful mother-in-law, however, and can hardly complain if she suffers from a slight loss of memory in that respect. It was such a pity that Timothy's mother and father could not come to the wedding, for I'd have dearly loved to find out if Louise has been as lucky as I was. You met them some weeks ago. What were they like?" Elizabeth asked as they reached the top of the stairs once more and turned toward the nursery wing.

Sylvia smiled mischievously. "They were exactly as I had pictured them. His mother was just like Timothy. She was charming and must have been very beautiful when she was younger, but quite indecisive. She left all the decisions to his rather dominating father, except, of course, housekeeping matters, which a competent staff handled completely."

"What a shame that the earl's gout started up again, for they would undoubtedly have enjoyed their son's wedding," Elizabeth said. "But now I believe I understand why Lady Fortheringham and his sister, Caroline did not come either. If the earl is inclined to dominate, he most likely would not allow the ladies to come when he could not himself be present."

"I believe he blamed Timothy's gambling for his indisposition, and Louise said he had exacted a commitment from Tim that he would not gamble again for a year. They were all completely happy, though, that Tim was marrying Louise. Don't you think she'll make him an excellent wife?"

"Most certainly." Elizabeth's hand was on the doorknob of the nursery. "Let's be quiet now, in case they're still sleeping," she murmured softly.

Sylvia loved the nursery at Colchester Castle, for before her first child was born, her sister had had the walls painted a pale blue, and then she hired an artist to paint scenes of birds, animals, trees, and flowers all the way around. It gave one the feeling of being in a delightful forest, for the carpet came right to the edge of the wall and was the color of new grass in spring.

Elizabeth need not have been so cautious, for the minute she opened the door there was a loud shriek and a small body came hurtling across the room to fling itself into her quickly opened arms. Then she swung the little boy high into the air.

"Should you be doing that in your condition?" Sylvia asked, having heard that women who were breeding were supposed to be careful, and many retired to couches for the duration of their confinement.

The gruff voice of David's old nanny came from the other side of the room. "No, she should not be lifting him like that, but there's no convincing her. Perhaps you can talk some sense into your sister, young lady."

The kindly face wore a frown that quickly disappeared as she looked down at the little girl in her arms to see if the noise had disrupted her sleep.

"If it's any consolation, Nanny, Dr. Radcliff agrees with you, but I'm afraid I lifted my son up instinctively. There was no harm done this time, but I'll take more care in the future," Elizabeth promised as she lowered John to the ground and led him to his waiting nanny.

"I don't know about that young doctor. You've been fortunate so far, and not needed much help, but his lordship's mama would feel much happier if you went to stay with her in London two months before this next one is born. She told me so just yesterday." The outspoken old nanny looked quite worried. "She knows a fine, older doctor there who would make sure you were cared for the way you should be."

"Nanny, we've been over this before," Elizabeth said patiently. "Just because Dr. Radcliff is tall and slim, and has thick sandy hair and a face that makes him appear boyish, does not mean that he isn't one of the finest doctors in the country."

"I've wondered about that each time I've met him," Sylvia broke in. "If he is so good, what is he doing wasting his time here as a country doctor? Surely he'd be better off in London?"

"He came here at David's suggestion, for the villagers and local gentry needed the services of a doctor, and this way he can practice medicine here, yet still be free to pursue special studies in London when he wishes," Elizabeth explained. "He went into medicine, he told me, because he wanted to help stop so many people from dying before their time."

Nanny grunted disbelievingly as Elizabeth turned toward the door.

"I must return to our guests before they think me a negligent hostess, for many of them will shortly be departing. Are you coming, Sylvia? The dancing must surely have commenced by now."

"You know, I've never really thought of Tom Radcliff as a dedicated doctor before," Sylvia remarked as they retraced their steps along the corridor. "He's always been here as just a friend, having dinner or talking to David. Just this morning, though, he suggested that if I was staying on, he might take me for a ride in the country. Can I assume it would be safe for me to go with him alone if he should ask me again?"

"Of course you'd be safe with Tom. He and David

met when they were both serving under Wellington in the Peninsula. Although Tom held the rank of major, he was not a fighting man, but had joined the army to gain experience after training at the University of Edinburgh and at several of the London hospitals.

"David told me that he would not be alive today were it not for Tom's skill on more than one occasion. They became good friends during those years, shared tents, batmen, cooks, a rare bottle of brandy, while the armies were on the move, and they grew to trust each other implicitly.

"Tom is now a fellow of the Royal Colleges of Physicians and of Surgeons, so he is not exactly just a country doctor."

"I'm quite impressed," Sylvia said, "for most of the young men Louise and I met in London were more concerned with their own appearance than anything else. If a cravat had not been tied to perfection, or a hair was out of place, it was an absolute tragedy."

Elizabeth smiled, remembering some of the gentlemen she had met in London before marrying David, then warned, "But don't accept anyone else's invitations without asking me first. You and Louise have been accustomed to going everywhere together, and consequently don't realize how forward some young men can be if they catch you unchaperoned."

Sylvia chuckled. "I'll be very, very careful, big sister," she promised, "and I won't do anything you wouldn't have done at nineteen."

The tart rejoinder Elizabeth was about to make was never uttered, for they had reached the door to the ballroom and her sister was drawn laughing into a group of young men and women choosing partners for a cotillion.

Watching them, Elizabeth smiled, realizing she had become overprotective of her younger sister, but she had sound reason for desiring to shield her. The castle would be lively for the next day or so, as wedding guests would linger longer than they intended, particularly her own mama and papa, for Sir Edward Danville was at his best when drinking and dining well at someone else's expense. The problem would be persuading her parents to go home and leave Sylvia in her care, for Sir Edward had indicated that he was low on funds just now, and he might try to seek redress by looking for an elderly, rich husband for his young daughter. It would not be the first time he had used this means to line his pockets.

She decided not to let her parents know that Tom Radcliff had shown some interest in Sylvia, slight though it was at this time. Tom was of good family, she knew, for David had told her some years ago that he was the third son of the Earl of Lynmouth, and a grandson of the sixth Marquess of Bradington.

As the old marquess had died a little over a year ago, and Tom's father had become the seventh marquess, Tom could now use the title of Lord before his name, but apparently preferred to stay with the title of doctor, which he had earned by his own hard work.

So far as Elizabeth could tell, there was no estrangement, but Tom seldom visited his family except when he was in London, for they resided on a large estate some twenty miles to the south of the city. They probably loved him but could not understand this dedicated young man.

2

"Elizabeth looks well able to survive a third birthing to me," Sir Edward Danville grumbled as his carriage rolled down the castle's private road at the start of their journey home. "She has a nanny to look after the children, and what good would Sylvia be if she did need help? That housekeeper of theirs, Mrs. Fowler, could run the place with both hands tied behind her back—and as for Sylvia being helpful, she knows even less than you do about running a house, if that's possible."

Lady Danville sighed. She knew she should not have allowed herself to be persuaded into letting Sylvia remain at the castle. "Her nanny is older than I am, and young children can be somewhat of a handful, my dear," she said querulously. "Sylvia has always been most capable with little ones—in fact, they both were. Do you remember when—?"

"All I remember is what Colchester said when I told him the wedding should be at Danville Hall," her husband snapped. "Downright ugly, he became, insinuating that I couldn't be trusted. That I'd not give him a true accounting of the monies spent if Sylvia was married from her own home, as she should by rights have been."

"It was Louise who married, Edward, not Sylvia. Even I can remember that, for they wore different-colored gowns for once," Lady Danville murmured dreamily. "And didn't they look beautiful?"

"Of course I know it was Louise, you numbskull. Just a slip of the tongue, that's all. And no matter which one it was, he had no right to insist she be

married from Colchester Castle," he said angrily, fling-
ing himself across the coach into the opposite corner
from his wife.

She blinked as though surprised, for he rarely looked
directly at her; then she said blandly, "But, my dear,
David did find you out at the time of his own wedding
to Elizabeth. If you hadn't asked him for almost twice
as much money as it actually cost, he might have
agreed to have Louise's wedding at home." Lady Danville's voice was not accusing in the slightest, for she
had long since grown accustomed to her husband's
peccadilloes. Just as long as he did not curtail her
personal spending, she did not really mind anymore.

"And, after all," she went on, "just think of all the
aggravation it would have been to plan for a wedding
the size of Louise's. Elizabeth's was much smaller
because it was not her first, of course."

"The minute we get home, you can just write and
tell Sylvia you don't feel well and we need her to
return. I may have two wealthy sons-in-law, but the
only good it does me is not having to buy fancy clothes
for the minxes anymore," he grumbled.

"Now, Edward," Lady Danville began, "you know
it's been all of seven years since Elizabeth cost you so
much as a penny, and David has promised to . . ."

Her voice faded as her husband jumped up and
banged on the roof of the carriage. "Women," he
snorted as the coach came to a halt. "They never give
a man a minute's peace with their prating and gab-
bing. I'm going to ride my gelding as far as the inn,
and by that time you may have learned to curb your
tongue."

Lady Danville looked startled for a moment as he
stepped hurriedly from the coach; then she sank back
against the squabs and prepared to have a peaceful
snooze.

The bay they had saddled for her was a beauty, and
Sylvia set off at a gallop across the Colchester lands,
trying to blow some of the cobwebs out of her head. It
had rained steadily now for two days, and she had

begun to feel as cooped up in the house as were the children, whom she had gladly relinquished to their nanny as soon as they became fretful.

Elizabeth was taking her afternoon rest when the first hint of a break in the clouds appeared, and Sylvia simply could not wait to get out into some fresh air, so had ordered a horse saddled at once. There was only a young lad in the stables at the time, and he did as she instructed. If he thought it strange that she was going out without a groom, he kept his thoughts to himself, as he had been taught.

Sylvia had stayed with Elizabeth and David before, of course, but always with Louise too, and they had done everything together. As she looked around, she was forced to admit that, of the two of them, Louise had the far better sense of direction. Nothing looked familiar to her, and she began to wonder if, indeed, she was still on David's lands or if she was trespassing on those of a neighbor.

"Hey. Where d'ye think you're going, missy?"

The rough shout took Sylvia completely by surprise, and it was all the bay needed. Startled, the horse took off across the middle of the field. The pounding of hooves behind her did little to help her gain control, and it took all her strength and expertise to prevent the bay from jumping the high hedge on the far side—a hazardous jump indeed, for she had not the slightest idea what lay beyond. As she gradually slowed the horse to a walk, she turned to see who had caused her discomfiture.

"You're on private land, miss, and for all you knew, it could've been set with traps."

Sylvia was about to make an angry retort but held her tongue when she saw that it was a slightly built man, about David's age, and though he spoke with a voice of authority, his clothes were decidedly the worse for wear. He had hazel eyes and russet-colored hair, and the lower portion of his left jacket sleeve was empty.

"I beg your pardon, sir," Sylvia said quietly, "but I had no intention of trespassing, and would have rid-den around had you not startled my horse into bolting across the field. I hope I have done no damage. I am Miss Danville, and I am a guest of my sister at Colchester Castle. Are you in the habit of setting traps on your land?"

"The land isn't mine," the young man grunted, checking his rather frisky mare, "and I'm a sort of guest also. I'm keeping an eye on it for an old army friend. I'm Jonathan Wainwright, and I'm sorry I startled you, but you'd be safer to stick to the lanes. I suppose you're not used to riding this beauty."

"We were doing quite well until you called," Sylvia snapped, annoyed that he had made no move to doff his cap; then she flushed as she realized that with only one hand he would have had to release the reins in order to do so. She gave him an embarrassed smile. "And if you think I'm lost, you're quite right. Could you, perhaps, point me in the direction of Colchester Castle?"

When the frown left his face, he looked ten years younger. "It would be my pleasure to escort you there, Miss Danville," he told her a little more politely, "but I should warn you that it's not safe to ride out alone in these parts. You never know when you might run into some of them radicals or reformers that roam around."

"I'm sure you're right, and I'll probably get a scold when I get back," Sylvia confessed, "but I didn't even think about asking someone to accompany me."

"Well, if you'll follow me, miss, I'll take you back a different way. You crossed Squire Bradford's land to get 'ere, and 'e's none too pleased when folk disturb the birds 'e's raising for 'is next shoot."

Sylvia followed Wainwright as he led her past what looked like a shack and, nearby, a young woman stopped what she was doing and waved. "That's me sister, Edith," he explained. "She's raising some 'ens and a pig, and growing some vegetables."

"Is that the only house on your friend's property?" Sylvia asked dubiously.

Wainwright nodded. "It's in need of repair and was

probably built as a shelter for hunters, but I patched the 'oles in the roof and it's dry enough now."

They rode in silence along a quiet lane that was hardly more than a path, until, in the distance, Sylvia caught sight of Colchester Castle. "I'm sure you've better things to do than see me home, and I'll be all right now," she began, then noticed a rider coming toward them from the direction of the castle.

"I think I'd best stay and pay my respects to the earl," Wainwright said dryly, "or 'e'll wonder what I'm about."

Colchester slowed as he drew near, and looked at Sylvia with raised eyebrows. "I would have thought you knew better than to ride out without a groom, my dear. Would you care to introduce me?"

"This is Jonathan Wainright, David. I'm afraid I got lost and Mr. Wainwright insisted on bringing me safely back," Sylvia said a little lamely.

"My sister and I are living for now on Captain Kingston's property a few miles back, my lord," Wainwright explained, "and keeping an eye on things for him."

"You were with him at Waterloo?" It sounded more like a statement than a question, for Colchester had not missed the empty sleeve.

"His staff sergeant, sir," was the equally terse reply.

"Was Squire Bradford stretching the property line a little? Is that why he wanted someone here?" Colchester asked.

"That was one of the reasons, sir," Wainwright said with a grin. "There's no problem now."

Colchester frowned. "What are you living in? Surely there isn't a habitable house on that property?"

"There's enough for us, sir. A roof over our 'eads is better than many 'ave"—Wainwright's eyes had softened at the show of concern—"and we live off the land."

With a nod, Colchester took Sylvia's rein. "Thank you for bringing my wayward sister-in-law back safely. I'll be over to see you tomorrow," he said abruptly, then started toward the castle. "Do I need to say any more about taking a groom?" he asked Sylvia, his eyes twinkling.

Sylvia shook her head. "I simply never thought about it," she said, "but I'll not do it again, I promise. You're not angry with Jonathan Wainwright, are you, David?"

He looked surprised. "Of course not. I know Kingston, and he must think quite a bit about that young man to want to help him. I'll take Tom over there with me tomorrow, for I think he'll be interested in meeting him."

They reached the castle, where Elizabeth waited, smiling. "I told him you'd be home any moment, but he had to come and look for you," she told Sylvia, slipping an arm around her shoulders. "And they say women worry the most."

"Things are not like they used to be, my dear," David said seriously. "There's a lot of unrest in the country, some of it deserved, but much of it stirred up by troublemakers. We'll see many changes these next few years, mark my words, and for now it is best that young ladies do not go riding unaccompanied." He leaned over and placed a tender kiss on his wife's cheek. "Is it tonight Tom is coming for dinner?"

Elizabeth nodded, then explained to Sylvia, "Tom's housekeeper is scrupulously clean, but not the best cook, so we have him here for an informal meal at least once a week."

Sensing that the two of them wanted some time alone, Sylvia excused herself and went upstairs to bathe and change. She looked forward to meeting Tom Radcliff again, for he had promised to take her for a drive, and this would be a good opportunity for him to make arrangements if he was still of the same mind.

Although Elizabeth had mentioned an informal meal, Sylvia found herself taking extra care with her appearance. This in itself took considerable time, for she was not very adept at arranging her hair in an attractive style. Louise had been the talented one in that respect and had always dressed it for her and picked out the clothes they would both wear, for until her marriage they had always dressed and worn their hair alike.

She was still trying to make a curl stay in place when she heard Elizabeth going down the stairs, and she impatiently flung down her hairbrush in disgust and decided it would just have to do. If she ever married someone of means, she resolved, she would have her own abigail, as Elizabeth now had.

They were in the drawing room drinking sherry when she finally came down, and Tom Radcliff bent low over her hand and did not seem to notice if her hair was a little unruly.

David seated her opposite Elizabeth, in one of the lovely old leather chairs that flanked the warm, blazing hearth, for even in late summer a fire was necessary to offset the chill of the castle walls. As he handed her a small glass, he said, "I was just telling Tom about the fellow who brought you back today. Didn't he say he lived with his sister?"

Sylvia nodded. "She was standing near to a rather decrepit-looking cottage, tending a small garden, and she smiled and waved to us as we passed. He told me she is growing vegetables and keeping hens and a pig."

"They must be country bred, then," David remarked, "and he didn't seem unhappy with his lot, but he lost part of an arm at Waterloo, Tom, and that's why I'd like you to go over there with me tomorrow. It's more than four years since he was injured, but you might want to make sure it's healed all right."

Tom nodded. "I'd be glad to, and if he's willing, I could probably help him to still get some use out of it. Did he seem to be the type who would like to try making it work again?"

"It's hard to tell, Tom. He had a gun with him, so I imagine he's shooting and trapping game for their table. He'd hardly carry it if he was not capable of using it," David said thoughtfully.

Elizabeth was about to change to a more suitable dinner topic when Sylvia asked, "How could he possibly use an arm he's lost?"

Tom leaned forward and explained, "Ever since the war ended, I have been working with some of the men who have been disabled, trying to somehow get them walking again if they lost a leg, or fitting a device on their shoulder or arm if part of that limb was gone. Even limited use is better than none, and it keeps the remaining muscles from atrophying," he said.

"Tom spends only part of his time caring for our sick," Elizabeth put in. "Then he leave us in the hands of a doctor several miles away, and works in London for a month or so at one of the big hospitals there."

"But surely there are few new patients with such injuries so long after the war," Sylvia started to say, but stopped as she heard the butler's discreet cough.

With Elizabeth on David's arm and Sylvia on Tom's, they walked into the dining room, where places had been set informally at one end of the long table, and the dancing flames from the fire rivaled the glow of the branches of candles in their silver holders.

As David sampled, then poured the wine, he asked, "What was it you were asking, Sylvia, when Shackleton announced dinner?"

"If we are to digest our food, I believe we should find a lighter topic of discussion," Elizabeth said pleasantly but firmly. "As none of us were in town last Season, and there was so very much going on, perhaps you could tell us some of the things that happened, Sylvia."

"Well, of course, the most interesting occasion for us was when we were officially presented at what would have been a Queen's Drawing Room. You see, as there is no longer a queen or even a princess, we were all wondering what would happen," Sylvia said.

"In the end," she went on, "whatever committee makes a ruling on such things decided that there had been a precedent set by King George II. He apparently started to hold drawing rooms after the death of Queen Caroline, so it was all right for the Prince Regent to hold one all by himself. It was a most awful crush, though, and with all the windows closed because of the Prince's fear of drafts, many young ladies became quite faint."

"I hear he's not been feeling at all well this summer, and it's not really surprising, after losing his mama just last year and his papa getting worse all the time," Elizabeth said sympathetically. "Lavinia told me that this last Season had not been nearly so gay as previous years, for so many of the *ton* have been finding it more and more difficult to entertain as lavishly as they used to."

"It was quite gay enough for us. In fact, we turned down a great many more invitations than we accepted. But it's over now, and I suppose that Papa will send word very soon that I am to return to Danville Hall." Sylvia did not look at all happy at the prospect.

"Now, don't start getting yourself upset," Elizabeth said firmly. "I don't intend to let Papa treat you the way he treated me, and if I have to, I'll send you to stay with Lavinia again even before the Little Season starts."

"The Little Season?" Sylvia repeated the words as though she could not quite believe them. "But surely the agreement was that David would pay for one Season only? I couldn't possibly let him pay for more, when it's quite obvious that I'm not going to meet anyone there."

She spoke much more loudly than she realized, and David looked across from the conversation he was having with Tom. "Did I hear my name spoken?" he asked, smiling understandingly at his young sister-in-law.

"This would not be quite the same," Elizabeth said gently, looking over to David for support. "What I had in mind was that, as Lavinia lives alone in what used to be my house on Grosvenor Street all the year round, you would be returning the favor she did in bringing you out, by keeping her company for a little while. If she wishes to go out in the evening, you would not, of course, want her to go alone."

The two men were all attention now, a half-smile playing on Colchester's face as he listened to his wife using her most persuasive powers on someone else for a change.

"But it would mean more gowns," Sylvia protested, adding softly, "although some of my old ones could be retrimmed so that no one would notice them." She shook her head firmly. "Papa would never permit it. He said if we didn't find husbands last Season, then he would find them for us, and I'm sure that's what he intends."

"Your father will not refuse me," David said firmly. "I'll send him a note, and the two of you can start making plans. It's all decided."

"Is the house in Grosvenor Street no longer yours, Elizabeth?" Sylvia asked. "I heard Papa saying that you had lost it when you got married again."

"It never really was mine, my love. It was left to me by my first husband, for my use as long as I did not marry again. When I did, it reverted to his heir, Robert Trevelyan, and he in turn gave his Aunt Lavinia the use of it, for he now has a much larger town house that belonged to his wife's family," Elizabeth explained. "Now, after all that, you're surely not still refusing to stay there again in a few weeks' time?"

"Of course not, as long as I'm not expected to get into the whirl of balls every night." Sylvia felt a little scared, deep down, for she would be alone this time and Louise had given her more moral support than she had realized.

"That's settled, then," David said with a grin. "What a fuss these women make over the slightest thing, Tom. Were you not wanting to ask something before we were interrupted?"

"I just wanted to know whether you're planning to go over to see Wainwright in the morning or afternoon," Tom said, "for if Sylvia is free, I was hoping to take her for a drive in the afternoon."

"Well, in that case we'll go in the morning, of course, but I thought you had to make some visits to patients in the afternoon?" David cocked an eyebrow when he saw his friend flush and Sylvia look quite embarrassed.

"I have only one visit, and . . . Now, look here, you

old rogue, I'll do my own inviting, if you don't mind," Tom said indignantly, then turned directly to Sylvia and asked gently, "Will you forgive our clumsiness and come for a ride with me tomorrow, my dear?"

"Thank you, Tom. I'd like that very much—and I'll even come in and see your patient if it will serve to cheer him up," Sylvia gladly agreed.

"Will two o'clock be all right?" David asked with a grin, dodging a blow his wife aimed at him.

Sylvia smiled at Tom and nodded. He was a very nice young man, and both she and Louise had found him pleasant company on previous visits, for he had not treated them as children but as young ladies even then. She would look forward to the drive tomorrow, and perhaps many more drives with him in the weeks before she left for London.

Tea was brought in, with port for the gentlemen, for Elizabeth had never believed in separating the ladies and gentlemen at an informal gathering. She disliked doing so at formal dinners also, for invariably the gentlemen became too interested in their conversation and drank so much port that they were a trifle bosky before they rejoined the ladies.

As she handed a cup of tea to Sylvia she asked softly, "Would you like me to assign a maid to act as abigail for you while you're here? I forget that you're no longer a sixteen-year-old and may need help dressing."

"Would it be possible?" Sylvia asked gratefully. "Louise always arranged our hair and I did all the brushing. Does it look terrible?"

Her sister laughed. "Not terrible, but nor is it the way it usually looks. It should have occurred to me before, but the two of you never wanted anyone, so I just didn't think. You shall have help from now on."

"We didn't want anyone because we would just sit and talk about an evening for ages before we got into bed. It was very special." Her eyes held a sad, wistful look, and Elizabeth reached out a hand and touched her cheek.

"You'll always love her, but one day you'll find

someone who will make a place for himself in your heart, and then it will not seem so empty anymore. I missed you both so very much when Papa sent me away to marry Lord Trevelyan, but his sister, Lady Lavinia, and my stepchildren helped."

Lady Lavinia was the younger sister of Elizabeth's first husband, the fourth Marquess of Dewsbury, and Lavinia had risked his wrath to befriend and defend his seventeen-year-old bride. His revenge had been to make no provision whatever for Lavinia after his death.

To her delight, however, Elizabeth had invited her to live with her in the London house, and Lady Lavinia had been able to renew all her old acquaintances from the days of her own come-out, many years before. It had been through one of these old bosom bows that Elizabeth had met Colchester.

After Elizabeth and David married and left for Colchester Castle, Lady Lavinia's nephew, the present Marquess, to whom the house had reverted, had made up for his father's meanness by giving her the use of the house plus a generous annual allowance for the rest of her life.

Sylvia felt selfish, for Elizabeth had been so very young when she had married for the first time. But when she looked into her sister's face, from which love and happiness now shone, it gave her new hope.

Elizabeth rose. "I'm going up to make sure the children are asleep now. Do you want to join me and leave the gentlemen to their port and tobacco?"

3

Maude, the maid sent to assist Sylvia, had been chosen for her ability to dress hair rather than for her own looks, for she was a small, plain little thing, but most anxious to please. Sylvia took to her immediately, especially when she found that the clothes she had set out had all been beautifully ironed. After helping her don her gown, the work-roughened hands had gently tamed her unruly locks to frame her face beneath her wide-brimmed straw hat, giving Sylvia a special feeling of confidence for her first ride with Tom Radcliff.

Elizabeth noticed the vast improvement as soon as her sister came into the drawing room, looking very elegant in a gown of delicate rose-colored jaconet muslin trimmed with cream lace at the throat, cream gloves, and a hat bound with rose ribbons that fell in long streamers down her back. "I'm truly sorry that I did not think to send a maid to you before, my love. You and Louise always looked so well that I assumed you had equal ability to make the best of yourselves."

"It always seemed to us that we had been given different talents so that we might share them. When it came to needlework, both plain and fancy, Louise was all thumbs, so I, in turn, did whatever sewing was required for both of us." Sylvia touched the artfully arranged black curls that lay against her cheek. "I could never have achieved this had you not lent me Maude."

"She's yours for as long as you need her, and I'm sure Tom will appreciate her efforts," Elizabeth said, looking pleased with herself. "He'll be back in just a moment, for as soon as he arrived, David just had to take him to see a foal that was born this morning when they were out. David's very proud of his stables, and this little fellow has an outstanding pedigree."

Sylvia was not at all concerned, for she was in no hurry and admitted, "I'm always a little early anyway. I've never been able to get used to keeping gentlemen waiting a fashionable fifteen to twenty minutes."

"And a good thing, too, young lady," David's voice boomed as he and Tom entered the drawing room. "I always thought it 'a rag-mannered custom and have even been known to leave after waiting ten minutes for a chit who was tardy."

"As Sylvia is ready, we should go now, for one of your grooms is quite unnecessarily walking my horses, and I'm sure you've other things for him to do," Tom said to his friend; then, giving Sylvia a look of warm approval, he took her arm and steered her toward the door. "I have a second patient to visit, so I don't expect we will be back for some time."

Sylvia did not know quite what she had thought to ride in, but it was certainly not a spanking new curricle like the one waiting outside, drawn by a pair of matched grays. It seemed a more suitable conveyance for a young blood in London than for a doctor in the country, but she was not about to complain.

He helped her up and they started out at a steady pace down the well-kept lanes near the castle, and she soon realized why the grays did not need to be walked, for they were a handsome pair, but more solid and reliable than the highly strung animals seen so frequently in town.

"Were you waiting long?" Tom asked. "David was anxious for me to see his new foal, and it was impossible for me to refuse."

She shook her head. "My sister told me where you were and it really didn't matter at all. It was kind of you to invite me to come with you."

"Not kind," Tom said, "but a rare treat for me. I drive these lanes alone most of the time, and it is a pleasure indeed to have such a pretty young lady for company."

Sylvia was slightly embarrassed by his gallantry, for she had thought of Tom only as a friend of David's. She quickly changed the subject. "Did you manage to see Jonathan Wainwright this morning?" she asked.

"Yes, and I'm glad I went, for the surgeon had botched up the job and he's still experiencing some pain there." Tom frowned, for he had seen many such cases in the London hospitals. "I believe I can take care of that, and then, once he is more comfortable, I will measure him for a sort of brace to which a device can be attached for picking things up and generally just aiding the other hand." He suddenly seemed embarrassed. "What on earth am I thinking of, telling you all this? It's hardly a suitable topic of conversation for a drive with a young lady on a sunny afternoon."

Sylvia put out a hand and touched his arm. "Perhaps I'm not the usual young lady you take on drives, but please continue, for I am extremely interested and not at all squeamish. You sound as though you're quite accustomed to handling cases like his. Is that what you do in London?"

Tom looked at her with a newfound appreciation. From a rather nice sixteen-year-old she had grown into an unusually thoughtful young woman, he decided. "It's part of it," he told her. "You see, field surgery had to be done of necessity in a hurry, and in many cases bits of metal and even pieces of cloth were left in the wounds. Some never healed, and caused fevers from which the patient died. Others healed on the outside only, with similar results, and still others caused pain in the area years later, and the patients thought that it was inevitable and that they must live with it."

Sylvia had begun to see Tom in an entirely new light. "And I thought until recently that you were just a country doctor—well-qualified, of course, or David would never have let you look after Elizabeth and the children. By the way, what did David want with Wainwright?" she asked, for she had been curious, but found it easier to ask Tom than her brother-in-law, who, at times, overawed her, though she loved him dearly.

"Just to be sure that he and his sister are all right, and to offer them work if they need it. He's sending some men over tomorrow to do more permanent repairs on the shack they're living in, and Wainwright will probably repay him in services when he can." He looked at Sylvia's surprised face. "Your sister married a man with a heart as big as his purse."

"I know, and I'm very glad now that I got lost yesterday, but I wasn't at the time. Wainwright scared both me and my horse, coming up behind me so quietly, but he was kind in a gruff sort of way."

Tom pointed ahead to where an old stone house was set back from the lane. "That's Mrs. Waterhouse's home we're coming to. She's been bedridden for a number of years, and has a girl to look after her. I stop by once a week to check on her and leave her some medicine. She'll enjoy seeing a young, pretty face."

He negotiated the turn off the lane, and let his horses pick their way up the dirt track to the house; then he alighted, tied the reins to a post, and helped Sylvia down.

Sylvia and Louise had been quite accustomed to visiting the sick in the village near home, but they were usually people who had known them all their lives and did not hesitate to tell them what little imps they had been when they were younger. She had no qualms, however, about meeting strangers, and followed Tom to the front door, which was opened before he could knock by a young girl covered almost from head to toe in a huge apron. She bobbed a curtsy to Tom but looked wide-eyed when she saw his companion.

"Good afternoon, Annie. Please tell Mrs. Waterhouse that I am here and that I have brought a visitor to see her," Tom said, and steered Sylvia into the small hall while the girl scurried up the stairs to do his bidding.

They could hear the murmur of voices from above, and then, a moment later, the girl was back, taking Tom's hat and pointing the way.

Mrs. Waterhouse was a grossly heavy, motherly-looking woman, and she greeted Tom with a big smile. "How nice of you to call, Doctor," she said, "and you've brought your lady friend with you, I see."

Tom laughed, not at all embarrassed. "Not exactly, Mrs. Waterhouse. Tell me how you're feeling today, and then I'll tell you who this young lady is."

The older woman's eyes clouded for a moment. "I'm about the same, I suppose, but I've not been sleeping very well at night. It's probably because I do nothing but lie around all day."

"And the pain?" he asked, leaning over to check her pulse.

"My chest hurts a bit sometimes," she admitted, "and it's hard to catch my breath, but I ring the bell and Annie helps me sit up a little higher."

"And then it goes away?" Tom asked, and when she nodded, he leaned over to press an ear to her chest, saying, "Breathe deeply for me . . . and again."

He straightened up. "I think you'd better sleep with an extra pillow under your head and shoulders. That might ease it a little for you, and don't forget to take your medicine at the right times," he advised, then said, "and now I would like you to meet Miss Sylvia Danville, who is Lady Colchester's sister."

"Oh, my!" Mrs. Waterhouse exclaimed. "The sister of a countess. I'm very pleased to meet you, my dear. I've seen your lovely sister and her bairns many a time around the village, and, of course, I can still remember what the earl looked like when he was a baby." She paused to catch her breath before adding in an almost awed tone, "But I never thought I'd have one of them actually in my house."

Sylvia laughed. "I'm pleased to meet you, Mrs. Waterhouse. Dr. Radcliff is very kindly taking me out for a breath of fresh air, and stopping to see you was an added bonus."

Mrs. Waterhouse started to reach for the bell. "I'll call Annie and have her make you a nice cup of tea," she began, but Tom put out a restraining hand.

"Another time, perhaps," he said with an understanding smile. "I have other patients to visit this afternoon, and Miss Danville wants to see a little more of our countryside. I'll come again next week, but if you need me in the meantime, just send Annie to get me."

"I hope I won't need to do that, Doctor. It's been grand seeing you again, and you too, Miss Danville, and perhaps he'll bring you with him next time." She leaned back against her pillow, obviously feeling a little tired, and they left her to rest for a while.

When they reached the foot of the stairs, the maid was waiting and Tom took his hat from her and admonished, "Don't hesitate to come and get me if she has any problems, Annie, and just see that she takes her medicine every night."

"What is her ailment, Tom?" Sylvia asked when they were in the curricle once more.

"A weak heart, burdened by her tremendous weight over a long period of time. If we had accepted tea, I know it would have been accompanied by plates of cakes and pastries that she would have been completely unable to resist. Her husband died many years ago, leaving her quite well-breeched, more's the pity. She's lonely and consoles herself by eating, though she knows it will be the death of her," he said with a sad shake of his head.

They drove for a while in a comfortable silence, enjoying the fresh summer air and the smell of the newly cut hay, and watching the field laborers in their smock-frocks as they swung their scythes, and the birds that followed closely behind them.

"My other patient lives almost three miles away," Tom said, "which gives me time to find out how you are going along now that your other half has left."

"How did you know it feels like that?" Sylvia asked in surprise.

"It's not so uncommon, my dear," he assured her, "even when twins are not identical. There's been a closeness between you since before birth, and when the separation comes, it can sometimes be quite devastating to the one who is left behind. If it's any consolation, it will ease as you start to live a life of your own, make new friends, and particularly when you marry. I am sure Louise is missing you also, but she has a husband to console her, and new things to enjoy every day."

"You're not a twin, so you can't be speaking from personal experience. Have you read about it in some of your medical books, then?" she asked, puzzled by the way he understood so well.

"A little is recorded," Tom admitted, "and it is very understandable. Your sister's plan to send you to London in a few weeks is an excellent one, and as I shall be returning to the city about that time, I hope you will give me the pleasure of escorting you—perhaps, also, of calling on you while you are there?"

Sylvia felt as though a weight had been eased from her shoulders. Just to find there was someone who realized how she felt helped, and she smiled her thanks. "Of course, I would like that very much," she agreed. "That is, if Papa does not send for me to return home first."

"Your sister is a very determined lady once she makes up her mind," Tom said with a grin. "I've no doubt things will work out as she plans them. And now, let me tell you a little about the patient we are about to visit. He is a young man of ten years, and he was injured when working in the fields with his father. A farm implement fell on his leg, breaking some of the bones. I did something I've been experimenting with, and I hope it will serve to keep the leg straight until the bones knit together again.

"First I put the bones back in their proper place and put splints on both sides of the leg, then bandaged completely over the splints with several layers of cloth. After that I mixed some plaster of paris with water and put it entirely over the bandage to form a casing. I stayed with the youngster until it had hardened completely, and emphasized to his family that it must not get wet. Now I want to see how he is getting along."

"How did you learn to do this?" Sylvia asked curiously.

"I didn't learn how. It's just an experiment. One of the things my colleagues and I work on in London," he told her.

"Will he be able to walk normally if you are ever able to get the thing off?" Sylvia inquired.

"I believe so. About five or six weeks from now, I will soak the plaster and remove the entire thing. Fortunately, in this case, I heard about it in time. Too frequently, I am afraid, children are injured and their parents feel they cannot afford to complain or they might all be put out of work, so the youngsters receive no attention and have to suffer for the rest of their lives."

"He'll not be back at work already, will he?"

"Probably," Tom said ruefully. "But we've had no rain this last week, so there's a good chance that he's not got the leg wet and ruined all my handiwork. We're almost there, so we'll soon find out."

Young Jack was quite hard at work when they reached the farm, and though the plaster was dirty, it was still in place and the little boy was wearing it with immense pride. He could move around every bit as fast as his brothers and sisters, but it was sad to see how painfully thin they all were, their clothes patched and mended and their feet bare. It was a hard life for young and old, with nothing better to look forward to.

"There's not much danger of him getting the plaster wet when he bathes, for they probably all wash from one small bowl of water," Tom said as they were leaving. "I had quite a time getting the leg clean enough to work with, for the dirt was ingrained.

"I don't wonder that more and more of them are leaving the farms and going to work in the towns. Unfortunately, though, they don't realize that it's just as bad, if not worse, in factories, for at least on a farm they see the sun and feel the fresh air. Some of the factory owners actually refer to child labor as free labor, for they often pay a man only one wage for himself and his whole family."

They took a different way back, and stopped to have a refreshing drink at a clear stream where minnows ran through their fingers as they cupped the cool water. Sylvia thought of how shocked Lady Lavinia would be if she saw her removing her gloves and drinking from her hands in front of a gentleman. She was a dear soul, but very, very proper, and sometimes Louise had teased her about it.

Thinking of Louise brought once more an odd feeling of unease. Louise should be having a wonderful time in Paris by now, but for some reason Sylvia felt that she wasn't, that something was upsetting her twin. A silence had fallen that Sylvia was unaware of until she looked up and saw Tom watching her.

"You're not by any chance worrying about your sister, are you?" he asked. He had been leaning against a tree and studying the expressions on her face as she carefully dried her hands on a towel he kept in the carriage.

Sylvia looked up at him in surprise. She had been taken unawares, for she had no idea that the worry showed on her expressive face. "Just a little bit," she admitted with a wry grimace, "and I don't quite know why. I like Timothy well enough and don't think for a minute that he would do anything to harm her, but I have an odd feeling that something is not quite right."

"An instinct?" he asked.

"I suppose so. But I could be actually feeling something that is troubling her without knowing what it is. We often did, you know," she tried to explain, "like the time, at a ball, when a young man insisted she go out into the garden with him for some fresh air, and though I didn't see her go, I took my partner to the very same place and was just in time."

Tom grinned. "A very useful instinct, I would say, if you're both at the same party, but not when the English Channel separates you."

He helped her into the curricle and they returned to Colchester Castle at a slower pace, with Tom pausing frequently to point out famous landmarks by which she could tell where she was. They stopped briefly at an orchard and visited the owner, coming away with a basket of apples, then Tom showed Sylvia the walls that marked the southern edge of Colchester's property.

"Now you have no excuse for wandering off David's land to the south, at least. If you'd like to come with me again tomorrow, I shall be visiting patients on the eastern side, and will show you where the lands adjoin the neighbors' there," he suggested, and Sylvia readily agreed, for she had completely enjoyed the afternoon and felt more relaxed than she'd been since the wedding.

After saying good-bye to Tom, she paused for a moment before climbing the stairs to her bedchamber. It had been a delightful ride and she could not remember the last time she had felt so at ease when alone with a young man. Was it, perhaps, the balmy weather? —for it had been warm and sunny all afternoon. Or was it, perhaps, the fact that he was such a good friend of the Colchesters that she need have no qualms as to his behavior?

It was probably a little of each, she decided as she started briskly up the broad staircase, but mostly it was the way he talked so freely to her about subjects that most young men avoided. She was not missish and she was genuinely interested in his work, and it had been a pleasure to be treated as a sensible young woman instead of a giddy girl who needed meaningless words and flattery to make her happy.

He was not as handsome as David, of course, but he had a nice face and a warm smile, and he made her feel that she was bright and intelligent and worthwhile. That was it, of course! The young men she met in London had treated her like a delicate ornament instead of respecting her as a person with ideas and a point of view of her own.

She gave a little sigh of pleasure at the thought of seeing him again tomorrow, then brought herself abruptly down to earth as she remembered all her father's past scheming. If she did go to London again, and she did meet a young, wealthy suitor, Papa would more than likely approve her marriage. But if she allowed herself to fall in love with a poor country doctor, Papa would never agree.

Her pace had lessened and her shoulders drooped as she reached the top step and started down the corridor toward her bedchamber. As she entered the room, Maude looked up from the dresser drawer she was tidying. The dinner gown her mistress would wear tonight was already ironed and hanging outside the armoire. "Will you be going for a drive again tomorrow, miss?" she asked.

Sylvia's frown turned into a big smile. "Yes, Maude," she said. "And I'll wear my pale green gown with the primrose embroidery. Do be sure it is clean and ironed, won't you, for I want to look my very best."

"That I will, miss," the girl said happily. "I'll take it down and do it now. And I'll freshen the green ribbon for your bonnet at the same time."

When Maude left the room with the garment in her arms, Sylvia almost danced over to the dressing table. She would enjoy herself tomorrow and take one day at a time. She was not in love with Tom, but she liked him very much and she'd let events take their course, wherever they might lead.

4

For two weeks now Sylvia had accompanied Tom Radcliff when he made his rounds of housebound patients. Today as he sat in his surgery listening to the problems of one of the villagers, he realized that he missed her. She possessed an excellent memory and could recall, without any prompting on his part, what was wrong with each patient, and, to their delight, she always greeted them by name.

He had invited her to join him initially because he knew that there were few young people of her age and class in the immediate neighborhood. Also, he fully understood how much she missed her twin, and when he realized she did not go into a decline at the mere mention of his work, he found himself looking forward to her companionship.

It had been a long time since he had known a young lady with a brain in her head she was willing to use. There had been one, several years ago, a young nurse who was both beautiful and intelligent, but she had succumbed to a fever and not sent for him until it was too late to save her.

He wondered if Sylvia's freshness would remain when she returned to the frivolous life of London, in which he himself participated on occasion, albeit somewhat reluctantly.

He had made the offer to escort her there in a few weeks' time because he was going to the city in any case, but now he began to look forward to taking her to some of the many parties and social occasions which she would, of course, attend. That was, however, provided her parents agreed to let her go there.

She had asked him one day, when they were going to see a patient, if he would teach her how to drive his curricle. It had been with some hesitation that he had agreed, for, like many others of his gender, he did not feel it a suitable pastime for a lady. By the end of the second lesson it had been quite apparent, however, that she was not at all cow-handed and just needed practice to make an excellent whip. Of course, the country lanes were comparatively easy to drive along. He sincerely hoped she would not expect him to let her practice in London's heavy traffic, for he would be forced to refuse, though it would go against his conscience to do so.

A solution to this problem occurred to him one day when he had the reins, but could see by the way Sylvia watched his hands that she was itching to try again.

He would escort Sylvia, riding alternately on horseback and within the Colchester carriage, and would leave his curricle behind, for it would be far easier for him to get around in the city either on horseback or by hackney.

They had been visiting an elderly gentleman who lived alone except for a manservant, and who liked to have a game of chess with Tom when he called to check on his condition. This time, though, it was Sylvia who played with him, and Tom was pleased to note how much more lively his patient became with such a pretty, proficient opponent.

She looked quite lovely in a lavender gown of sprigged muslin, with sleeves that puffed at the shoulders, then had fitted undersleeves reaching down to the wrist. A straw bonnet with lavender ribbons framed her lovely face, with its sparkling blue eyes and ready smile.

The sherry of which the two gentlemen usually partook had been gladly dispensed with today in favor of afternoon tea, and they had both enjoyed watching her delicate hands pour the beverage, adding milk and sugar and offering a plate of sweets to the two of them. When they left, the old eyes had an added sparkle, and he extracted their promise to come back the following week for a return game.

"How dreadful it must be to live all alone like that with only a servant to talk to," Sylvia remarked sadly as they drove away.

"He has a considerable library," Tom told her, "and his books are like companions to him. Also, he and his man have been together a great many years and are much fonder of each other than would appear. But he certainly enjoyed your company, my dear."

"He was very charming, and I shall enjoy going back next week," she said softly, "if, of course, you will take me."

Tom turned his head to look at her, sitting demurely beside him and watching the movement of his hands as he controlled the grays. They had no more calls to make today, and there was no reason to spring the grays, for they should be home about their usual time, so he released the reins to her so that she could get a little more practice. The lane they were traveling along was narrow but smooth, and they were going at a moderate pace when a young puppy sprang out from behind a hedge and ran directly in front of the horses.

Sylvia saw the flash of something tan-colored on the left side of the road, but before she had time to do anything, the horses reared. She saw, with relief, that the pup was already leaping into the hedge on the left. Then she heard a scream.

It all happened so quickly that she didn't realize what had occurred until it was over, for Tom had grabbed the reins as the horses reared, and was attempting to bring them under control when a small boy came running out after his dog. Within seconds he was under the horses' hooves and Tom was straining every nerve to bring them to a halt without overturning the curricle.

It was fortunate that the grays were an unusually steady pair, for they calmed quickly and Tom was able to jump down and run back to where the boy lay quite still in the middle of the lane, while his puppy ran frantically back and forth.

Sylvia had watched Tom tie up the horses on numerous occasions, so she scrambled down from the vehicle and went to the nearside horse. Murmuring soothingly to him, she led the pair over to the side of the lane and tied the gray up to a limb of a tree. Then, reaching beneath the seat of the vehicle, she picked up Tom's leather bag and went back to where he knelt examining the youngster.

"Is he very bad?" she asked, her voice trembling a little.

"It would seem as though his left leg is broken, and it rather looks as if a hoof caught him on the side of the head. He's breathing, but he's unconscious," Tom said tersely. "There's a farm just a field away, owned by a family called Beardsley. If you can help me get him through that break in the hedge, I'm going to carry him over there. I believe he's one of theirs."

Tom lifted the youngster and carried him to the hedge, then carefully placed him in Sylvia's arms before scrambling over and taking him from her. Then he started slowly across the field, with the puppy running ahead, then coming back, then running ahead again. A few minutes later, ignoring the rips the sharp twigs made in her gown, Sylvia climbed through and caught up to them. At first Tom did not appear to know she was there; then he said, "The horses need to be tied up at the side of the lane. Do you think you could manage it?"

"I already did," she told him, and kept on walking by his side, his bag in her hand, looking anxiously at the face of the child. He was an attractive youngster of about five years, with a mop of curly red hair and a mass of freckles that stood out against the white of his face.

As they neared the farmhouse a woman in a white apron came running toward them. "It's little Willie," she cried, holding the apron to her face. "Oh, dear me, what happened, Doctor?"

"His dog ran into the lane and he came after it, right under my horses," Tom said briefly. "I'll need a table or something flat to place him on so that I can discover the extent of his injuries. Can you go with her, Sylvia, to help?"

Without answering, she gently took the weeping woman's arm, turning her around and asking quietly, "You're Mrs. Beardsley, aren't you?" and when the woman nodded, she urged, "Come along and help me get a table ready for the doctor."

Sylvia hurried her toward the back door of the house and, once inside the big kitchen, glanced around to see what would be suitable. The large kitchen table held dirty dishes from tea, so she started to take them over to the sink, and when Mrs. Beardsley saw what she was doing, she pulled herself together and helped.

"What else will he need?" the worried mother asked. "Hot water?"

"It wouldn't do any harm to put a kettle on," Sylvia said quickly, having not the least idea but knowing it would give her something to do. "And if you can find as many old cloths as possible, I'm sure he'll need those too. Willie is your son, isn't he?"

The woman nodded, put the kettle on the fire, then went to a cupboard and had started taking out teacloths and towels when Tom came into the room with the child.

As he placed him on the table, Sylvia handed him the bag she'd been carrying. Tom looked surprised, then said, "Good girl," and reached inside for a pair of scissors.

"You're not going to ruin his trousers, are you? We can take them off," Mrs. Beardsley started to say, coming forward, but Tom shook his head and made the first snip. "He has a broken leg, Mrs. Beardsley. It's better this way."

Standing by the table, Sylvia reached over to ease the fabric away from the leg, then took the cut-up garment and handed it to the mother while Tom carefully felt along the tiny limb.

"I'll need two flat pieces of wood for splints, and some torn-up cloths to bind it. Will you see what you can find?" he asked Sylvia, and she took Mrs. Beardsley to one side and asked her for what he needed.

They found some wood in the laundry, and began to tear up an old sheet into strips, and soon Tom had the small leg encased so that the boy would not injure it further when he came around. Then he gently felt the youngster's temple, where a bruise and swelling were forming.

Tom looked at Sylvia and answered the question in her eyes. "I think it must have been only a glancing blow, for the skin is scarcely broken and there's no imprint of a hoof. I'll have to wait here until he comes to, I'm afraid, and it may be some time."

"And the curricle can't be left in the lane indefinitely," Sylvia put in. "If you like, I can go get it and bring it up to the house. I'd be very careful."

Tom eyed her gravely, then smiled. "Don't try to turn them around. Lead them back onto the road before you climb up, and you'll see an entrance to this farm just a little further along."

Sylvia felt a surge of pride that he trusted her to do this for him. She walked back across the field, tearing her gown even more as she pushed through the hedge again, and was relieved to find the curricle still where she had left it, and the grays quietly munching on grass at the side of the lane.

She followed Tom's instructions carefully, holding the grays to little more than a walk, and it seemed no time at all before she entered the farmhouse yard, jumped down, and tied them up under a clump of trees.

Even so, much had happened since she left the warm kitchen. Willie had come around and was whimpering fretfully while his mother tried to soothe him, and Tom was checking his vision and his hearing for signs of impairment.

Finally he straightened up, rubbing his back, for he had been crouched over the youngster for some time. "I think he's a very fortunate young man, and he should be all right except for having a nasty headache, Mrs. Beardsley—and, of course, a broken leg. I'll carry him up to bed for you, and give him something to make his head stop aching, and then tomorrow I will return to see to that leg properly. In the meantime, leave it just as it is. Don't touch it."

He picked the youngster up in his arms and followed the mother, while Sylvia waited downstairs.

"Now, don't forget, under no circumstances are you to touch his leg, or the bone will come out of place," he was saying to Mrs. Beardsley as he came back into the kitchen. "Before you go to bed tonight, if he's very fretful you may give him another of these powders, in water, and I'll be back early in the morning."

"Won't you stay and have a cup of tea, Doctor?" The farmer's wife was recovering rapidly from the shock, and was anxious to offer hospitality.

"Not this time," Tom said with a smile. "Miss Danville is already late home, and Lady Beresford will be anxious."

A big smile came over Mrs. Beardsley's face. "You're her ladyship's sister, miss? I'm right glad to have met you, that is, I mean . . ."

Sylvia took her hand. "I know, and I'm sure Willie will be all right. He gave us all a fright, didn't he? But I really must be going now. Perhaps I'll come by one day to see how he's getting along." She could almost hear the thoughts going through the good lady's head as she pondered just what she would say to her family and friends.

Tom took Sylvia's arm and led her outside, then smiled as he saw his horses nibbling daintily at some leaves. "You are going to drive me back to the castle, aren't you?" he asked, looking at her with a new warmth.

"You'll still let me?" she asked a little tremulously.

"Of course. The accident was not your fault in any way, and you handled yourself exceptionally well, both with the cattle and with young Willie. I must say, you're an unusually levelheaded young lady."

His hand was beneath her elbow, helping her up and handing the reins to her, and she went at a slow pace until they were back in the lane; then she let the grays out a little, for they were anxious to be on their way.

Tom became very quiet on the way back, and Sylvia, trying to concentrate on her driving and give a good showing, remained silent also until they had turned into the driveway.

It was by now close to the dinner hour, and he knew that he would have to go in and make his explanations to Elizabeth and David, for they must have been quite worried about their charge.

The curricle had scarcely come to a halt before the front door opened and David came out and ran down the steps. "Where on earth have you two been until this hour?" he asked abruptly. "Elizabeth is beside herself with worry, and I don't need to tell either of you how bad that is for her in her present condition."

"For goodness' sake, stop berating them as though they were children, David," Elizabeth called from the open door. "Dinner will be in about fifteen minutes, Tom. Why don't you come in and join us, then you can both tell us all about it."

David had handed Sylvia down and was escorting her up the steps when a boy appeared as if from nowhere to take charge of the curricle and horses, so Tom had little option but to follow the other two. As he reached the top step and started through the open door, he was surprised to hear Elizabeth give a little scream.

"Your gown is in shreds, Sylvia. What on earth happened?" she gasped.

Sylvia looked down, lifted her torn skirts with a dainty hand, then shrugged. "It's not really in bad condition when you consider that I scrambled through a hedge twice," she said with deliberate casualness, "is it, Tom?"

David glanced back at Tom's jacket and breeches, which also looked somewhat the worse for wear, then turned to the butler, who was standing by impassively, awaiting instructions. "Please ask Cook to postpone dinner a half-hour, Shackleton, and we'll have sherry now in the drawing room," he said quietly.

Not until the ladies were comfortably seated and the drinks had been served was another word spoken;

then, as the door closed behind the butler, David said grimly, "Now, for God's sake, give me an explanation, Tom."

Sylvia, who had been desperately trying to keep a straight face, now started to laugh helplessly, for it had never occurred to her that her brother-in-law, who was now glaring at her, would immediately think the worst.

"There was an accident—" Tom began.

"I knew something would happen when you decided to teach her to drive," David growled. "Women just can't handle cattle."

Tom glanced across at Sylvia's indignant expression and gave her a solemn wink before clearing his throat and continuing. "As I said, there was an accident. We were on our way home when a pup ran into the lane by Beardsley's farm, startling the grays. They reared and I grabbed the reins from Sylvia, but—"

"Told you so," David snapped, "women—"

"David, if you don't stop interrupting, I'm going to take Tom into the hall and get the full story from him there," Elizabeth said indignantly.

Giving his wife a sheepish grin, David nodded for Tom to continue.

"The Beardsleys' youngest came flying out after the pup, and the next thing we heard was a cry and he was under the carriage. By the time I had the grays under control, he was unconscious in the middle of the lane a few yards back," Tom told them with a shake of his head. "If you or I had been driving, it would have been just the same, David."

With an apologetic grin at Sylvia, David nodded. "I suppose it would," he agreed. "Youngsters never look, they just come charging out."

"How is he?" Elizabeth asked. "Were any bones broken?"

"His leg's broken, but it'll be all right," Tom said. "However, he took a kick on the head from one of the hooves and was unconscious, so I couldn't leave till he came round."

"What a miserable ending to your afternoon," Elizabeth said, then looked at them strangely, "but that does not explain what happened to my sister's gown."

Tom looked at Sylvia and raised his eyebrows. "Your turn, my dear, for I'll be darned if I know," he said.

"To be honest, I really didn't notice that I'd done so much damage," she admitted. "There was an opening in the hedge that Tom went through, and I handed the little boy over to him. I never even thought about how much wider my skirts were until I was stuck; then I just gave a good tug to free myself." She grinned a little ruefully. "Then I went back the same way to get the curricle and bring it to the farmhouse door, and I did the same thing again, but it just didn't seem important at the time."

"It wasn't, compared to the little boy's life," Elizabeth agreed. "If you want to run upstairs now, I believe Maude has a fresh gown waiting for you." As her sister hurried from the room, she turned to Tom. "You have accepted my invitation to dine with us, haven't you?"

"As my own has probably burned to a cinder by now, I shall be delighted. That is, if you will excuse my rather shabby attire." He glanced down at his jacket, then said, "While she is out, I must tell you how proud you would have been of that young lady. Without my asking, she led the grays to the side of the lane and tied them there; she calmed down Mrs. Beardsley, who was quite distraught, and got her helping find the things I needed; and she went alone to get the curricle and drive it up to the farmhouse."

Elizabeth smiled happily. She had secretly hoped that Tom and Sylvia might grow fond of each other, and now it seemed there was a good chance of its happening.

"Did you write Papa about sending Sylvia to stay with Lavinia for a while, darling?" she asked David, who had been watching her easily readable face with interest.

He grinned. "Of course, and I had a note back from him just today, saying that we should send her there by all means. He quickly forgot his desire to have her return home when I suggested that he might have to repay the costs of her come-out if he did not stick to our agreement."

Tom raised an eyebrow, and Elizabeth hastened to explain. "When we married, David told him that he would cover the costs of the twins' come-outs, miscellaneous gowns, and so on, and their weddings, as long as he allowed them to marry suitable men of their own choice. You see, my father has a propensity for gambling—and for arranging marriages to pay off his debts."

"Then the visit to London is definite?" Tom asked.

"Almost," Elizabeth assured him. "I've written to Lavinia, in London, asking her to formally invite Sylvia to stay with her for a few months, and I know she will be most happy to do so. Do you still want to escort her to town, or is your business there less urgent?"

"Even more urgent now," Tom said with a wide grin. "I'll inform them at the place I usually lodge, and make arrangements to have my practice covered while I'm gone. Don't worry, I'll be back long before your next child is ready to make his appearance."

The door opened and a now immaculate young lady entered. She dropped a low curtsy. "Will my transformation suffice?" she asked.

"Stop fishing for compliments, missy," David growled. "You're going to have a head bigger than your sister's if you're not careful." He ducked as a pillow came flying at him from his wife's couch. "I didn't say which sister, did I, my love?"

After the trials of the day, the four of them enjoyed a lighthearted game of whist after a delicious supper, and when Tom stepped into his curricle to return home, he found that he was humming softly to himself. He always enjoyed his work in London, but this time there would be an added reason for being there.

5

As expected, Lady Lavinia's invitation came promptly, begging Sylvia to come and stay with her in London, for she sadly missed the bustle of the Season and the twins' companionship.

As soon as Elizabeth had read it, she insisted on examining her sister's wardrobe, and immediately sent for her own dressmaker to augment it, though Sylvia insisted that she would herself alter slightly and retrim some of her gowns, to make them look like new.

She worked on them in the mornings so that she could still accompany Tom on his rounds, for she meant to see all his housebound patients at least once more before she left.

Mrs. Waterhouse had tea all ready this time, and ate most of the cakes herself, as Tom had said she would; Willie was up and about, using a homemade crutch to aid his broken leg, and suffering no ill effects from the bump on his head; and Sylvia had a last game of chess with Mr. Johnson, the elderly gentleman, who insisted on presenting her with a handsome volume of Byron's poems to take with her to London.

The lines on Jonathan Wainwright's face seemed lighter, and he smiled more often now that Tom had eased the constant pain he had been stoically bearing. He was practicing wearing the brace Tom had made for him, though he was taking Tom's advice and doing it by slow stages so as to allow the muscles to rebuild. His sister loved children and was helping Nanny with the little ones at the castle.

Sylvia had accomplished everything she had meant to do before leaving, and now it seemed like a new beginning for her when she stood outside David's carriage ready to start the journey to London. Maude was traveling with her as her abigail, and Tom would ride inside some of the time, but on horseback part of the journey, for he told her he found it much easier to get around London without his curricle. One of the trunks on top of the carriage was, however, filled with his books and clothes.

He greeted Sylvia with a look of admiration when he rode up to the coach. "You look very lovely this morning, my dear," he said, and her cheeks flushed to a shade somewhat lighter than the deep rose of the carriage dress she was wearing.

Her bonnet was in a soft gray velvet, the brim lined with rose to match her gown, and her muff and ribbons were in the same soft gray velvet. On her feet, however, were fine-quality boots, for she would need to walk after sitting several hours at a stretch, and she did not intend to do so in dainty, soft-soled slippers.

After she had hugged Elizabeth and the children for what must have been the tenth time, and flung her arms around David to whisper her thanks for his kindness, she stepped into the carriage, where Maude waited, and they started out. Two drivers sat on the box, armed with shotguns, and outriders rode on either side of the coach. Tom intended to ride only for an hour or so, then tie his horse to the back of the coach, next to Sylvia's mare, and join her inside for a while.

They had left the castle behind and were on the open road when Sylvia tried to strike up a conversation with her maid, who was sitting with an extremely glum expression on her face.

"Have you ever been to London before, Maude?" she asked brightly.

"No, ma'am, I 'aven't, and I 'ear tell it's a terrible place for young girls to be," the girl replied, her eyes opening wide at the thought of what she had been told could happen to them.

"Do you mean you didn't want to come with me?" Sylvia was surprised, for she had only just noticed that the girl seemed unhappy. "You should have told me, and I would have had someone else come in your stead. I would not have made you join me against your will."

"I'd 'ave lost my job and been back to scrubbing floors if I 'ad, ma'am," Maude said.

"And that would have been even worse than London?" Sylvia suggested with a twinkle in her eyes.

"Much worse, for I'd not 'ave been with you, ma'am, and I've been 'appiest since I worked for you."

"Oh, I don't think you'll find London as bad as you believe. Lady Lavinia's household is a happy one and you'll make friends with the other servants, I'm sure." Sylvia suddenly thought of something. "Did you, perhaps, leave a gentleman friend behind at the castle?"

"Oh, no, ma'am!" the girl exclaimed, quite shocked. "I don't let any of 'em get their 'ands on me."

With a smile, Sylvia picked up the book she had brought with her. Although she had not expected brilliant conversation from Maude, the journey promised to be exceedingly dull unless Tom spent much of his time inside. She almost prayed for the weather to be inclement so that he could more easily be prevailed upon to do so.

Cook had packed a basket of food for a picnic luncheon, so they made their first stop close to a small village through which a pretty stream meandered. Sylvia was glad to get out of the carriage and stretch her legs, walking down to the banks after she had eaten her share of the cold chicken and ham pasties. It was a delightful, peaceful place and it reminded her of the time she and Tom had refreshed themselves at a similar spot not very long ago.

She turned around and saw him coming toward her, as if he had also remembered, but the first words he spoke were in a more serious vein.

"I'm afraid we'll have to change our plans a little," he said quietly. "One of the villagers just told Will Coachman that a group of Reformers have been seen marching this way, and I think it would perhaps be prudent to avoid them if we can."

"Would they really try to stop us?" Sylvia asked in some surprise. "From what David has told me, they're just trying to make their voices heard in Parliament."

"I'd rather not take any chances, with you in the carriage, my dear," Tom said firmly. "We'll turn off and take a lane that runs in a more easterly direction for a few miles, and then get back onto this one a little further along. I just wanted to let you know in case you should worry when we make the turn."

"Whatever you think best, Tom," she said softly, "but don't mention anything about it in Maude's presence, for she is already quite nervous about going to London. Do you want to leave now, or do we have time for a drink of lemonade and a piece of Cook's seed cake?"

He smiled. "Oh, I think we have time for that, and afterward I believe I'll tie up my horse and ride inside with you for an hour or so."

She had noticed lately that his eyes held a new warmth when he looked at her, and she found herself unaccountably flushing and feeling a little breathless when he paid special attention to her needs, as in this instance.

He took her arm and they walked back to the carriage together, helping themselves to a little more food before Maude packed it away and they were ready to resume their journey.

But they had waited too long. They had just started out and had not yet reached the lane where they were to turn off when a group of about thirty men, most of them dressed in work clothes, came walking toward them.

Sylvia heard their voices in the distance and glanced across at Tom, who reached up and knocked on the roof, an obvious signal, for the coachman immediately reined in the horses and the carriage came to a halt.

Sylvia leaned toward the window and saw that there were more than a dozen poorly dressed men who just stood and stared as if they had never seen a carriage before. Tom's hands were firm but not rough as he grasped her shoulders and pulled her back against the squabs. Glancing toward the other window, she saw there were men on that side also, peering in.

"Why did you signal Will to stop?" Sylvia asked, frowning.

"Because I want no one hurt if I can help it. If one of them was injured by a horse's hoof or a carriage wheel, they'd put the blame on us and try to retaliate. There's sure to be a leader among them, so we'll just wait and see if anyone comes forward. There are four of our men outside with shotguns, don't forget, but they have orders not to attack first." He took her hand in his and pressed it reassuringly.

" 'Ere's where all t'money goes, lads. In fine carriages an' fancy uniforms. These are t'ones as sit in Parliament an' put up t'price of bread so 'igh we can't afford it," one angry voice shouted.

"Hunt and Liberty," a dozen or more men yelled, while "We want representation," could be heard in the background, and "Our own man in Parliament."

Maude had a kerchief to her face and was sniveling loudly. "I'm going to be sick," she whispered.

"No you're not, my girl," Sylvia said, more sternly than she'd ever spoken to her before. "Sit up straight and pull yourself together."

The maid looked at her with frightened eyes, then blew her nose hard and put away the kerchief, though her lips still trembled.

"Is there anything we can do?" Sylvia asked Tom quietly.

"At the moment they're all noise and no action, and I hope it will stay that way. I'm still counting on there being a leader who will have the sense to call them off before they become too incensed," Tom said, giving her a comforting smile.

"No corn laws," a voice closer to the carriage called; then someone shouted, "Let's show 'em we mean business." Angry-looking faces moved closer to the windows and Tom put an arm around Sylvia's shoulders as they felt the coach rocking slightly back and forth.

"Stop that at once." The voice held a note of authority. "You heard me, take your hands off that carriage now."

The men at the windows dropped back and the coach was steady once more.

"Now, move along with you, in single file. We've more to do than harass innocent travelers, you fools." The voice sounded nearer now, and the faces looked sullen, but the men were moving along past the windows as they'd been told to do.

Then there was no one there except one man, dressed in plain country clothes and wearing a tall white hat, which he doffed as he bowed low to the occupants of the carriage.

"My sincere apologies, sir, ladies," he boomed. "The lads get carried away sometimes, but we don't need violence for our cause, just honesty, fair wages, and a voice in our country's government. Your restraint was much appreciated, for I know you're well-armed, and I promise to give them the rough side of my tongue when I catch up with them. Good day to you."

With a flourish he replaced the hat on his head and strode off after the others.

Tom gave a double rap on the roof with his cane, and the coachman opened a small hatch.

"There's no point in going out of our way now," Tom said. "Let's stick to our plan, and we'll make up for lost time if the road is good enough. I want to reach the inn by six o'clock at the latest."

When they were settled once more and the carriage was moving at a steady pace, Sylvia asked, "Did you notice that ridiculous white top hat he was wearing, Tom?"

"I did," he replied a little grimly. "He was one of the many educated leaders they have behind them, and just what I was hoping to find leading that mob. Hunt started by wearing a hat like that, and now all the leaders do so in order to stand out. Do you know that you weren't even trembling? Does nothing ever frighten you?"

"Of course it does. I was trembling inside while trying to seem calm outside, for I was quite fearful that we would be turned over," she admitted softly. "What would you have done if they had succeeded?"

"They wouldn't have," Tom assured her. "The outriders and guards had orders to shoot only if they became violent and attacked the coach or the horses. We were outnumbered, of course, but four shotguns, two rifles, and my own pistol would have more than evened things up."

A muffled sniff came from the corner where Maude still huddled, and Sylvia reached into her reticule and withdrew a bottle of hartshorn. "Take a sniff of this, Maude, and you'll feel much better," she instructed, and the girl did as she was ordered, then returned the bottle. A moment later she sat up straight, as though determined to be as courageous as her mistress.

They had actually lost no more than ten minutes, although it had seemed much more than that at the time, and with no further delays they reached the inn where they were to spend the night just a little before six o'clock, as Tom had hoped.

He jumped down first and helped both Sylvia and her maid down; then Maude stayed behind to be sure the luggage needed for the night was removed. As they entered the hostelry, which was small but had an excellent reputation for food and comfortable beds, the robust landlord came forward to greet them.

"Welcome, my lady, my lord," he said. "Do you require rooms for the night?"

"One for the lady and her maid, and one for myself," Tom told him, "and a private parlor for dinner in about an hour's time."

"Excellent, sir. I trust you had a comfortable journey?" he asked as he led them up the narrow stairs. "We heard a rumor that a band of radicals overturned a coach about twenty miles up the road."

"Really?" Tom said in feigned surprise. "We just came from that direction and saw no overturned carriage. Are you sure you are not mistaken?"

"Then the rumor must have been false. I thought so myself, for those folk are not usually prone to violence. My wife was all for sending for the yeomanry, but I told her it was probably all a tale. Now," he said, throwing open the door of a pleasantly furnished room with a dormer window, a fireplace, four-poster bed, dressing table, and bedside commodes. "Will this be suitable for you, my lady? There's a cot in the dressing room for the maid."

"Perfectly," Sylvia told him as he entered and put a light to the fire that was already laid, then looked around to be sure that all was in order.

As the door closed behind him, she sank gratefully onto the bed. It had been a long day and she had been much more frightened than she cared to admit even to herself.

Not five minutes later, when Maude and the inn-keeper's wife came in with hot water, they found her fast asleep.

"I think a large glass of sherry before your supper is going to be doctor's orders for you tonight, my dear," Tom said as he poured a full glass and handed it to Sylvia. "You respond remarkably well to crises, I find, but I want to make sure you get a good night's sleep."

Sylvia took a sip, then chuckled. "I've already had almost an hour's sleep, but had to pay for it by wash-ing in cold water. Maude had not the heart to wake me until it was almost time for me to join you."

"How is she feeling?" he asked. "Not that I intend to give her a glass of sherry," he hastened to add, "but I was quite surprised at how upset she became, and how well you handled her."

"Oh, someone has been filling her head with terri-ble tales of what can happen to a young girl in Lon-don, and if it were not for the fact that she'd be back to scrubbing floors if she left my service, I'm sure she would never have come with me." Sylvia gave a short laugh. "As Mama was on her best behavior at the wedding, you probably did not realize that she has the vapors every time Papa threatens to cut her allowance, and as that is almost a monthly occurrence, you can imagine, I'm sure, how much practice Louise and I have had at handling them."

"Be grateful you did not inherit that trait, my dear, for it is inherited, though accentuated when it achieves its objective every time." He looked thoughtful, for he was beginning to realize that the twins had really had only each other to rely on in that household once Elizabeth was married. No wonder the separation had been so traumatic for Sylvia.

"I'm thankful that Maude recovers faster than Mama, for she appeared completely back to normal when I left her, but I hope she does not tell the kitchen help that our carriage was stopped, or the innkeeper will wonder why you did not tell him."

Tom suddenly looked as starchy as David did on occasion, Sylvia decided, and she wondered what he was about to say. She did not have long to wait.

"I am not in the habit of telling tales to innkeepers, no matter how ingratiating they try to be," he said shortly, and took another sip of his wine.

Sylvia's instinct was to make a sharp retort, but she knew that if she did, their budding friendship might be shattered, and she most decidedly did not want that to happen. Wisely, she held her tongue and concentrated on the quite delicious dinner of roast pheasant, served with a variety of vegetables, including potatoes, and conserves.

After a few minutes of silence, Tom looked at Sylvia's downcast face as she concentrated a little too carefully on her meal. "I'm sorry, my dear, if I sounded too abrupt," he said gently. "I meant no criticism whatsoever of you, but what you said reminded me of something that happened years ago that I prefer not to talk about."

She looked into his eyes and saw something there that made her heart give a little lurch. He might be just a poor doctor whom her papa would never allow her to marry, but for tonight, she decided, she was going to pretend he was an eligible suitor and already a little in love with her.

She smiled softly. "I understand, though I didn't for a moment. I never thanked you for being so calm and comforting when those men were on the verge of tipping the carriage, for I know that they were about to do so," she said huskily. "I'm so very glad you volunteered to escort me to London, for I do not care to think what it would have been like had I been alone."

Tom remembered how she had felt when he placed his arms around her to shield her in the carriage, and he longed to do so again, but knew that she was very innocent and he must not frighten her. He would take it very slowly while they were in London, and perhaps when she had had her fill of parties and balls, he could bring her home again and court her the way she deserved. Not that he would not still escort her to the various entertainments, for he intended to be at her side as much as he possibly could.

"Thanks are not necessary between us, my dear," he assured her. "I'm only glad I was there at the right time to be of service. We should be at Lady Lavinia's house before dinner tomorrow night if all goes well. Do you want me to order a picnic for lunch again, or would you prefer to stop at an inn?"

"I'd prefer a picnic if possible," Sylvia told him, imagining sitting on the bank of a stream with him again, "for there will not be many more opportunities to have picnics once the colder weather sets in."

"I'll arrange it before I retire for the night," he assured her, "and if it's anything like this dinner, it will be quite delicious. Would you like to have tea now, or would you prefer to try a glass of port with me?"

"Oh, tea, please," she said quickly, "for if I have any more wine I may fall asleep here and waste that wonderful feather bed upstairs."

Tom's thoughts immediately went along lines he could not admit to, causing him to ring the bell a little too savagely, for the innkeeper was there in a second, anxiously inquiring if everything was to their liking.

"It was perfect," Tom assured him, "but now the young lady would like tea, and I would like a glass of port."

The innkeeper hastened to do his bidding, and while

she waited, Sylvia concentrated hard on keeping awake, for she had suddenly become very tired indeed.

Tom, now under control, smiled and raised an eyebrow. "If he doesn't hurry with that tea, I can see that I may have to carry you up those stairs," he told her. "What time would you like to leave in the morning?"

"I will be ready at whatever time you say," she assured him. "I assume we'll have breakfast here before we set out."

"I'll order it tonight for eight o'clock in the morning, and then we should be able to get the coach packed and be back on the road before nine," he said. "And I'm sure you'll be very glad when we get to Grosvenor Street."

"Not really," she told him with a warm smile. "You have made it one of the most comfortable journeys I have ever undertaken."

He grinned. "Well, it's not everyone who can place you in the very center of a radical meeting, is it?" he asked. "I'm afraid I cannot promise any such excitement on the return journey."

"Oh," she exclaimed. "Are you going to escort me home also? You really are much nicer to me than I deserve, Tom, and I'm hoping that you will be a frequent visitor at Lady Lavinia's house, for I know she'll be most happy to see you there."

Just then the tea and port arrived, and they sipped them slowly, both of them quite weary after the excitement of the day, but neither wanting to be the first to suggest leaving.

Finally Tom saw Sylvia's eyelids drooping, and he went over and drew her up from the chair. "As you are to be down here by eight o'clock in the morning, my dear, you really must get some sleep. And if you would like the rest of your tea, I'll be glad to carry it up for you." He reached for the cup, but Sylvia put a hand gently on his arm.

"It's all right, truly," she murmured. "I'll go quietly and leave you alone to contemplate your folly in offering to be my escort to town and back. But don't think to get out of it now, for you agreed to do so and it's much too late to back out."

Her eyes were half-closed, and he thought she wouldn't even know if he placed the lightest of kisses upon her forehead, but when he did so her blue eyes opened wide and her smile was even wider. "You do the nicest things, Tom," she murmured. "Do you think anyone would mind if I stayed here all night?"

"They might not, but I would," he told her regretfully. "Come, I'll help you," and he took her by the hand and led her up the stairs and into the waiting arms of her maid.

"She's exhausted, Maude," he said. "The sooner you get her into bed, the better. Don't let her forget that she's having breakfast with me at eight and we leave at nine in the morning."

"Yes, sir," the maid said. "I won't forget."

6

Lady Lavinia Trevelyan had been eagerly awaiting the Colchesters' coach all day, flitting to each of the windows and gazing hopefully along the street more times than she cared to count, and so it was a disappointment to her that when it did arrive she was in the kitchen making last-minute changes to the dinner menu for that evening.

She heard the sound of the doorbell, however, and came as quickly as she could without actually breaking into an unladylike run. But Sylvia was already inside, and she flung herself into Lady Lavinia's arms with a cry of delight, for this was her favorite adopted aunt.

When the hugs were over, Lady Lavinia looked around for Colchester, but all she saw was a young man who looked vaguely familiar, but she wasn't quite sure why.

"Did you have a comfortable journey, my dear," she asked, "and where can Colchester be? I was sure he would not permit you to travel all this way alone."

"I didn't travel alone, dear aunt," Sylvia said happily. "You've met David's friend Dr. Tom Radcliff, haven't you?"

"Oh, of course I have. I'm delighted to see you again, sir. Come along into the drawing room. It's too late for tea and too early for dinner, but I had the butler open a bottle of claret in case Colchester should be in need of a stimulant when he got here." Lady Lavinia chattered nervously on as she led the way, until Sylvia took her by the arm and made her sit beside her on a sofa.

"Now, let me tell you why Tom is here instead of

David," Sylvia said calmly. "Tom is a doctor, as I know you will recall, and he comes to London several times a year. By the luckiest of chances he happened to be coming at the same time that I was, and he offered to escort me so that David need not leave Elizabeth alone for several days."

"How very nice of him," Lady Lavinia said, beaming happily. "You will stay to dinner now that you're here, Dr. Radcliff, won't you?"

"It's very kind of you, my lady, but I'd best get settled into my own accommodations before I socialize. I'll gladly accept that glass of claret, however, while the coach is being unloaded," Tom reminded her, "and then Will Coachman can drive me to my place with my baggage."

Lady Lavinia jumped up quickly and returned with the tray and glasses. "Please help yourself, and perhaps Sylvia needs a little something after the tedious journey."

"It wasn't the least bit tedious, Aunt Lavinia. In fact, it was quite exciting, but I'll tell you all about it tonight after Tom leaves, and I will have just a very small glass, Tom, to keep you company." She smiled her thanks as he handed her a glass.

"We're going to have such an interesting time, my dear, for when I let it be known that you are staying with me for the Little Season, everybody wanted to see you again," Lavinia said excitedly.

"But I'm not here for the Little Season," Sylvia protested. "I've come to keep you company during the next month or so, and I don't expect to go out very much at all."

"Well, I don't intend to stay home every night," Lady Lavinia retorted, "and I can't very well go out alone, can I?"

"You're outmaneuvered, my dear girl," Tom said with a chuckle, "so you might just as well give in gracefully."

He stayed about a half-hour, then left, promising to come by in the morning to see if there was anything Sylvia or Lady Lavinia needed.

Lady Lavinia had planned a quiet dinner at home, and perhaps a game of cards, but after listening to Sylvia's account of what had happened to them on the road the previous afternoon, she insisted Sylvia retire for the evening.

"I have never heard of anything so shocking in all my life, and had I been in your place I would have been prostrate for a week afterward. Dear me, when I think what might so easily have happened to you with ruffians of that sort, I feel quite beside myself," she said with a little shudder, clasping Sylvia's hand as if for reassurance. "You may not realize it now, my dear, but you must be quite exhausted after such happenings. If you have an early night, you'll wake up refreshed in the morning and ready to meet all the people who are so anxious to see you again."

Sylvia did not feel at all tired, and would actually have preferred to stay talking a little longer, for as soon as she had entered this house again, memories of the last time she was here, with Louise, came rushing back. Aunt Lavinia's excitement at seeing her had helped push them somewhere to the back of her mind, but she knew that as soon as she was alone they would return.

There was no arguing with the dear lady, however, who Sylvia knew wanted only the best for her, so she bade her good night and made her way up the stairs to the bedchamber that had been prepared for her. It was, of course, the same one that she had shared before with Louise.

Maude was almost finished putting her clothes away, and had set aside a number of gowns to take down and iron for tomorrow. "Will you be needing your riding habit in the morning, ma'am?" she asked.

"Not yet, Maude. I'll wear the lilac morning gown, I think, but you may as well iron the habit also, for then it will be ready in case I do get the opportunity to ride. The deep yellow gown will be the most suitable in the afternoon, I believe," she said, "for there'll probably be guests for tea."

She walked over to the armoire and opened the

door. "You can press this green-and-white lace gown also, for it will be appropriate for anything that Lady Lavinia plans to do in the evening." She heaved a sigh, realizing that her aunt was right and that she was very tired. "I'm afraid I had quite forgotten what a lot of dressing and undressing one does in town. No wonder Elizabeth insisted I have so many new things made."

Maude put the clothes aside and started to ready her mistress for bed, helping her into the nightrail she had already set out. "Would you like me to brush your hair, ma'am, for it'll make you feel more sleepy," she suggested, unpinning it and starting to do so. "Then I'll get you a glass of warm milk."

"Thank you, Maude, that would be nice, and then I won't need you until morning. You can bring me a cup of tea about eight o'clock."

It seemed so strange, she thought, when she was at last alone, to be here in this house without Louise. But she would get used to it, as she had done at Colchester Castle. It was understandable, she told herself, after they had been so close all their lives. Louise now had her own life to live, and she herself would live hers eventually.

But why was she so sure that her twin was not happy? Why did she feel something was wrong?

She sipped the warm milk until she started to feel drowsy, then put down the glass and snuggled under the covers. It did not seem more than two minutes later, though it was, in fact, several hours, when she awoke from a dream in which Louise had been holding out her arms and begging for her help. Sylvia was covered in icy perspiration and she could still see the fear on her sister's face.

After that she slept only fitfully, tossing and turning on the comfortable feather mattress until Maude came in with her morning tea, and she had taken hardly more than a sip of the delicious beverage when Lady Lavinia came bustling into the room.

"I just wanted to be sure that you slept well, my dear," Lady Lavinia assured her, peering through her rather shortsighted eyes at Sylvia's face, "and you must surely have, for indeed you look full of that lovely flush of youth. I can't say the same for myself, though. I didn't sleep a single wink for thinking about your experience with those dreadful men."

"I'm sorry I told you and upset you so, Aunt Lavinia." Sylvia was contrite. "It was not nearly so dreadful as it sounds, and you must put it out of your mind completely and not think of it again. I came to no harm, and now I'm longing to know what you have planned for today."

Lady Lavinia sat on a small chair by the bed. "Well, this morning I decided to forgo my usual visit to the shops and stay in, for there'll be time enough tomorrow for that, and I'd be surprised if your young doctor did not call to see how you are. Then, this afternoon I will be at home to my friends and I expect quite a few of them will come for tea and to renew their acquaintance with you."

"And will you be going out this evening?" Sylvia asked.

"Oh, yes, for Lady Dartmouth is having one of her delightful musical evenings that I would not miss for anything. You must accompany me, for I know you will enjoy it so much," Lady Lavinia told her enthusiastically.

Sylvia smiled and tried to look pleased, for though a musical evening was not her favorite form of entertainment, she would never have let Lady Lavinia know. The twins had always liked her, but during their stay with her for the Season they had grown to love this gentle little lady who had the heart of a lion within her tiny bosom.

"Now, I know that you must be eager to be up and dressed, so I'll not delay you further, my dear," Lady Lavinia twittered. "Cook is preparing a substantial breakfast, so I'll see you downstairs in about half an hour."

As soon as she left, Sylvia rose, stretching lazily, then rang for Maude. Once she was on her feet, she found that despite her restless night she really was eager to be up and about, and a little hungry for the delicious breakfast she knew would be waiting below.

Lady Lavinia was right, for Tom Radcliff arrived in the late morning and sat talking to her for some minutes before Sylvia came in. He was more observant than his hostess had been, and when she left to tell Cook there would be a guest for an early luncheon, he turned to Sylvia with a puzzled look.

"Did Lady Lavinia wear you out last night, my dear? I would swear you look more tired than you did when you first arrived here yesterday," he remarked with a frown.

"You have sharper eyes than my aunt, Tom, but I'm not one of your patients, so you needn't fear I will go into a decline," she said a little more sharply than she intended, then, realizing it, smiled apologetically. "I'm sorry. It's nice of you to be concerned about me. The truth is, however, that not only did we not go out, but Aunt Lavinia insisted upon such an early night that, once in bed, I had difficulty sleeping."

He grinned. "That's sometimes the case. Lady Lavinia told me that tonight you are to attend a musical evening. My only hope is that you do not fall asleep in the middle of it, or it will not make a very good impression upon Lady Dartmouth."

She laughed. "Why don't you come too, and then you can give me a little nudge if I should do anything so dreadful as to nod off," she suggested, then could have kicked herself, for she realized that despite Tom's friendship with David, she knew nothing about his background—and did not care—but the *beau monde* might feel differently.

"Lady Lavinia has already asked me, but I regret to say I have a previous commitment," he told her. "I'm having dinner with two of King George's physicians. The following night, however, I am to have the pleasure of escorting you both to Sally Jersey's ball, which officially opens the Little Season."

Sylvia sighed with relief. If Sally Jersey had invited him, then he must be acceptable, for she was one of the patronesses of Almack's, the exclusive assembly rooms where only the *ton* were permitted to dance sedately and partake of the meager refreshments.

Luncheon was a happy meal, with Tom and Sylvia telling Lady Lavinia stories of his more eccentric patients, and before he left he invited Sylvia to go riding in the park with him at eight o'clock the next morning. She accepted with alacrity, for this had been one of the things she and Louise had enjoyed doing most when in London, and unless they had been extremely late home the night before, they would be up and out on horseback as soon as it was light enough to see where they were going.

The door had hardly closed behind him when the house became a hive of activity. Additional chairs were placed in the drawing room, and under the direction of Bates, the butler, the maids were set to repolishing the large urn and silver trays in case the slightest hint of tarnish had dared to form since they were used a week ago.

"Cook is baking ratafia cakes, almond tarts, and gingerbreads, which I believe were the favorites of you and Louise, and there's a rich seed cake and a lemon cake already baked and cooling on the kitchen table," Lady Lavinia reported as she bustled in to oversee the preparations. "Are you going to run up and change into that lovely yellow gown I saw hanging outside the armoire, my dear?"

There was plenty of time before anyone would be there, but Sylvia knew that the excited little lady would be on edge if she wasn't ready and waiting a full half-hour ahead of the first callers, so she went quickly upstairs to do as she was bidden. Then she sat in a corner of the drawing room out of everyone's way as her aunt inspected every crack and crevice to make sure not a single speck of dust had been missed.

As the afternoon progressed, Sylvia, who was seated at the tea urn pouring oolong into the dainty china cups, could not help but admire her aunt's accomplishment as a hostess, for though she had never married, she had as a young girl been well-schooled in such duties by her own mama.

When the guests arrived, she personally greeted them, asking after their health and their families, even though she had probably seen them only days before. Then she took them to meet anyone they might not have met for some time, and finally seated them with their friends, signaling a maid to procure tea from Sylvia and pass the huge trays of food for their selection.

Then, as guests announced their reluctant need to depart, she was on her feet once more, expressing her pleasure in their visit and the hope that they would come again soon, while escorting them to the door. Sylvia hazarded a guess that she and her sisters were probably the only ones who had any idea which of the gossiping, tale-bearing guests Lady Lavinia did not really care for, as she put it, for her aunt had been taught she must never express anything as strong as a dislike for anyone.

"How was the musical evening?" Tom asked as they set out for the park with a groom trailing far behind.

"Not too hard to bear," Sylvia told him with a grin. "The soprano screeched only when she tried to hit the very highest of notes, and the piano recital was really quite passable."

They rode in single file through the narrow streets, for at that hour, though there were few riders or carriages about, there were many carts carrying anything from bolts of cloth to fruit and vegetables to various shops and markets.

Tom was leading the way, and he put up a hand to signal her to stop while a stagecoach rattled by, with passengers packed together on top, where luggage was also piled illegally, and many heads peered out from the inside. The coachman was shouting at and cruelly whipping the four horses, for it seemed they had made a late start.

When they reached the park a few minutes later, Sylvia said, "I don't know who fared the worse on that coach, the horses or the passengers. Did you see how tightly packed together they were, and how one woman seemed forced to cling to the side rail or be thrown off? Surely the coach was overloaded?"

"Coach travel is fraught with hazard, I am afraid, and passengers are thrown off quite frequently," Tom told her gravely, "and they will continue to be as long as Parliament permits one passenger for every sixteen inches of seating, or four per row, both inside and out."

"But that is ridiculous, Tom," Sylvia protested. "Even four people of my size could not sit in so small a space."

"Without other means of relatively cheap travel, they have no alternative. What is more, many stages overturn," he said grimly. "They are dangerously high off the ground, inclined to rock at high speeds, over-loaded, and are driven quite frequently by coachmen who drink intoxicants to keep out the cold."

"Could a coach like David's turn over so easily?" Sylvia asked, frowning, for she had thought the only hazard to travel was that of being held up by highwaymen.

Tom grinned. "Not while I am escorting you," he said, "for I would not allow it to happen. You've nothing to worry about, for I doubt that you'll ever need to travel by stage." He looked around carefully. "There's no one else in sight. Would you like to try a gallop?"

"Dare we?" It was just what she had hoped for, but had expected to see others riding at this hour.

"Nothing ventured, nothing gained," Tom said, and forged ahead, with Sylvia close behind him.

They were fortunate to meet no one, and Tom was the first to bring his horse to a slower pace, Sylvia following suit a moment later. The groom was no-where to be seen, but neither of them noticed.

"Did you find out last night the condition of King George's health?" Sylvia asked as they made their way slowly back toward the entrance.

"I'm afraid he's quite deteriorated," Tom said, "and the physicians told me that his hair and his beard, which now reaches his chest, are as white as driven snow. He does not, of course, know that the queen is dead. He has been blind and deaf for some time, but he is now weakening and wasting away, something that is only to be expected of a man who is eighty-one years old."

"It's sad, though," Sylvia murmured. "I'm sure I'd rather die than live the way he has done for these last twenty years and more."

"The choice is not ours to make," Tom said quietly, "but there is little doubt that the Prince Regent will be King George IV before long, and what an extravagant king he will be. Already he has plans for enlarging Buckingham House to serve as his royal palace."

"I wonder what will become of Carlton House then," Sylvia mused. "I suppose he will get his own way in the end and divorce Princess Caroline, for he turned down the idea of a formal separation. I wonder if he really will marry again."

Tom smiled. "I'm not sure whether he will be allowed the divorce, for it would not be popular with the common people. They like her much more than him, I'm afraid. As for his marrying again, I know there's a rumor that he will do so, but if he did, I believe it would be only to produce an heir to the throne. He'd be foolish to do so for any other reason, for he's had little joy in his relationships with women."

"You sound as if you are against marriage, Tom," Sylvia teased. "Have you had little joy in your relationships also?"

He turned to stare at her in surprise, then started to laugh. "My relationships are none of your concern, you minx, but I am certainly not against marriage. I believe it to be an excellent institution, but," he said firmly, "to deliberately change the subject, I was wondering if you and Lady Lavinia are going to the Worthingtons' card party tomorrow night."

Sylvia laughed. "Was I treading on hallowed ground?" she asked, then said, "I believe we are going, for Aunt Lavinia loves a game of cards."

"Do you play often?" he asked, mildly curious.

"I play whist on such occasions, provided it's for the

lowest possible stakes, but Louise and I have always refused to play piquet," she asserted firmly.

"For any special reason?" Tom asked, for it was a popular game for two people.

"Because of Papa." She was serious now. "He loves gambling passionately, and piquet is his favorite game, though he must not be very good at it. You see, Papa's gambling is the reason we have lost all the land we once owned, and the house would have gone long ago if he could have used it as a stake. It's good that the deed does not permit it."

"You've pretty good reason not to play the game, then, I would say," Tom said quietly, "and I'm sure you'll be able to play whist there, or even not play at all if you do not wish to do so."

"Are you going to be there?" she asked hopefully.

"I'm afraid not, but your aunt has asked me to an early dinner tonight, and to escort you to Sally Jersey's ball, so I'll see you this evening, and as your escort I'll expect at least one waltz," he pronounced, reining in his mount, for they had reached the Grosvenor Street house.

"Of course," Sylvia said, secretly delighted, "I'll save the one before supper for you, and then you can take us both in to what promises to be an excellent meal, for she is known not to stint, I believe."

"It will be my pleasure," he said, smiling fondly at her, for he meant it. "And now, if you like, I'll help you dismount, then take your mare back to the stable. It was a delightful morning and I hope you will allow me to take you riding again."

"Yes, please," Sylvia said guilelessly. "Anytime you wish." Then, leaving him with both mounts, she ran lightly up the steps and into the house.

7

It was almost a week since Lady Jersey's ball, and Sylvia had seen little of Tom, for he was working with one of the surgeons on an experimental project, often well into the night.

And the worst thing was that it had been such a delightful evening, or so she had thought at the time.

She had worn one of the new gowns that Elizabeth had insisted on having made, a frothy affair of pale blue satin covered with silver lace, and with long silver ribbons falling from a bow beneath the bodice and down the front almost to the floor. In her hair were matching silver combs, and when Tom had arrived to escort them, he had looked spellbound as she had come slowly down the stairs, being careful not to trip.

After a light meal they had left for the ball, and Tom had danced a delightful dreamy waltz with her, and had later taken both Sylvia and Lady Lavinia in to a supper that made them regret having eaten even so much as a morsel beforehand. He had been most attentive, making sure she did not feel even the slightest chill when they stepped out into the brisk early-morning air afterward.

But it was then that he had told them he would be engaged for almost the whole of the following week, and though Sylvia was disappointed, she knew that his work was his real purpose in coming to town, and that she could not complain.

However, she had missed him more than she would have believed, and this morning felt unaccountably restless. The weather was so dull and cloudy that Lady

Lavinia had felt disinclined to visit the shops as she had originally intended.

"Are you thinking of paying calls this afternoon?" Sylvia asked her aunt when they had finished a rather late luncheon. "If not, why don't we go for a drive somewhere, perhaps to Kensington Gardens, or to Kew?"

Lady Lavinia shook her head. "Not Kensington Gardens, my dear, for of late it has become the popular place for the cits and their families to gather. No one of quality goes there anymore. As for Kew Gardens, much of their beauty depends on a sunny day, so you could hardly call today quite suitable."

"Aunt Lavinia, I've never known you to appear so condescending," Sylvia said with considerable amusement.

Lady Lavinia flushed. "It's nonetheless true, Sylvia, for I went there one day and was most embarrassed. Hyde Park is now the only place to drive. But I really should return some overdue calls, so perhaps we could do our duty first, then take a ride in the park?"

She looked a little anxious, so Sylvia leaned forward and put a hand on her arm, her blue eyes twinkling. "I was only teasing, and I'm sure you must have the right of it, dear aunt. Of course we must return the calls, and then if we have time we will see if any of your friends are in the park."

They ordered the coach to be brought around, and soon were on their way to the first of several calls, where they sipped tea and nibbled on cakes and biscuits, and discussed which people had attended which party the night before—and particularly what they had worn.

They stayed no longer than a half-hour at the houses of three of their acquaintances, and then, as they stepped into the carriage once more, Lady Lavinia took one look at Sylvia's face, and they both began to laugh like naughty schoolgirls playing truant. "You can now take us to the park," Lady Lavinia told her coachman as she tried to muster a little dignity. He muttered something to himself that was quite unintelligible, then whipped up the horses.

At first the park was quite full with carriages and gentlemen on horseback exchanging greetings or stopping to converse, and as they made their way slowly through, stopping to talk, or waving to first one and then another carriage, they did not notice that a mist was descending.

"I had a letter from Elizabeth today, and you won't believe what my little nephew did last week," Sylvia told her aunt. "He was in the study with David, whom, as you know, he adores, and had crept behind a large chair. He was so quiet that David forgot all about him and left to go out riding, closing the door behind him."

"Oh, dear," Lady Lavinia murmured. "Poor little fellow. He must have screamed the place down before someone heard him."

Sylvia laughed. "Not he," she said. "Nanny missed him and swears she looked in there but saw no sign of him. Then she and Elizabeth searched the castle and were becoming quite frightened, when out he toddled, for Nanny had left the door ajar when she looked in there. He was carrying a page he had torn from one of David's priceless antique volumes. He was very proud of himself and happily led them back to the chair, behind which they found the binding with the rest of the pages scattered around."

"What a little monkey he is," Aunt Lavinia declared. "But what did David say?"

"He apparently took it very well, saying it was his own fault for not keeping an eye on him. Of course, he spent the rest of the afternoon putting his antique books on a high shelf that little John will not be able to reach until he's old enough to know better," Sylvia said with a laugh.

Lady Lavinia smiled indulgently, for she was very fond of Elizabeth's children. Then she glanced around and was startled to see that most of the carriages were leaving. An early-winter mist had begun to swirl around them, giving the park a strangely eerie appearance.

She leaned forward and instructed her coachman to take them home, then turned and saw Sylvia holding her arm and gasping with pain. "What is it, my dear?" she asked, frightened when she saw how pale Sylvia looked in the gray light. "Did you hurt yourself?"

"I must have, when the coach swung around," Sylvia gasped. "I don't remember doing so, but it's making me feel quite faint."

Lady Lavinia put an arm around her niece's shoulders and urged the coachman to hurry; then, as soon as they reached Grosvenor Street, she helped her down and told the coachman to wait while she wrote a note.

A footman assisted them up the front steps and into the house and they made Sylvia comfortable on a sofa, whereupon Lady Lavinia went to her writing desk and started to reach for a piece of paper.

"What are you doing?" Sylvia asked, still holding her sore arm but attempting to sit up. "Whom are you writing to?"

"I'm sending for Tom to come right away, of course," Lady Lavinia said gently. "If he's home, I know he'll be here in ten minutes at the most."

"Oh, no, please don't. I'm beginning to feel much better now, and I believe the pain is easing," Sylvia said earnestly. "I don't want Tom to come rushing over here and making a fuss."

"Are you sure, my dear?" the older lady asked, pausing and looking carefully at her. "You do seem much better than you did, for the color is returning to your cheeks, but I still think he should take a look at that arm."

"We can ask him about it later. Please don't disturb him now," Sylvia begged. "I'm sure it's nothing, and I probably felt faint because I've been having a few too many late nights. I think I'll stay home this evening, and you can make my excuses to Lady Winchester."

"If you say so," Lady Lavinia said a little doubtfully, "but I think we'd better get you into bed right away."

Sylvia made no argument against that, and allowed herself to be assisted up the stairs to her room, where

Maude helped her off with her gown. To her surprise, there was not a single mark or swelling on her arm.

"Does it hurt when I touch it?" Lady Lavinia asked, and Sylvia shook her head.

"It doesn't hurt in the slightest now, but I didn't imagine it, I know," she insisted. "I don't think I'll come down for dinner. Maude can bring me up a little soup."

"I'll bring you the soup, for I'm not going out tonight and leaving you here like this," Lady Lavinia said firmly, but Sylvia laid a hand on her arm.

"Please, you must go, or I will feel dreadful at keeping you from something you always enjoy." Sylvia was adamant. "Maude will stay with me in case I need anything."

With a worried sigh, Lady Lavinia left her and went to change for the evening, stopping by again before she left to make sure that Sylvia had eaten something and was comfortable.

Maude was sitting close to the bed, just staring at her, and finding this somewhat disturbing, Sylvia asked her to go downstairs and see if they had some of the sleep-inducing herbal tea her nanny had always given them, and when the maid brought it she dismissed her for the night, telling her she did not wish to be disturbed until the morning.

Sylvia sipped the familiar beverage slowly, remembering all the times either she or Louise had been given it before, and soon it took effect and she slipped into a deep, dreamless sleep.

She awoke almost twelve hours later, feeling completely refreshed, to find Maude standing beside the bed, a cup of hot chocolate in her hand and a worried expression on her face.

"Are you all right, ma'am?" the girl asked.

Sylvia stretched lazily before sitting up in bed, puzzled by the maid's question. Then she remembered. "I feel wonderful this morning, thank you, Maude. And I'm very, very hungry, so get out my pink morning gown and I'll dress and go downstairs as soon as I finish this."

As Maude brushed and arranged her hair, she glanced outside and saw to her relief that blue skies and bright sunshine had replaced the fog.

"Hurry, Maude," she smilingly urged, "for you'd not want me to faint this time from hunger, would you?"

Putting in one more pin, the maid stepped back, and Sylvia thanked her and left the room, hurrying down the stairs to the dining room, where food was already waiting on the sideboard.

She helped herself to a generous portion of bacon, eggs and kidneys, and two slices of heavily buttered toast, and had just started eating when Lady Lavinia came in.

She looked at Sylvia's plate and smiled. "By the look of it, you are feeling much better this morning, my dear. I did not look in last night when I returned, for I understood that you were sleeping and did not wish to be disturbed."

"I fell asleep almost as soon as you left, but I feel wonderful now, and cannot think what got into me yesterday," Sylvia said, looking quite radiant. "But whatever it was, it's gone now. Did you enjoy last evening?"

"I had a lovely time. Just about everyone was there, and they were so sorry to hear you were not feeling well." She helped herself to a reasonable portion and smiled when Sylvia got up to replenish her plate. "My goodness, you are hungry this morning, but of course you did not have dinner last night, did you?"

"Only a little soup," Sylvia replied, "but I am making up for it now."

"If you're feeling well enough, I thought perhaps we might go to my modiste this morning," Lady Lavinia said. "There's been a chill in the air recently, and I thought I might order a few warmer clothes for outdoors. You'd think one would grow accustomed to the cold as the years go by, but instead I seem to feel it a great deal more."

"I'd love to come with you, and I think that while we're out I might look for a pair of gloves to match one of the gowns Elizabeth insisted on buying for me." Sylvia frowned. "It's an unusual shade of pink, and we knew it was no good trying to match it outside of London."

"Very well, my dear. Do you think you might be ready to leave by ten o'clock?"

"I not only will be ready but also will have written at least two letters by that time," Sylvia said, smiling. "But don't hurry, for the letters are much overdue."

A little over an hour later, they set out for the modiste, where Lady Lavinia ordered the garments she needed, picking out the styles from a book the modiste assured them had come straight from Paris.

After that they went to a glovemaker, where Sylvia was successful in procuring a pair to her liking.

Lady Lavinia was nothing if not thrifty, and these establishments were not quite in the fashionable area of town, so she saw none of her friends and acquaintances until they started back home.

"Let's go back by way of Park Lane, my dear," she suggested. "We may meet people we know, and I am sure they will be glad to see you up and about again. It's such a beautiful day, and almost everyone will be abroad after the poor weather yesterday."

As she spoke, several open carriages passed on the other side of the street, but she had turned toward Sylvia and caught only a glimpse of the last one. She saw enough, however, to wonder why Lady Tarrington, in the last carriage, one of her bosom bows, had not even waved to them. The lady was quite elderly, however, so she concluded that her sight was failing.

Then, just before they turned into Upper Grosvenor Street, they came face-to-face with her good friend Lady Moorehead, Colchester's mama. After a moment's hesitation, Lady Moorehead waved, but there was something about the expression on her face that puzzled both Sylvia and Lady Lavinia.

"I wonder what can be the matter with Mildred?" Lady Lavinia asked, frowning. "She looked almost grim, and I can't help wondering if she was coming from my house, for this street would be out of her way otherwise."

"Well, you are at home this afternoon, aren't you, so perhaps she'll come back then," Sylvia suggested.

"Perhaps she will, but I'll tell you now that if I were not expecting guests, I would go to Hanover Square this afternoon to see what was wrong," Lady Lavinia declared, quite disturbed.

Luncheon was ready when they reached the Grosvenor Street house, and they sat down immediately to eat, for the fresh air had given them an appetite, despite the large breakfast Sylvia had consumed.

As usual, the maids were rushing around, dusting and rubbing up the silver, and Cook had baked enough cakes and tarts for a crowd. At two o'clock people started coming, but there were only half as many people as usual, and none of Lady Lavinia's close friends put in an appearance.

When the last one had left, Lady Lavinia, looking quite grim, steered Sylvia into the study while the maids cleared away.

"I have never been given the cold shoulder by my friends," the little lady said with quiet dignity, "but I believe that is what has happened today, and I cannot for the life of me think what it is all about. Can you understand what it could be, Sylvia?"

"I've never seen anything like it." Sylvia was almost in tears. "That your friends could snub a dear, kind person like you, I cannot believe. What kind of friends are they?"

"Careful of their own reputations, I would say. They have not actually snubbed me directly, Sylvia. It's almost as though they're waiting to see what happens, for every one of them can quite easily say that she was not well or had something urgent to do this afternoon.

"Then there was Mildred, this morning. I've almost a mind to get out the carriage and go and ask her what this is all about," Lady Lavinia started to say; then her face seemed to crumple. "Almost a mind, but I'm afraid I don't quite have the courage," she finished bleakly.

"Well, I have the courage to go," Sylvia said angrily. "How dare she snub you?"

Lady Lavinia shook her head. "She didn't. She greeted me, but I see now that there was obviously something wrong. That is a little different, my dear."

"That kind of greeting was not the sort you give an old friend," Sylvia declared angrily. "I don't care if she is Elizabeth's mama-in-law, she's no right to behave in that way. If you'll call the carriage, I'll go and see her right now."

Lady Lavinia shook her head. "No, you won't, my dear, for that would make matters worse. The only trouble is, I don't know whether we should go to Lady Leicester's dinner party tonight or not. I don't think I could bear it if we were openly ignored."

Sylvia had been looking forward to it, for Tom was taking them and she hadn't seen him for almost a week. "Let's get ready for it, anyway, and we can decide what to do when Tom comes for us," she suggested.

Lady Lavinia smiled weakly. "You're right. That's the best thing to do, but we needn't start to dress yet. Why don't we go and lie down for a half-hour, and perhaps by then we'll both feel better."

She had hardly stopped speaking, however, when the doorbell rang and a moment later Tom was shown into the room.

"Good afternoon, Lady Lavinia," he said with a gentle smile, taking her hand and squeezing it.

Then he turned to Sylvia, who was so happy to see him that she was smiling warmly. Her smile faltered, however, when he did not smile in return, but looked at her with the coldest expression on his face that she had ever seen. She had reached out her hand toward him, but at the sight of his face she withdrew it.

"I hear that you were indisposed last evening, Sylvia," he said icily, "and I trust that you are now feeling better. What exactly was wrong with you?"

Sylvia did not answer, but just stared at him, for she could not believe he was speaking to her in this way. Lady Lavinia replied for her.

"We were driving in the park yesterday afternoon when she suddenly became quite ill, Tom. It was the strangest thing. One minute she was talking and laughing, and the next she was clasping her upper arm in pain, and her face was deathly white."

"And she was too ill, then, to go out yesterday evening, I understand," he said to Lady Lavinia. "As a doctor, I can only say that sounds like a very strange illness."

"You should have seen her," Lady Lavinia said. "I had to help her out of the carriage and into the house, and was all for sending for you, but she wouldn't hear of disturbing you."

"And a little after that she started to feel fine, I suppose," he said, still ignoring Sylvia.

"Well, yes," Lady Lavinia admitted. "She did start to feel better, or I would have ignored her and sent for you anyway."

"What is this all about, Tom?" Sylvia asked sharply. "If you're disputing the fact that I was ill, it's your privilege, and I have to admit that it was all very strange, for I've never felt like that before. But I see no reason why you should walk in here and behave as though I am some sort of leper."

Tom turned and looked at her, then addressed Lady Lavinia once more. "I suppose she went to bed and asked not to be disturbed until morning?" he suggested.

"Tom," the little lady said with a frown, "I am in agreement with Sylvia. I'd like to know what all this is about too."

"It's quite simple," Tom said wearily. "Once you went out for the evening, she presumably got up, dressed, and met a certain gentleman. She went with him to a particularly unpleasant gaming hell, and she won a considerable amount of money at piquet. She was seen there by a member of the *ton* who has seen her several times, and when she ignored him, he spread the word around."

He turned to Sylvia. "You should have shared your winnings with him, my dear. It was very foolish to ignore him."

She had gone every bit as white as she had been the day before, and suddenly hugged herself and shivered with cold. She was remembering the pain she had felt yesterday in the park, and knew without a shadow of a doubt that someone had hurt Louise at that moment, perhaps hit her to make her do what he wanted. Louise must be in London, and she had to find her and help her.

Tom saw at once how white she had gone, and he was watching the expressions pass across her face. "It wasn't me, Tom. I don't care who says he saw me, I never left this house last night. Do I know the man I was supposed to be with at this den of iniquity?" she asked quietly.

"Yes, you do. It was Sir Roger Albertson," he told her, and immediately regretted causing the fear that came into her eyes. They were all still standing, and he instinctively slipped an arm around her shoulders and held her close.

"I have never played piquet in my life. I told you that once before, and I even told you why," she said softly.

"I know," he said with a sigh. "I've been thinking about that."

"And deciding I was a liar," she said with a wan smile. "What am I supposed to have been wearing, by the way?"

"A very revealing tight-fitting gold dress," he told her, looking down at her white face. "The kind of gown that suited the place."

8

"Tell me once again what happened yesterday afternoon," Tom said gently, his arm still around her shoulders.

"For what purpose?" Sylvia muttered, trying to move away from him, but his grip tightened because he had no intention of letting her go. "You won't believe me, for I admit that it does sound most odd even to my ears."

"Tell me," he coaxed. "I will believe you. There are many things here that don't make much sense, and I cannot help if I don't know the whole of it."

She looked at him more hopefully. "The fog was swirling all about us, and Aunt Lavinia had just leaned forward to instruct the coachman to turn around, when I felt the most awful pain in my left arm, just here," she said, touching the place.

"What kind of pain? A stabbing pain, a dull ache, or the way it would feel if someone hit you with something?" he asked, frowning in bewilderment.

"The last seems more like it. It hurt terribly and I felt for a moment as though I was going to faint," she recalled.

"How long did it last, Sylvia?" His voice was soft and persuasive. "Did it gradually diminish, or did it go away all at once?"

"It diminished slowly over about ten minutes, I would say. Just about as long as it took to get back to the house, for by the time I went up to my room it had gone altogether," she told him.

"May I see?" he asked.

"You can, but there's nothing to see. There was no

red mark, no bruise or anything." She was wearing a long-sleeved gown, and she unbuttoned the cuff and pulled up the sleeve, to show creamy skin without a bruise or a single blemish.

"You think it was Louise last night, don't you?" he said.

Surprised, she nodded. "Then you do believe me after all," she said, breathing a sigh of relief.

"I do now," he said. "I was upset at first, for I never thought about Louise, assuming that she was still in Paris. What I thought was that you'd done something for a lark and it had misfired, for you'd been seen, therefore damaging your own reputation and also that of Lady Lavinia."

"How did you find out about it, Tom?" Lady Lavinia was anxious to know, for people had avoided her but no one had told her why. Tom must have found out from someone.

"It was being bruited about the clubs, but only as a rumor so far, for the fellow couldn't quite be sure it was Sylvia. What we have to do now is to give her an alibi, and then face down everyone as though we know nothing whatsoever about any tales being spread," he told them firmly.

"What do you mean?" Sylvia asked. "Pretend we didn't notice people ignoring us?"

"I mean that you should both get ready for this evening as though you know nothing about it, and look completely surprised if anything is mentioned. Someone is bound to ask how you are feeling, Sylvia, and when you say you feel much better, Lady Lavinia will immediately say how much better you look than last night, and that you were sleeping like a baby when she peeped into your room." Tom glanced over to Lady Lavinia and raised his eyebrows.

"I know it's telling a lie, but I believe it's in a good cause, for I am sure that if I had looked in, that is exactly what I would have seen," Lady Lavinia said firmly.

"I'll stay close to both of you all evening," Tom promised, "so that no one can say anything unpleasant without all of us hearing it, and I guarantee that they'll all decide the fellow was mistaken, that it must have been someone else, not Sylvia."

Sylvia still looked worried. "Are you quite sure it will be all right, Tom? I couldn't bear it if we got there and everyone snubbed Aunt Lavinia."

"They won't, because I intend to call on Lady Moorehead, David's mama, and be sure she knows that the rumor is not true. With her behind you, no one will dare be rude," he promised.

"That's right," Lady Lavinia confirmed. "No one ever dares contradict her, for they know that she is very straightforward and not at all malicious. I am quite sure now that she must have been here this morning to find out the truth and try to put an end to the shocking story."

"Very well," Sylvia agreed, "we'll show them a united front and they'll not dare repeat that lie anymore."

"I think we should go up and dress now, and let Tom go back and change also, or we'll all be late to Lady Leicester's, and that would never do tonight," Lady Lavinia put in.

Tom rose. "Walk to the front door with me, please, Sylvia," he asked, but Lady Lavinia broke in.

"You needn't do that, for I'll go up now and give you a little privacy in here. I'll see you in a couple of hours, Tom."

She walked to the door, pulling it closed behind her, and Tom took Sylvia into his arms, his hands gently stroking her back until it seemed as though she was melting against him. She could feel his breath on her ear as he murmured, "I should never have doubted you, my love, but I heard the rumor and let myself get carried away. It won't happen again."

She felt his words and his touch flow into and strengthen her, then made a request. "Will you help me try to see if Louise is in town?"

"Of course I will," he promised. "I thought that went without saying. Don't forget, tonight all you do is just hold your head high and let the two ladies make it clear that someone who frequents such places is not a reliable witness."

Sylvia looked up at him, her eyes shining. "Thank you for believing me," she said. "Now you must go or you'll be late."

She watched him hurry out of the room, then made her way up the stairs. It would be a difficult evening, but the fact that she had done no wrong should make it easier to behave as Tom had suggested.

Her deep yellow gown, which she had earlier decided to wear this evening, was hanging outside her armoire, but she realized this was no longer appropriate. As Maude came hurrying in, she handed her a simple gown of solid white crepe, with a silver-and-white bead trimming that seemed only to emphasize the color, or lack of it.

Sylvia dressed carefully. She had not worn a white gown since early summer, when she and Louise had come out, but tonight called for her to look as opposite as she could to the woman in gold, so she was deliberately dressing to look as pure and innocent as possible.

"An excellent choice, my dear," Lady Lavinia said when she saw Sylvia standing waiting in the drawing room. "You look just as sweet and guileless as you are."

"What do you suppose will be planned for after dinner?" Sylvia asked. "Not charades, I hope."

"I really don't think so." Lady Lavinia looked thoughtful. "I believe they usually have a professional singer and pianist, and call for talented guests to perform also. I know Elizabeth can't sing a note, but how about you?"

"It must run in the family," Sylvia said quickly. "I've never been able to carry a tune."

"Good. If she asks me, I'll tell her, so as not to embarrass you," Lady Lavinia assured her. "I'm so glad that Tom is taking us tonight, for I doubt that I would have had the courage to attend otherwise. You see, nothing like this has ever happened to me before."

"Of course it hasn't, and I hope it never will again," Sylvia said. "I believe that's Tom now."

He entered the drawing room looking immaculate and much more handsome than he had seemed when Sylvia first met him, but then she had been too young to think of such things.

"I called on Lady Moorehead, and she says you are not to worry, she'll quash this ridiculous rumor, and I really believe she will," he told them. "And now, are you ladies ready to leave? I noticed your carriage outside."

He offered an arm to each of them, and they were soon on their way to Lady Leicester's dinner party. It seemed only minutes later that the carriage door was opened by a footman and they stepped out.

Sylvia was sure that Lady Leicester had heard something, for there was, to her observant eyes, a moment's hesitation before the hostess stepped forward to greet them.

"Lavinia, my dear, how are you?" she gushed, "and . . . Sylvia, isn't it? So nice to see you again, and Dr. Radcliff. Such a pleasure."

Her loud voice had carried across the drawing room, where the guests were gathered, sipping sherry, and several heads turned in their direction.

Then Lady Moorehead, gowned in soft turquoise, stepped forward. "Dear Lavinia," she said, throwing her arms around her friend and kissing her cheek. "And, Sylvia, I do hope you are feeling better, my dear, for we sadly missed you last evening. How was she when you got home, Lavinia? Sleeping comfortably, I hope?"

This was Lady Lavinia's cue. "Sleeping like a babe, though a little flushed, and I hadn't the heart to wake her," she said, her voice a little louder than usual.

A hush had fallen over the other guests, but suddenly they all seemed to start talking at once, and the three ladies, with Tom at their side, moved forward to join them.

Tom took a glass of sherry from the waiter's tray and handed it to Sylvia, then took one for himself, but before he could even take a sip, a young lady who had made her come-out with the twins was at his elbow.

"Dr. Radcliff, it's so nice to see you again. I suppose you are making sure that Sylvia doesn't suffer a relapse," she said a little tartly.

For the life of him, Tom could not remember who she was, though he recognized her high-pitched voice and babyish face immediately.

"He's been quite wonderful to me, Margaret," Sylvia said, guessing Tom's problem, "and his recommendation was fewer late nights. It seems I need more sleep than I've been getting these last weeks."

Tom nodded. "The trouble is, she's an early riser, and you cannot burn the candle at both ends for long, you know," he said in his most doctorlike voice. "She took a sedative last night, however, and woke as fresh as ever this morning."

"You simply must give me the name of that sedative, Doctor," Margaret said so loudly that some of the guests turned around. "I probably need it every bit as much as Sylvia did."

"It was just a simple herbal tea my nanny always made for us, and it worked the same as it always did when we were young," Sylvia said.

"And the cook here just happened to know the exact mixture?" The voice was scornful. "That's a little difficult to believe, surely."

"Not at all." Sylvia smiled, for she was enjoying baiting this girl who had always been jealous of her and Louise. "You see, Lady Lavinia's cook worked for my mama and papa when we were young. She and Nanny were the best of friends."

"I see," Margaret said tightly. "I thought it was something the good doctor had given you, that's all." She turned and flounced away.

"That gal is growing up every bit as spiteful as her mama." Sylvia recognized the voice of Lady Moorehead. "But I suppose it's no more than one might expect. How are you, my dear?"

"Very grateful, my lady, for your support," Sylvia

said. "It was most kind of you, and I do appreciate it."

The older lady put a hand on Sylvia's shoulder. "We're family, my girl, and if this young doctor here says you were home all night, then that's where you were."

Tom's smile turned into a wide grin. "Really, my lady. That sounds somewhat compromising, to say the least."

"You know what I mean, Tom. I can't stand tale-bearers, and I never could. David would tell you that, for when they were little they knew not to carry tales or they'd get the worse of it." She looked closely at Sylvia. "Do you think it was your twin, my dear?"

Coming so unexpectedly, the question brought tears to Sylvia's eyes. "I don't know, my lady," she whispered. "If it was, then she must be in terrible trouble."

Lady Moorehead smiled at Sylvia and squeezed her shoulder. "Now, don't go jumping to conclusions. If there's anything really wrong, we'll find out soon enough. David and my James can handle anything," she assured her, then saw Tom's face. "With the help of this young man, of course. Now I believe we're being asked to go to the dining room."

To her relief, Sylvia found that Tom had been seated across from her, and both Lady Lavinia and Lady Moorehead were not far away, while Sir James Moorehead was on her left. She was not without friends around her.

"How was my favorite stepdaughter-in-law, if there is such a thing, when last you saw her?" Sir James asked, his friendly voice warming the rather nervous Sylvia. "We saw too little of her at your twin's wedding, but we hope to pay them a visit before the next child is born."

"Elizabeth was very happy, and appeared to be taking everything in her stride, as usual," Sylvia told him, "and your step-grandchildren were just as lovable and as mischievous as you could wish."

"Do you miss them?" he asked with a twinkle in his eye, "or are you enjoying London too much for that?"

"I really came here only to keep Aunt Lavinia company," she tried to explain, though she realized he was not deceived, "or at least that's the official reason."

He became serious. "I am aware of the unofficial one, my dear, and my lady and I will do all we can to help you in that regard. In the meantime, I hope you're having fun here. Make the most of it, for you're young and innocent only once, you know."

"How is David's grandmama?" Sylvia asked, to change the subject. "I understand she now lives with you and Lady Moorehead."

"She is becoming quite forgetful, I'm afraid. She never was as deaf as she pretended, but this time it's not an act. Of course, she's really quite old now," he explained.

"I'm sorry to hear that," Sylvia said, meaning it, for she and Louise had enjoyed the cantankerous old lady when she had come to Elizabeth's wedding. "David always pretends he can't tolerate her company for a moment, but I believe he loves her in his own way."

"Well, she has placed him in some very embarrassing situations over the years, but he's always been her favorite. When the memory goes, I'm not sure whether it's a good thing or a bad one, for we all have some memories we'd like to forget," he said a little ruefully. "Do you know if Tom is going to be in town long? There's something I want to talk to him about."

If good manners only allowed it, Sylvia thought, he could ask Tom himself, for he was seated directly across the table, but courtesy demanded that at a formal dinner you only converse with the person to your immediate right and left.

"I'm afraid I don't know, Sir James," she replied. "He is not here purely on a social visit, but is working, I know, with some of his colleagues, and also patients in the hospital. I've asked him to take me there, but he absolutely refuses."

"Quite right, too, my girl. It's no place for you to go, for many of them are in a bad way, and the conditions are deplorable," Sir James said fiercely.

"You're here to have fun, not to see things of that sort."

"I suppose so," she agreed, "but Tom has taken me to visit some of his patients near Colchester Castle, and I enjoyed that."

"I imagine you did, and they enjoyed seeing you, I'm sure, for your pretty face would cheer them for the rest of the day," Sir James said kindly.

It was now time for them to talk to the partners on the other side, and Sylvia turned dutifully to the young man on her right, whom she was sure she had not met before.

"I understand you're the one everybody's been talking about," the rather supercilious young man said. "Is it true?"

"I have not the slightest idea what you mean, sir," Sylvia said, looking at him with distaste.

"No need to look at me like that. I'm not the one that started it," he said gruffly. "Something about a gaming den, as I recall."

"As I have never been in a gaming den in my life, I really cannot help you, sir," she replied stiffly. "I'm afraid you've made a mistake."

She glanced across the table and saw that Tom was looking at her; then he smiled as if to give her reassurance.

"I'm sorry if that's the case," the young man blustered, "but it was somebody here that told me. He pointed you out, in fact."

"Then he got the wrong person, sir," Sylvia said firmly. "I believe we'd better start again. I have not had the pleasure of meeting you. My name is Sylvia Danville, and yours is . . . ?"

"Peter Finlay, miss," he said. "It's my first time in London and I don't know many people here yet. In fact, this is the first dinner I've attended. Have you been here before?"

"Yes, I have," she said pleasantly enough. "My sister and I came out in the summer, and I'm now visiting my adopted aunt, Lady Lavinia, for a month or so."

"Well, perhaps I'll call on you, take you for a ride in the park or something. Where does she live?" he asked.

"She has a house on Grosvenor Street, number sixteen, but if I were you I would leave a card first," she suggested, "for my aunt is not always at home."

"That would suit me, as long as you were there," he said, grinning. "Then I could decide for myself whether it was you they were talking about."

"I think you must have had a little too much to drink, sir," Sylvia said quietly. "Why don't you finish your meal and I'll do the same, in silence."

She turned her head slightly and applied herself to her food, and to her surprise, Peter Finlay did not say another word. She sincerely hoped that would be the end of it, but had an odd feeling that it would not.

"Is everything all right, Sylvia?" Sir James asked, for he had noticed that she was no longer conversing with her other dinner companion.

"Perfectly all right as long as he keeps his comments to himself, Sir James," she told him. "I think he must be slightly in his cups."

Sir James raised an eyebrow. "Whatever you say, but let me know if he gets out of hand."

She smiled a little weakly at him, then continued with her meal, but it was a relief when the dinner came to an end and the ladies left the gentlemen to their port.

Lady Moorehead led Sylvia to a place at the far side of the drawing room where a couch and several chairs were arranged in a comfortable grouping, and Lady Lavinia followed closely behind. Within a few minutes, several of the older, more influential ladies had joined them, and though none of them mentioned the rumor, for it would have been in extreme bad taste to do so, their presence signified quite clearly that they believed it to be false.

Sipping their tea and asking after Sylvia's welfare, they left no doubt as to their feelings in the matter, and soon others were joining the group. Even before the accompanist and the soprano arrived, it had become clear that they had all given Sylvia the benefit of the doubt.

For once, the soprano was in excellent voice, Sylvia thought, or else it was just her own relief that made the woman sound better than she was, for Sylvia actually enjoyed the arias she sang, and did not even mind it when several of the younger ladies present gave their own somewhat shakier renderings of popular ballads.

The gentlemen came in at that point, adding a few tenor and baritone voices to the concert, and when Sylvia realized that Peter Finlay was no longer present, she relaxed and enjoyed the rest of the evening.

Gradually, guests started to make their farewells to Lady Leicester, and Lady Moorehead leaned over to her friend Lavinia and said quietly, "I think we should make sure to be almost the last guests, so there is no opportunity for talk after we leave."

Lady Lavinia nodded her agreement, and passed the word on to Sylvia, and as the chairs emptied around them, Sir James and Tom came over and joined the three ladies.

"Is everything all right, Sylvia?" Tom asked. "Did you have any problems?"

She shook her head, but Sir James spoke up. "I made a point of speaking with Finlay, my dear, and he indicated he had imbibed too much, sent his apologies, and left, but I do not believe he was in the least inebriated."

"Who's that?" Tom asked, frowning.

"The young fellow sitting on Sylvia's right," Sir James explained. "What did he say to you, my dear?"

"He mentioned the rumor and asked if I was the one. And he said he would call on us at Grosvenor Street," she told them. "Of course, I said I didn't know what he was talking about and that he should leave a card, for we were often not home. Then he said something about wanting to see me alone. That was when I turned away from him and did not speak to him further."

"I'll make sure the staff know not to admit him,"

Lady Lavinia said. "What a pity you had to have someone like him beside you!"

"I think you behaved just right," Tom said to Sylvia. "If you should hear anything further from him, make sure to tell me, won't you?"

As Sylvia promised to do so, Lady Moorehead rose. "I think it's time we thanked our hostess for a delightful party," she said. "I'll call on you tomorrow afternoon, Lavinia, if I may, after I've visited one or two of my other friends." She turned to Sylvia. "You handle yourself very well, my dear, for one so young, but I should have expected it, for Elizabeth did also. I don't think you'll need herbal tea to make you sleep tonight."

She was right, for Sylvia almost fell asleep on the short ride back to Grosvenor Street, but awoke enough to enjoy the warm hug Tom gave her before he left.

"Would you like to ride in the morning?" he asked, and when her eyes lit up at the opportunity, he grinned. "I'll be here at eight o'clock sharp," he said, then got back into the coach to return to his own lodgings.

As they climbed the stairs, Lady Lavinia smiled. "Something good may have come of this after all, for I believe that young man is getting quite serious about you."

Sylvia turned to look at her, and there was a sudden glint of tears in her eyes. "He mustn't, for Papa would never let me marry someone without title or wealth," she said sadly, then hurried into her bedchamber.

9

Sylvia was up and dressed in her riding habit before Maude appeared with her hot chocolate, much to the maid's dismay.

"Why didn't you tell me you were going riding, ma'am?" the girl asked.

"You had a late night, Maude, and I am still capable of getting myself dressed. I hope you can do something with my hair, though, for I cannot, and it looks just like a bird's nest," Sylvia said ruefully.

"You sit down 'ere, ma'am, and I'll 'ave it looking nice in a jiffy," Maude said. "It's all tangled, but I'll try not to pull."

Within minutes it was neat and orderly. A shako matched the riding habit she was wearing, and the maid pinned it firmly on her mistress's head and stood back. "You look a real treat, ma'am, and no one would know you'd 'ad only five hours of sleep."

She'd had less than that, thought Sylvia, for she had not fallen asleep for some time last night. It had not been the events of the evening that had kept her awake, however, but Tom's protective attitude toward her and the remark that Lady Lavinia had made.

She expected her papa to arrive in town at any moment, for he had been unusually quiet, and she feared that he would be once more looking for a wealthy husband for his last unmarried daughter, to provide him with additional funds. He would make it clear, she was sure, that a country doctor just would not do.

It was almost eight o'clock now and she did not want to keep Tom waiting, so she went quietly down the stairs so as not to waken Lady Lavinia, and reached the door just as the bell rang. She was tempted to open it herself, but knew that Bates would be quite shocked, so she stood to one side and waited.

"Prompt as usual, I see," Tom said, taking her arm and leading her down the steps to where a groom waited with both horses. "You do want to go to the park, don't you?"

"Is there anywhere else we can gallop?" she asked hopefully.

"Not within several miles," he told her, "and by the time we got there it would be time to come back."

"The park it is, then," Sylvia said, accepting his assistance in mounting. "It's so good to be out at this hour, when the air smells cleaner."

Tom chuckled. "The air is cleaner around here, for the streets have just been swept and there's not been enough traffic yet to dirty them again. Did you sleep well after your rather trying evening?"

"Not really," she admitted. "I kept wondering when Papa might suddenly show up, for I'm sure he will before long."

"He probably will, and I'm sure you'll be glad to see him again, for it has been several months, hasn't it?" Tom asked.

"Yes, it has," she said a little sheepishly. "I wouldn't mind at all if he just wanted to see me, but I know that is not why he'll come."

"It may be different this time," he said comfortingly. "Stop worrying about something that hasn't happened yet. Look, the park is almost empty and we should be able to get a good gallop without danger of anyone seeing us."

They crossed the road and went in, noticing some riders in the distance and just one carriage nearby. They waited until the carriage had passed before heading in the opposite direction.

"I'll race you to the patch of oaks," Sylvia called, and set off at a gallop, while Tom stayed back a moment to give her a head start, for he knew that his mount could easily overtake the pretty mare.

They galloped until the horses showed signs of tiring, then walked them back along the familiar path, while the groom followed some distance behind.

"Didn't Lady Moorehead say she would be calling on your aunt this afternoon?" Tom asked.

"Yes. She said she was going to make several calls first and then come to let Aunt Lavinia know what, if anything, was being said about me. Why don't you pay a call at the same time?"

"I think I will," he said, "for I'd like to be sure that the rumor has been well and truly killed. And I'll stop off at my club later, where I first heard it and was so shocked."

"I can't understand how you came to believe it was me, Tom, for you know I don't gamble, and certainly don't play piquet." Some of the hurt that Sylvia had felt when he was so angry showed on her face.

"Neither can I now," he said ruefully, "for it didn't make sense at all. And it's possible that it wasn't Louise either, you know, for the man had probably had a drink or two and couldn't tell one brunette from another."

"It's possible, but I don't think so, for why did I suddenly feel that pain in my arm?" she asked him. "It hurt terribly at the time, but you saw for yourself that there was no bruise or mark of any sort."

Tom shook his head. "I don't know, but whatever it was, we'll get to the bottom of it, don't worry. And now I am just starving to death, so I'll take you home and then go and get something to eat."

"I'm sure Aunt Lavinia wouldn't mind if you came in and had breakfast with us, Tom." Her eyes brimmed with laughter as she tried to tempt him. "Cook makes the most delicious ham steaks, bacon, kidneys, and eggs—just the way you like them."

"Stop it, young lady," he cried. "You're only making me feel worse, and I can't use up my welcome, for I am coming by this afternoon also."

"So you are," Sylvia said, laughing as he helped her dismount. "The groom will take my mare back to the stable, so you'd best hurry before you become weak from hunger."

He brought her hand to his lips. "Until this afternoon, my dear," he said, then watched her run lightly up the stairs and through the door that Bates held open.

He did not hurry back to his rooms, however, for he was wondering what Lady Moorehead would have to say this afternoon, and thinking that he might need to pay a visit to that gaming den himself. He was quite sure now that it had not been Sylvia, but he was not at all sure about Louise. The man who had been there also, Sir Roger Albertson, was a ladies' man and a rake—and he was known to Louise. He was, in fact, her cousin by marriage.

Lady Lavinia was nothing if not conscientious, and she felt a strong sense of responsibility for her guest. That afternoon, before her friend Lady Moorehead arrived, she sat down at her desk and penned a note to Elizabeth. She wrote of the strange occurrence in the park and of the rumor that had circulated and been effectively quashed.

As a footnote, she mentioned the budding romance between Tom and her charge, and quoted Sylvia's exact words of the night before, for she felt sure there must be some misunderstanding on the girl's part. She herself had accepted Tom as David's friend, had come to like the young doctor, and could not see why Sir Edward Danville might have objections to an alliance. That was, of course, if the relationship should develop further.

Carefully sealing her missive, she rang for her butler, and instructed him to have it sent off right away.

A few minutes later she heard the sound of the doorbell, and looked up when Bates entered the library.

"It was the gentleman you are not at home to, my lady," he told her, "Sir Peter Finlay. When I told him that neither lady was in, he left his card for Miss Danville."

"Just the card, or did he write something on it?" she asked, trying to sound casual.

"He wrote something, my lady," he said, and handed it to his mistress.

"Thank you, Bates. Just be sure not to admit him at any time," she instructed.

When he had gone, she looked at the engraved card but did not turn it over, for she would no more have thought of doing so than of reading someone else's mail. She set it down on the desk to give to Sylvia.

A few minutes later, Lady Moorehead arrived, was shown into the drawing room, and Lady Lavinia went to greet her.

"Come, my dear, can I offer you a cup of tea or have you had as much as you can tolerate for now?" she asked.

"None of them served the finest oolong, as you do, Lavinia. I'll take a cup by all means, and I deliberately refrained from eating so that I could better enjoy your cook's rich seed cake and almond tarts. No one in town serves as good an afternoon tea as you do, you know."

Lady Lavinia flushed with pride. "What a nice thing to say, Mildred, but I'm afraid the credit is due to Elizabeth, you know, for she stole our cook from her papa, who always grossly underpaid her."

She rang for Bates, and within minutes a delicious afternoon tea was set before them. Picking up the silver teapot, Lady Lavinia poured a cup and handed it to her friend before asking, "Were you able to find out anything about that horrid rumor?"

But before Lady Moorehead could reply, the door-bell rang and Bates announced, "Dr. Radcliff, my lady."

"How nice to see you, Tom," Lady Lavinia said as he took her hand and bowed low over it. "I'm sure Sylvia will be down in a moment. You're just in time for tea."

"I trust you are well this afternoon, my lady?" he inquired, smiling at her warmly, for he had liked the birdlike little lady since the first time they had met, some years ago, and admired her for the way she cheerfully accepted her lot in life.

"Very well, Tom, thank you. Of course, you know Lady Moorehead."

He turned to take Lady Moorehead's hand. "David is very fortunate, my lady, to have you for a mother," he said, "and what is more, he has told me so many a time, both in Spain and in France, as well as here."

Lady Moorehead flushed prettily. "How nice of you to tell me, Tom, for I'm afraid David often forgets, but I do know how he feels. Shall we wait until Sylvia arrives before we relate our findings?"

"We'll not have to wait long," Lady Lavinia murmured, "for I hear her on the stairs now. She was expecting you, I'm sure."

A moment later Sylvia entered and was about to close the door behind her, for privacy, when Lady Lavinia stopped her. "That horrid man who was your dinner partner last night called just now, Sylvia. He was not admitted, of course, but he left his card for you, and you'll find it on the desk in the library."

She went to get it at once, and the others waited until she came back, the card in her hand and a puzzled expression on her face. "What does he mean, Aunt Lavinia?" she asked.

"I don't know, my dear, for I would not read a card addressed to you. Do you want to tell us what it says?" Lady Lavinia looked concerned.

" 'Unless you admit me tomorrow, I will prove to your friends that it was you I saw,' " she read. "What on earth can he mean? He told me last night that it was not he who saw me, but someone else he had talked to before dinner, but I got the distinct feeling that he was lying. He cannot prove I was somewhere I was not, but he may not know that I have a twin," she said in a frightened voice.

Tom had risen when she came in, and he now put his arm around her and guided her to a couch. "Give me the card and have a cup of tea, my dear. He must have been lying to you last night. As you say, he cannot prove it, but I'd be very interested in finding out why he thinks it was you. Do you know what time he called, Lady Lavinia?"

"Earlier this afternoon is all I can tell you. Perhaps an hour ago," she said. "Bates can probably be more accurate."

"It's very strange, if he is the person who started the rumor, that he just happened to be sitting next to you at dinner last night, Sylvia. Perhaps he changed the place cards around beforehand," Lady Moorehead said. "Why don't you admit him tomorrow, Lavinia, and we can all be here to meet him, James as well, for I know that he would be furious if I didn't tell him about it."

"You don't think that perhaps just James and I should be here to receive him?" Tom began, but was immediately interrupted by Sylvia.

"No, we don't, for that card is addressed to me and I certainly want to hear what he has to say, provided I have some of you here for support. How dare you try to leave us ladies out of this?" Sylvia's eyes flashed as she looked at Tom.

Lady Lavinia cleared her throat to get their attention. "Lady Moorehead is right. We should all be here to give Sylvia support and find out what this young man wants."

"You're right, of course, and I bow to your better judgment, ladies," Tom said with a wry grin. "I think there's little doubt that he was at the gaming den and thinks he saw Sylvia, and now he's anxious to get some of that money that was won for himself."

"Then you must come for luncheon and just stay until he arrives," Lady Lavinia suggested.

"Come in by the back way and make sure the carriages are not walked in front of the house," Sylvia said, getting into the spirit of it. "I can be alone in the drawing room to receive him, and then, when he comes right in, you all follow behind him and he cannot escape."

Tom shook his head. "James and I will be in the room with you, but hidden from his immediate sight, for he could have a weapon and attack you, you know. Or he might even intend to kidnap you."

"My, my," Lady Moorehead said with a laugh, looking from one to the other of them. "You must both have been reading the same mystery stories that I have. Where would you two hide?"

"Mildred," Lady Lavinia said reproachfully, "this is very serious. This young man may very well try to extort money from Sylvia."

"I know, my love," Lady Moorehead agreed, "but I really don't know why, for the rumor is quite dead, or was in the homes I visited this afternoon. I even brought the matter up myself at Lady Towers' home, and the ones who had heard it said it was utter nonsense—someone trying to make trouble for two ladies on their own."

"The topic was dead at the club also," Tom said. "They're all talking of the high cost of tobacco, and this was never mentioned even once."

"This room has double doors, and Bates always flings them both open when he shows people in," Sylvia remarked. "Could you not hide behind each of the double doors and tell Bates to leave them open?"

Tom considered her suggestion for a moment. "I don't think so, Sylvia. He would be certain to turn and close them, for he would not wish passing servants to hear what he was saying. The draperies are a better idea, but it's a pity they're such light colors."

"Elizabeth would not agree with you," Lady Lavinia remarked, "for she spent a great deal of time and trouble getting rid of all the dark furnishings and replacing them with those softer greens and beiges when we first moved here."

"I've no doubt she did an excellent job," Tom said, grinning, "but I know she would forgive me for the thought. Let me see how thick they are."

He went over to a window and stood behind one of the curtains. "Can anyone see a shape or a shadow through the fabric?"

"No," said Lady Moorehead, "that will be all right as long as you make sure to keep out of the window itself, or he'll be able to see you from the outside as he comes up the steps."

Tom came back to the sofa. "Is it agreed, then? Shall we meet here tomorrow for luncheon?" he asked. "Or do you want to check with Sir James and let us know if he is free, my lady?"

Lady Moorehead smiled broadly. "I can tell you right now that once he knows of the plan, he'll cancel even a meeting with Prinny just to be a part of it."

"Come to the back door then, Mildred, at half-past twelve, and we'll have a leisurely lunch and perhaps a game of cards if he keeps us waiting," Lady Lavinia said, a pink flush tinging her cheeks at the very thought of such excitement.

"Then it's all arranged," Lady Moorehead said, rising. "Are you going to the Melbournes' ball tonight?"

"No, my good friend Lady Stratford is having a small party for her niece who is just out of black gloves, and she was so helpful with the twins when they came out that I felt we really owed it to her to attend," Lady Lavinia explained.

"Are you going without an escort?" Lady Moorehead asked, "for I really don't think it's a good idea."

Sylvia looked across at Tom, and he nodded. "If it would not upset Lady Stratford's seating arrangements, I'd be glad to accompany you," he suggested.

"An extra gentleman is never a problem to a hostess," Lady Moorehead said dryly, "but Lavinia could always send a note around to let her know. I'd feel better if they did not go alone. And if it's all settled, I'd best be on my way, for James does fuss so if I don't take a rest before I go out of an evening."

After hugs and kisses, she swept out of the room and into her waiting carriage, and Sylvia turned to Tom. "This all seems terribly dramatic. Do you think it is really necessary?" she asked.

"Would you not agree that he quite openly threatened you?" he asked her, and when she nodded, he went on. "If he'll do that on a card anyone could have read, then what do you suppose he'll try when you're alone?"

"You're right, but he didn't appear very threatening last night at dinner. I just thought he'd had a little too much to drink." She shrugged. "Let's not speculate about it further. I believe we have to leave at eight o'clock tonight, so . . ."

"I'll be here," he began, but Lady Lavinia, who had come back from seeing her friend out, put up a hand.

"We'll send the coach for you at seven-thirty, Tom, and then you'll come back for us at eight. It will be much more convenient that way," she said, "and I must say that it is kind of you to offer at such short notice."

"My pleasure, my lady," Tom said, with a bow. "Until tonight."

"I don't know about you, Sylvia," Lady Lavinia said when they were at last alone, "but I'm going to follow Mildred's example and have a rest before we go out. It's been quite an exhausting day."

"Sir Peter Finlay is asking to see Miss Danville, my lady," Bates informed his mistress.

Tom and Sir James rose quickly and slipped behind the curtains, while Lady Moorehead went through the door leading to the dining room and reluctantly closed it behind her. Both Lady Lavinia and Sylvia stood up, as had been arranged.

"You may show him in, Bates," Lady Lavinia said calmly.

He left the room and returned a moment later. "Sir Peter Finlay, my lady," he announced, and the small, insignificant-looking young man who had sat beside Sylvia at dinner the other night entered the room.

He paused when he saw Lady Lavinia.

"I had hoped to see Miss Danville alone," he said. "I won't keep her a moment."

Bates had closed the doors behind him, and Finlay stood as though uncertain what to do, for he had not been asked to take a seat.

"In our circles, young ladies do not see strange men alone, sir. She is my niece and you may state your business in front of me," Lady Lavinia said firmly.

All at once the uncertainty disappeared. "All right, if that's the way you want it," he said with a sneer. "I was the one who saw her the other night, dressed like a strumpet and winning every hand."

"My niece never left this house on the night in question, young man. You may have seen someone who looks similar to her, but she was here all evening," Lady Lavinia stated emphatically. "I saw her myself, fast asleep, at one o'clock in the morning."

"That's what you say," he snarled, "but I know differently and unless she shares some of her winnings with me she'll be very sorry, very sorry indeed. I'm not greedy, I only want half. Five thousand pounds will do very nicely for now."

Up to this point Sylvia had remained silent, allowing her aunt to do all the talking, but now she could not help herself. "She won ten thousand pounds, this woman you saw?" she asked in amazement.

"Don't come on like that with me, missy. You know how much you won, and we can go right upstairs to wherever you keep it and get it now." He made as if to grab Sylvia's arm, but she had earlier been practicing just what to do in such an event and now stepped quickly back behind a chair.

Finlay's back was toward the windows and Sir James and Tom came quietly forward, each grasping one of his arms and twisting them up behind him.

"You've made a big mistake, young man," Sir James told him. "This young lady has witnesses to prove that she was ill in bed on the night in question, and should you continue to go around maligning her, we shall have you arrested. Do you understand?"

"But I did see her, sir," Finlay protested. "I know I did. Perhaps I shouldn't have come here and tried to get money from her, but I'd swear in a court of law that it was her. That's why I got myself an invitation to that dinner the other night, so that I could take another look at her and make sure. I changed the place cards so that I'd be right next to her."

"The woman may have looked like her, Finlay, but it wasn't her, and I would strongly advise you to think twice before you make any further accusations. I am her doctor, and I can assure you that she was ill on the particular evening in question," Tom said.

Tom and Sir James released the young man, and he first straightened his clothes, then stood up tall, sticking out his chest. "You can't have me arrested yet, for you can't prove that I've said anything," he told them. "It's only my word against yours. I'm going to keep my eye on that place, and if she goes there again, I'll be waiting."

"You do that," Sir James said, "and make sure you accuse the right person next time."

Finlay had been moving away from them as he spoke, and all at once he darted toward the door and was out of the room in a flash, for neither Tom nor Sir James had any desire to detain him.

"I don't think he will make any further trouble for you, Sylvia," Sir James said, "but if he does, you know where to come."

10

"I was wondering if, provided you have no other pressing engagement tomorrow afternoon," Tom asked when he, Sylvia, and her aunt were taking an afternoon drive in the park, "you might permit me to take you to see the Royal College of Physicians, where I have been working this last month?"

"I would indeed be interested in seeing the place where you have been hiding yourself away so frequently of late," Sylvia told him, delighted that he had at last invited her there.

"You might also find it of interest, Lady Lavinia, for it has been housed in a quite imposing building in Warwick Lane since the late 1600's, but will not be there much longer. Sir Henry Halford, who, it is rumored, will be the next president of the college, is endeavoring to find a suitable new location."

"Much as I would enjoy seeing it, Tom, I'm afraid I will not be able to do so," Lady Lavinia told him regretfully, "but take Sylvia, by all means, for I believe the outing will be good for her, and she can then tell me all about it when she returns."

"Are you sure, for we can postpone the visit, my lady, if you would really like to join us," Tom assured her, while secretly hoping that she would not do so, for he had been trying to get Sylvia to himself for some time, and this would be a splendid opportunity.

"Quite sure, my boy," Lady Lavinia said, positively beaming at him for his kindness. "Isn't Sir Henry one of King George's physicians?"

Tom nodded. "He's been one of the foremost of

them for some time, and he's also physician and a personal friend of the Prince Regent."

"Is he one of the physicians you dined with the other night?" Sylvia asked curiously.

Tom laughed. "No, he is not. I'm afraid that he and I do not move in the same exalted circles, my dear."

Just then they saw Lady Jersey's carriage slowing in order to have a word.

"Lavinia, how lovely to see you, my dear. And, Sylvia, it's nice to see you up and about again, for I heard you had not been well. And, my dear Tom, I haven't seen you since the night of my ball, you naughty boy," she said loudly enough for everyone within several feet to hear. "Why don't you come to call on me next week? You may bring this lovely young lady and her delightful aunt with you, of course. I won't take any excuses. I'll expect you on Tuesday afternoon."

"It will be a pleasure, my lady," Tom told her, grateful for her attention, for after that no one would dare repeat those wretched rumors.

They drove on more slowly, for although no one had been snubbing them, now the occupants of other equipages went out of their way to stop and have a word.

There were fewer carriages in the park than before, as there was now a decided nip in the air. Most of the trees had lost all of their leaves, and the clip-clop of hooves was deadened by the gold-and-russet carpet they had laid underfoot. There was a faint smell of burning wood and a lovely soft mistiness around that was a portent of the winter that could not be far away.

Though the hardier gentlemen were not yet wearing the many-caped coats that would be seen everywhere in just a few more weeks, the ladies were already wearing pretty pelisses and cloaks over their gowns, and velvet bonnets had replaced the straw ones of the warmer days.

"Has the College of Physicians always been on War- wick Lane?" Sylvia asked, now eagerly looking forward to tomorrow's outing.

"Good heavens, no," Tom told her in some surprise, forgetting that she had not yet seen the place, and didn't know its history. "The college was founded in 1518, in the reign of Henry VIII, and the early meetings were held in the home of its first president, Thomas Linacre, who, incidentally, was also King Henry's physician."

"And what exactly do you do there, Tom?" Lady Lavinia asked. "I mean you, personally, for surely at this stage you do not need further study?"

He could not help laughing, for she was so very far from the truth of the matter. Leaning toward the two ladies, he tried to explain.

"If I studied every day to the end of my life, I would not know all there is to know about medicine. It's a wonderfully exciting field, for new things are being discovered all the time." His face seemed to light up as he talked. "Tomorrow Sylvia will see portraits of the faculty members who made their mark so long ago: Harvey, who discovered the circulation of the blood; Sir Edmund King, who learned how to transfuse blood from one animal to another; Sydenham, who first introduced the cool regimen in the smallpox, and many, many more.

"I go there to read, for there is a magnificent library, and I meet with fellow physicians and discuss cases, new methods, and cures. I also make it a point to attend the quarterly meetings of doctors and listen to eminent speakers from here and overseas. While people are still dying of illnesses we know nothing about, we have a duty, as doctors, to learn as much as we possibly can."

He stopped. "I'm sorry," he said with a rueful smile. "I should not have bored you so—"

"But you didn't, Tom," Sylvia interrupted, her eyes shining with admiration. "I think it's wonderful that you are so dedicated. I only wish women were allowed to be even half as useful."

Lady Lavinia sympathetically patted her niece's knee. "I only wish that all who call themselves doctors felt the way Tom does. But unfortunately he is very much in a minority, for most country doctors either have never studied at all or have been veterinarians who aspired to a more profitable profession."

"I agree with you entirely," Tom said. "But the day will come, I am sure, when only those who have studied and passed examinations will be permitted to call themselves doctors and practice medicine."

"I hope we all live long enough to see it happen," Lady Lavinia said dryly. "And now I believe we should start back, for we are expected at the Melbournes' tonight, and I think Sylvia should take a rest first."

"Aunt Lavinia," Sylvia protested, "I'm not some sort of invalid to need rest all the time. But if you want to lie down for a while, then by all means let's turn around."

Tom grinned. "I don't think that either one of you would come to any harm by stretching out for an hour before you have to start dressing for dinner. I know I'm going to, anyway," he said, and signaled to the coachman.

Sylvia was ready long before the appointed hour for her visit with Tom to the Royal College of Physicians. She had on a pelisse of light gray kerseymere lined with blond sarcenet with a wide sleeve that fell over her hand. The fastening down the front was trimmed with ruby-red velvet, which continued around the slightly full hemline and edged the high-standing collar and the long cuffs. On her black curls she wore a bonnet of the same ruby-red velvet topped with a high plume of ostrich feathers in the same shade, while the wide brim was lined inside with blond fabric and edged with a frill of blond lace.

"I was just coming to see if you were wearing something warm enough," Lady Lavinia said as she entered the drawing room, "but I need not have worried. That outfit is quite lovely and sets off your dark hair and rosy cheeks to perfection. Your young man will be very proud to show you off to his colleagues."

If only he really was my young man, Sylvia thought longingly, for he possessed the qualities she had always dreamed about in a man. He was kind, considerate, gentle sometimes and strong when he needed to be. But more than that, she had begun to get the strangest urges when he looked at her in a certain way. And he had looked at her in that way more often lately!

If only Louise was still here to talk to about them, for she couldn't mention them to anyone else, not Aunt Lavinia and certainly not Mama, for they were both too old to understand. Was this how Louise had felt with Timothy?

But though he seemed always to have sufficient funds, as a young doctor he could not possibly be rich enough to suit her papa, nor had he ever mentioned a wealthy father or perhaps an uncle. And, of course, he did not possess a title, which would be the final mark against him when Papa came to town.

"He's just a friend, Aunt Lavinia, not my young man," she protested mildly, but her cheeks became even rosier and there was a wistful expression in her eyes.

"I would not be too sure of that if I were you, my love. He spends an inordinate amount of time at this house for one who is just a friend," the older lady said coyly.

Sylvia's deep sigh said more than any words could have done, and Lady Lavinia took her niece's hands in her own. "Don't start worrying now, my dear. Just enjoy yourself and everything will work out for the best, you'll see," she told her. "And now I believe I hear Tom arriving."

A few minutes later he entered the drawing room and eyed Sylvia with appreciation. He had borrowed a friend's carriage and coachman, as he had left his own curricle in the country, and after promising Lady Lavinia to take good care of her niece, he swept Sylvia outside and into the waiting carriage.

She made such a delightful picture that he could not take his eyes off her, and for the time it took to drive from Grosvenor Street to Warwick Lane—almost forty-five minutes in the early-afternoon traffic, for it was off Newgate Street, near to St. Paul's Cathedral—he

did not need to do so. Today he had her all to himself
and did not have to concentrate on keeping a curricle
on a straight course; or hold a restive horse on a tight
rein; or make courteous conversation with a chaperon.
For once, Lady Lavinia had not thought it necessary
to have a maid accompany them.

"I hope you feel as well as you look, my dear, for
you positively glow, and render me quite speechless,"
he told her appreciatively.

Sylvia said nothing for a moment, for she was, in
fact, feeling quite breathless with excitement. They
had never been alone in a closed carriage before, and
his proximity had much to do with her condition.

"I've been looking forward to this afternoon so much,
Tom," she finally murmured. "Do you think I will be
able to meet some of your fellow physicians?"

"That depends upon who is about," he told her,
"but there is always someone that I know there. I'd
rather not share you with too many others, however,
for I, too, have been looking forward very much to
this outing."

"In what area of London is the college located?"
Sylvia asked when they had traveled for almost half an
hour.

"It's actually no longer in the most salubrious of
neighborhoods, for the Fleet Prison is no more than a
stone's throw away, but Christ's Hospital and St.
Bartholomew's Hospital are nearby, as is St. Paul's
Cathedral," Tom told her. "The unpopular area is one
of the main reasons for the search for a new site."

Sylvia looked startled, for she had not been into any
unpleasant areas before.

Seeing what he took for fear, Tom hastened to
reassure her. "You have no cause to worry, my dear,
for you must know I would not allow any harm to
come to you. We will be set down right at the door of
the college, and will not leave until the carriage is
waiting directly outside."

"I'm not at all afraid," she told him, "for I trust you
completely to see that no one harms me. I was just

surprised that such an illustrious place was in such a poor area of the city."

Tom reached for her hand, and the warmth from his came through her mittens and brought an even deeper flush to her cheeks. They rode this way until the carriage pulled up at one of the loveliest buildings Sylvia had seen.

Before entering through the octagonal porch, she looked up at the dome atop it that ended in an unusual cone.

"Christopher Wren is credited with the design, but Robert Hooke had a say in it also, and Inigo Jones designed the central building," Tom explained.

He led her inside and through to the vast library, where he was immediately greeted by two of his colleagues, John Marsden and William Forrest.

"So this is the young lady you've been rushing off to see every time our backs are turned," Marsden said, bowing low over Sylvia's hand.

"I, for one, can't say that I blame him." Forrest grinned and said to his friend, "Come along there, move over and give a fellow a chance"; then he also took Sylvia's hand and looked deeply into her eyes.

"Tom is a dedicated doctor, a man with a future, my dear. We both feel fortunate to know him," he told her, and though his mouth still formed a grin, his eyes held a look of admiration for his colleague.

More than a little embarrassed, Tom sought to change the subject. "She's really come here to see what I do with myself when I do not call for a number of days," he told them.

"You're surely not going to show her the room that has all the muscles in the human body, are you? I hardly think that would appeal to a young lady, but it is where you spend your time," Forrest asserted. "That and in here, of course."

Sylvia smiled and raised questioning eyebrows to Tom.

"It's true," he said ruefully, "for I am making a close study of the muscles in order to find out which ones can be used in place of missing limbs. I did not bring you here to show you that, though, so if you're duly impressed by the sheer size of the library, and the seriousness of my fellow physicians"—he bowed to the two young men—"I'll take you to the great hall where our quarterly meetings are held, and where you can see portraits of some of the finest doctors of our time."

Amid cries of "Shame," he led her out of the library and into a tremendous room lined with portraits and busts, some of which she recognized from museums she had visited.

He picked up a guidebook lying on a table. "The building used to be one of the regular sights for visitors to London, and this little book, published in France in 1693, actually recommended that tourists give at least threepence to the person who shows them around," Tom told her.

Without a word, Sylvia reached into her reticule and withdrew four pennies. "Let no one call me a clutch-farthing," she said with a straight face as she reached for his hand and put the coins in his palm.

Tom looked surprised for a moment, then threw his head back and roared with laughter. When he was serious once more, he reached for her and drew her toward him, his hands on her back holding her near so that her upturned face was only inches from his, and he looked deeply into her intense blue eyes.

"I can no longer remember the time when you were not close by, making me laugh and turning my visits to patients into joyous occasions," he murmured. "This is not an appropriate time or place to talk about it, but I just wanted you to know how I feel, and how much I hope you feel the same way."

She started to tell him how she felt in turn, but before she could voice the words he placed a finger on her lips. "Don't say anything now," he insisted. "Think about it for a few days, and then I'll find an opportunity to talk to you again."

He heard footsteps approaching, and released her so quickly that she reached out a hand to a table to steady herself.

"Ah, my boy," a voice came booming forth from the far end of the room. "I heard you were here with your young lady and I wanted to see her for myself."

Tom took Sylvia's arm and led her toward the owner of that resounding voice. "Sylvia, may I present Sir Henry Halford. Sir Henry, this is Miss Sylvia Danville, daughter of Sir Edward Danville and sister-in-law of the Earl of Colchester, whom I'm sure you will recall."

"Very pleased to meet you, my dear," Sir Henry boomed. "We're all very proud of this young man and his work with our wounded soldiers. He's a credit to the profession."

"I'm very happy to meet you, sir"—Sylvia dropped a curtsy—"for I have heard a lot about you."

"Only good, I hope," he boomed, then said, "Must get back to my work, my dear. Hope to see you again, and just you look after this young man of yours."

He turned and strode out of the room, while Sylvia turned her excited gaze upon Tom. "That was wonderful! I never thought I would actually meet a man who has looked after the King of England," she said in awe. "I'm so glad you brought me here today."

Tom smiled tenderly at her. "So am I, my dear. Have you seen enough? Do you want to go home now?"

"I suppose so, unless, of course, you will let me come with you to the hospital and see some of your patients there." She knew the answer in advance, but still thought she might just be able to persuade him when he was in such a delightful frame of mind.

"Definitely not," he growled. "You know my views on that. It's no place for a young lady of your breeding. I'll send for the carriage to be brought around."

Sylvia said nothing more, for she knew by now that there was no use arguing with him when he spoke like that, but she determined that one day she would see the inside of one of the London hospitals, and find out if there was anything at all she could do to ease the suffering of its patients.

They retraced their steps to the front of the building, waiting inside until they could see the carriage drive up and stop, and only then would Tom take her beyond the door and out to the street.

Tom handed her inside, then stepped in himself. sitting beside her this time, and as soon as the carriage began to move, he slipped his arm around her shoulders and drew her closer to him.

"Did you enjoy the tour," he asked, "or was it a little boring for someone who is not directly concerned with the college's purpose?"

"Tom, you must know I thoroughly enjoyed it," she said enthusiastically. "I certainly told you so often enough, and the best moment of all was when the king's own physician came out to meet me, a nobody."

He looked at her, "You're not a nobody and you never will be, my dear," he assured her. "You're one of the kindest, most understanding young ladies I have ever—" he was saying, when suddenly he heard her gasp as if in pain.

"Where do you hurt, Sylvia?" he demanded, turning her toward him so that he could see her deathly white face. "Tell me, my love, what is it?"

She put her hand up to her right cheek, which had suddenly gone a bright red, while the other was still white, then gasped again and reached for her left shoulder, crying out with the pain. Then she started to tremble.

He banged on the roof, and when the coachman answered, he called to him to drive as fast as he could back to the house. Then he cradled her in his arms, murmuring soothingly to her until at last the trembling stopped and she leaned against him, exhausted.

"Are you feeling a little better now?" he asked softly, and she nodded but kept her eyes closed.

"We'll soon be home and we'll get you straight to bed, my love. Don't try to talk about it now, just relax and let me hold you," he murmured, shocked at what he had just seen happen to her.

Although the coach was moving at a fast pace, it still took a half-hour before they reached Grosvenor Street, and when they did so, he lifted her in his arms

and carried her into the house, instructing the coachman to wait.

Lady Lavinia came running out of the drawing room.

"What happened, Tom?" she cried. "Was there an
accident? Is she going to be all right?"

"Show me to her bedchamber and let's get her
directly into bed," he said urgently. "And stay with
me, for I want to examine her and see if there's any
visible physical damage. I think it's somewhat similar
to the last time, but more severe."

He placed her on the bed and left the room until
Lady Lavinia and Maude had undressed her and put
her into a nightrail; then he went back inside and
examined her thoroughly while Lady Lavinia watched.

When he had finished, he said, "There's not a mark
on her, but she was in the most dreadful pain and I
actually saw one cheek go scarlet while the other one
remained white. I'm going to give her something to
make her sleep, and this time I think it would be best
if you could stay here with her all night. Would it be
an imposition . . . ?" he asked hesitantly, for he would
have liked nothing better than to stay with her himself, but knew it would be completely improper.

"I'll not leave her side for a minute," Lady Lavinia
interrupted determinedly. "No one is going to accuse
her of any wrongdoing this time."

"Tom," Sylvia said faintly, and he went over to the
bed so that he could hear her more clearly. "I'm so
sorry I spoiled your afternoon, but I'll be all right
tomorrow, I know I will."

He took her small hand in his, and Lady Lavinia
walked away to give them a little privacy. "You didn't
spoil it, my dear," he said softly. "We've just got to
get to the bottom of this, and then there'll be many
more afternoons like this one that we can enjoy
together."

He reached into his bag and brought out a small
packet, which he emptied into the glass of water that
the maid had left. Putting an arm around her and
raising her shoulders he said, "Drink this down, my
love. It will help you get a good night's sleep."

She drank the whole, shuddering a little at the unpleasant taste, then lay back. Tom felt her forehead, then touched her pale cheek with a gentle finger before rising and going toward where Lady Lavinia waited.

"It happened just a few moments after we had entered the coach and started for home," he said, "and I have to admit it's one of the strangest things I have ever witnessed. And just five minutes before, she was as happy as I have ever seen her.

"Don't try to give her anything except a little water if she should waken and ask for it. I'll be here early tomorrow morning to take a look at her again. She should sleep now all night, but if she should need me, don't hesitate to send for me. I know she's in good hands."

11

Lady Lavinia had linens brought through and spent the night on the chaise in Sylvia's room. The sedative that Tom had given her niece had worked well, and not ten minutes after she had taken the draft, the frightened expression had left her face and her eyes closed as she fell into a deep sleep.

When Maude entered the room, early the next morning, Lady Lavinia went back to her own bedchamber to freshen herself, and while she was there, she sat down at her escritoire and wrote another letter to Elizabeth, to be sent out right away.

She was just about to go in to breakfast, a little after eight o'clock, when Tom paid a call. "Is she still sleeping?" he asked.

"She must be," Lady Lavinia told him, "for Maude relieved me at six o'clock, and I gave her strict instructions to send someone for me the minute Sylvia awoke. I am a light sleeper and I heard not a sound from her all night."

"Have you considered letting her parents know?" Tom asked next, though he knew the answer beforehand.

A disgusted expression came over the good lady's face. "I considered the idea and rejected it immediately," she told him. "But I did write and tell Elizabeth about the first occurrence, and have sent a second letter to her this morning by special messenger, for someone in the child's family should know what is happening."

"Then we can expect Colchester late tomorrow or the next day," Tom said with grim satisfaction.

"I made no such suggestion," Lady Lavinia informed

him, "but, of course, he may very well come, for I know he thinks a great deal about the twins. I hope we don't experience any of the unpleasantness of last time this happened. Perhaps I had better send a note around to Mildred also. Colchester will probably wish to stay with her, for I know he gave up his rooms in town shortly after John was born."

She suddenly realized that she was wanting in her manners.

"I do beg your pardon, Tom, but can I offer you some breakfast? I was just about to go through and have something myself," she told him.

"Then I accept with pleasure, my lady, for I'm sure you would not wish to eat alone," he said with a glimmer of a smile.

They went into the dining room, and as soon as they had filled their plates and taken seats at the table, Tom made a suggestion.

"When you write your note to Lady Moorehead, it might be a good idea to ask her if she can ascertain if any more rumors of the sort that followed the last occurrence are circulating."

"That's a good idea, and I will, of course, tell her that I spent the entire night in Sylvia's room, for she can pass that information along if anyone should try to make mischief again," Lady Lavinia said firmly, adding, "as I have no doubt they will, for that unpleasant young man told us he would do so."

Tom just nodded and looked as though he was thinking of something else. Then he picked up a piece of ham with his fork, and said, smiling, "I'm only now realizing how foolish I have been, for when we have been riding early, Sylvia has frequently invited me to breakfast and I have refused. She did tell me that your cook makes an excellent meal with which to start the day, but mere words do not do it justice."

"You're always welcome here, Tom. Living in rooms, as you do when in town, must be most uncomfortable, and we would both be delighted to have you join us whenever you can," Lady Lavinia said kindly.

He took the last sip of his coffee and patted his lips

with his napkin. "If you don't mind, as soon as you are finished, I think I will prevail upon you to come upstairs with me while I take another look at Sylvia."

Lady Lavinia smiled and rose at once, and Tom jumped up quickly and opened the door.

"She just woke, my lady," Maude said as Lady Lavinia knocked and peered into Sylvia's bedchamber, "and you'd better come and talk to 'er, for she's wanting to get up and dressed."

"Come in, Tom. Perhaps your presence will dissuade Sylvia from jumping out of bed," Lady Lavinia said as she hurried across the room. "Now, my dear, you must not exert yourself so quickly. You've been quite sick, you know."

A pair of clear blue eyes stared at Tom as he came across the room, and a delicate hand tugged the covers up a little higher. "I don't remember very much except that I was in the carriage with you when I began to feel ill again," Sylvia told him. "My head still hurts a little, though."

"Your head?" Tom looked at her in surprise. "Show me where it's sore."

Sylvia put her hand to the back of her head, on the left side, but Tom could feel no signs of a bruise.

He looked into her eyes, lifting her eyelids, but appeared satisfied with what he saw there. Then he felt the place on her wrist where a tiny pulse raced.

"I know you feel restless and eager to be up, but I'd much rather you stay in bed today, my dear," he told her.

As she looked up at him, she suddenly remembered what a delightful afternoon it had been, meeting Tom's colleagues, and one of the king's physicians. And she felt a sudden warmth as she recalled the moment Sir Henry Halford had interrupted when she and Tom were so very close.

"What is it?" he asked, a little concerned.

"Nothing to worry about," she said with a smile. "I was just remembering yesterday afternoon. It was such a pity you couldn't join us, Aunt Lavinia," she said, then felt a little embarrassed as she realized what a good thing it was that her aunt had not been there. "I met some of Tom's friends at the college, was in the biggest library I have ever seen, and then was presented to Sir Henry Halford."

Tom turned to Maude, who had been standing close by, listening. "Why don't you go down to the kitchen and see if Cook can poach an egg very lightly and serve it with just a slice of toast and a pot of tea."

"Yes, sir, I'll go right away," the girl said eagerly, and hastened from the room.

"You're treating me like an invalid, Tom," Sylvia complained, "and apart from a little headache, I feel perfectly well now."

"I don't want you to take any chances, Sylvia. If only to please me, will you stay in bed today?" he asked, gazing at her intently.

She nodded, for when he looked at her like that she would do anything he asked. "You will allow me up tomorrow, though, won't you, bully?"

He grinned, delighted to see the mischief back in her eyes. "That depends upon how you are feeling, but you're young and healthy and I really don't expect any aftereffects."

He left her chamber then, for he realized she probably needed privacy, and a few minutes later Maude arrived with the breakfast, and Lady Lavinia came out of the room.

"She seems to have made a good recovery again, Tom, and she promised to do as you said and stay there, but I will stop by to keep her company from time to time," she told him. "Now I'll write that note to Mildred and send it around."

He started down the stairs with her. "If you want to do it while I wait, I'll take it, for I'd like to have a word with Sir James if he's home."

"Of course, if you wouldn't mind taking a seat in the drawing room, I'll not be long," the little lady assured him, disappearing in the direction of the study.

Not ten minutes later she was back, and handed him the sealed note.

"I'll see that she gets it, and I'll come back later this

afternoon to check on my patient again," Tom said as he slipped the note into his pocket; then he unexpectedly bent and kissed Lady Lavinia's cheek before leaving the room.

He was on horseback this morning, and a groom brought his mount around immediately. Resisting the temptation to take a quick turn in the park, for he had come directly to the house, he turned the other way and was in Hanover Square in less than five minutes.

He asked for either Sir James or Lady Moorehead and was shown into the breakfast room, where he joined them for a cup of coffee while he gave them the gist of what had happened to Sylvia the previous afternoon.

"Personally," he said, "I believe that Louise is here in London and being mistreated in order to make her do something against her will. There are case histories of identical twins reacting in this way when half a world apart, you know."

"And you think that last time this occurred she was being forced to play, and probably cheat, at piquet?" Sir James suggested.

"I should think that's part of it, for I understand from Sylvia that it's a game neither one of them would ever play of her own free will," Tom said thoughtfully. "But if Albertson is forcing her to do so, where is her husband?"

"And why are they not seen about town?" Lady Moorehead asked. "You do realize that unless Elizabeth is not feeling well, David will be here by first light in the morning, if he doesn't wake us in the middle of the night?"

Tom grinned. "Of course. Quite aside from his extreme fondness for the twins, this is a puzzle after his own heart, and he'll not be able to resist it."

"I'll go to the most notorious gabsters in town today, and if any rumor has started, you can be sure I will hear it," Lady Moorehead said. "And if I pick nothing up today, then I'll try again tomorrow, for if Louise felt as Sylvia did last night, she would not have been able to go out gambling anywhere."

Tom said, "Bravo! Now I know from which side of the family David got his brains. We'd not thought of that, though if it's true, then the sooner we find Louise, the better. But what can have happened to Fotheringham? Though he did not strike me as exactly an aggressive type, I don't believe he would stand by and see his bride physically abused by that bounder."

"There's no point in speculating when we have so little to go on," Sir James said, frowning. "Let's wait until David gets here, and then tomorrow night the three of us will go to this gaming den and see what we can find out." He turned to Lady Moorehead. "You wouldn't mind spending the evening with Lavinia and Sylvia, would you, dear?"

Lady Moorehead smiled knowingly and shook her head. She had been fully aware that this was what would happen, and she was anxious to help her daughter-in-law's twin sisters in whatever way she could.

The two men continued their conversation while Lady Moorehead went through to the kitchen to be sure they had all of David's favorite foods on hand. Then she instructed the housekeeper to make up a bed for him in his old room. She chuckled to herself at her words, for, in fact, all the rooms now belonged to her son, but he had insisted that she and James live there and "keep the place clean and aired," as he had phrased it. He and Elizabeth were too busy building a family to stay long in London these days, and of this she wholeheartedly approved.

Once everything was taken care of, she put a pelisse over her gown and went to make some morning calls, but though she visited some of the most notorious scandalmongers, she caught no hint of a rumor about Sylvia.

Colchester thought it had been all his own idea that he come to London right away to get to the bottom of Sylvia's problem, and was a little annoyed to find that everyone expected him.

After going first to his mother's house in Hanover Square, for it was not yet six in the morning and no time to pay a call on two unmarried ladies, he bathed and put on fresh clothes, then went to waken Tom and bring him back for breakfast.

"Just because you've been traveling all night is no reason to wake me from my sleep," Tom grumbled good-naturedly. "Did you get any rest at all last evening?"

"Of course I did," Colchester said, looking smug. "It was Elizabeth's idea that I come in the carriage so that I could sleep most of the way, and you of all people should know that I can fall asleep anywhere when I need to. Now, tell me just what this is all about, for Lavinia is a dear lady, but she writes a most confusing letter."

"I wouldn't be too fast to put blame on her this time, David," Tom warned, "for this is one of the most confusing things I've ever come across. I have heard of it happening at times, but no doctors seem to have an answer for it."

"Come to the point, Tom, for you're beginning to sound as bad as Lavinia," David growled.

While the two men sat in the drawing room drinking coffee and waiting until Sir James and Lady Moorehead came down to breakfast, Tom quietly and completely explained what had happened on each of the two occasions, including the run-in they had had with Sir Peter Finlay.

"And you think that it had to be Louise in that gaming den with Albertson? It couldn't have been someone like her, and Sylvia's illnesses just a strange coincidence?" David asked.

"There's only one way to find out, and that is to go to the place and try to catch Albertson in the act," Tom declared. "I only hope they didn't go there last night, but I'm afraid there's a good chance they did, for last night Sylvia was feeling completely normal and anxious to go out, so her sister probably felt the same way."

"The whole thing sounds like something out of one of those lurid novels my mama reads," David said with a slight shrug, "but you're the doctor, not I."

At the sound of Lady Moorehead's voice in the hall, the two men sprang to their feet.

"David, darling, how nice to see you, and how are my grandchildren and dear Elizabeth?" she asked, lifting her face up for her son's kiss.

"They're all getting bigger every day. That's why I came here right away. We need to get this whole thing cleared up and have Tom back home before Elizabeth's time gets much closer," he told her. "She won't let anyone except Tom touch her."

"And my grandchildren, John and Patricia?"

"A couple of little monsters by day, and angels when they're put to bed exhausted each night," he replied, his handsome face softening as he spoke of them.

They went through to the breakfast room and the younger men helped themselves to generous servings of finnan haddie, eggs, ham and bacon, with heaps of toast and piping hot coffee. There was a silence for several minutes while they savored the tasty flakes of fish.

"Now, does either of you know where this den of vice is?" Colchester asked the two men.

"Thanks to Sir Peter Finlay, we now know that it's at the end of Warwick Lane, almost at Amen Corner," Tom said, "and is up some stairs."

"It sounds like a pretty bad part of town. And just who might Sir Peter Finlay be?" Colchester asked. "From your tone, he sounds like someone we don't want to know."

"He is." Tom sounded grim. "He's the fellow who started the rumor in the first place. He was at the gaming den the first night, watching the young lady and Albertson fleece a young lord to the tune of some ten thousand pounds. Finlay had the nerve to go to Grosvenor Street and tell Sylvia that he wanted half."

"I assume you sent him off with a flea, or better still, a fist, in his ear?" Colchester said, his eyebrows raised in question.

"Not quite, for he could be very useful to us in finding them again if Albertson changes to some other place. He left threatening that he was going to keep an eye on the den, catch her in the act, and ruin her good name once and for all if she was not willing to share her winnings with him the next time," Sir James said.

"Sounds like a charming fellow," Colchester remarked. "I believe I'd like to meet him in one of those dark alleys near Newgate Street, and teach him a thing or two about threatening a sister-in-law of mine."

"I'd rather there not be any violence," Lady Moorehead said with a worried frown.

Colchester looked the picture of innocence. "Did you hear me say anything about violence, Mama?" he asked her. "Sir James may have said something of that sort, but I certainly didn't. And, to be honest, a lot is going to depend on what has happened to Louise when we finally find her. If she's been hurt, as we suspect, I shall not make any promises about what I'll do."

They finished breakfast and then the three gentlemen went for a horseback ride in the park, leaving Lady Moorehead to change into something suitable for the visits she intended to make that morning.

As an ex-army officer under Wellington, Colchester was all too familiar with the use of strategy, and within a half-hour, a plan had been devised, which had of necessity to be flexible, for they had no idea what the inside of the gaming den would be like. In all probability, tonight would be a reconnaissance expedition only, but they must be ready for any exigency. Once they were satisfied and agreed upon the time to start, they rode over to Grosvenor Street to meet with Sylvia and her Aunt Lavinia.

The hour was still early, so they were shown into the breakfast room, where Lady Lavinia offered them a cup of coffee, which they gladly accepted.

"Sylvia will be down in just a moment, gentlemen," Lady Lavinia told them.

"How is she feeling today?" Tom asked.

"Completely back to normal," she said, obviously quite surprised herself. "I wanted her to at least have her breakfast in bed this morning, but she wouldn't hear of it."

A moment later, there was the sound of light footsteps hurrying down the stairs, and Sylvia entered, looking quite radiant in a deep wine-colored morning gown.

"David," she exclaimed, then went over to him and reached up to receive a big hug. "How is Elizabeth?"

"She's probably been feeling better than you have these last few days," he told her, then added, "We just wanted to let you know that we are going to pay a visit tonight to this gaming den that you're supposed to frequent."

"You will look for Louise, won't you?" Sylvia begged, "and get her out of whatever trouble she's in?"

"We'll do that," Colchester promised, "never fear."

"It may be exceedingly difficult and dangerous." Lady Lavinia looked most anxious. "You will all be very careful, won't you?"

"Of course we will," David said, "and Mama asked me to tell you that she's going out this morning to ferret out and kill any rumor that may have been spread last night."

"Your mother is a wonderful woman, David, and I don't think you always appreciate everything she does for you," Lady Lavinia told him quite seriously.

Then, just as seriously, David said, "Yes, I do, and I agree that she is quite wonderful. I'm very proud of her."

Tom took Sylvia on one side to question her regarding her state of health.

"You look well, but I just wanted to make sure you were feeling completely normal now," he explained. "I should think that, with David now here, everything will be taken care of pretty quickly and you and I will be able to get back to our morning rides."

"I hope it will soon be over, for I'm more anxious about my twin than I am about myself," she said, then added more softly, "and I, too, will look forward to our rides again, once I know that Louise is all right."

Tom smiled. "We've every reason to think she will

be, very soon now. You must trust us to take care of
the matter. I don't want you to add worrying to your
problems at the moment."

"I won't," she promised, "but you will find her
soon, won't you?"

He took her hand in his, gazed steadily into her
anxious eyes. "You know we will, just as soon as she
surfaces again. Tonight is just for reconnaissance
purposes."

It was quite late, already past eleven o'clock, when
the three gentlemen stepped out of the Colchester
coach at the corner of Newgate Street and Warwick
Lane. Both of the coachmen, who were well-rested
after driving through the previous night, were there,
one to keep an eye on the place and the other to be
ready to bring the coach up at a moment's notice.

The gaming den was at the end of the lane, but not
difficult to find, for it was quite unlike the quiet,
well-guarded clublike gaming houses around St. James's
Street. The noise of voices could be heard almost from
the end of the street, coming from an upstairs room.

In single file, the gentlemen mounted the wooden
stairs and stepped inside a room that smelled of smoke,
gin, and cheap perfume.

"Good evening, gentlemen, come right in and make
yourselves at 'ome," a well-endowed woman with
henna-rinsed hair greeted them. "What will your fancy
be tonight?"

"We were looking for some friends of ours, but I
don't see them," Colchester said. "Is there another
room?"

"There are plenty of rooms for other purposes, but
this is the only gaming room," she said. "Let me find
seats for you, and a drop of gin, per'aps, or would
gents like you prefer brandy?"

Sir James nodded. "Brandy for me, I believe. What
about you, Tom?"

He agreed to have the same, and when the hostess
left to fill the order, they sat down at the table to
which they had been shown. Fortunately, it was strate-

gically placed and they could see right away that there was no sign of either Louise or Sir Roger.

A few minutes later, Addie, as the red-haired woman was called, came back with the drinks and took a seat at their table.

"What did your friends look like?" she asked. "We don't use names around these parts as a rule, but I'm sure you could describe them."

"I'll try," Colchester said. "A gentleman in his late forties, I believe, with dark gray hair and blue eyes. Very friendly with the ladies. And with him a young lady, very pretty, black-haired, blue eyes also, and with expensive French-looking clothes."

The hostess did not look very pleased. "I've seen them once or twice. He's nothing much to look at, but she's so gorgeous, and dresses so stylish in a flashy way that men can't watch their cards for looking at 'er. They were in last night, so I doubt that they'll be 'ere again tonight. She's the one as plays, and 'e just watches. Took a lot of money, they did, last night, from one of our regulars, and though it seemed all fair and square from what we could see, there were them that swore they were cheating somehow."

"When do you think they may be back?" Colchester asked.

"I 'eard 'im saying something about coming back the night after next, but don't blame me if you miss 'em, for the regulars don't like 'em winning so much, and they might just drive 'em away, if you know what I mean."

"I think I do. What did you say your name was?" Colchester asked with his most charming smile.

"Addie, sir," the woman said, smiling also. "Just ask for me if you want anything at all, and I'll be 'appy to oblige."

They stayed talking for a little while, so as not to make it appear as though they were in any hurry; then, slipping a generous coin into Addie's hand, Colchester and the others left the premises.

A few moments later the coach drew up and they drove away.

"I suggest we have Harry, my second coachman, hang around tomorrow night, and come and get us if he sees our quarry," Colchester said. "I doubt they'll be there, however. By the following night I hope to have reached Bert Eggers, my former batman, and a very useful fellow to know. He can set up a watch on the place and let me know as soon as Albertson shows up."

"It sounds like a good plan," Tom said. "I hope they don't have to do it for too many nights, but it's worth it, I know. Lady Moorehead is no doubt impatiently awaiting Sir James's return, but I thought perhaps you might like to come back to my rooms for a while. I have a much better bottle of brandy than we tasted tonight, and something I'd like to discuss with you."

"By all means," Colchester said, "for the night is still young. We'll drop James off as you suggest, and then catch up on what's been happening. It will be like old times on the Peninsula."

12

"I understand that Lady Lavinia is giving a dinner in my honor this evening," Colchester remarked to Tom.

They were sitting in one of the alcoves at White's after spending a fruitless morning at Tattersall's looking for a well-bred pony for young John. Having just partaken of a satisfying late luncheon, they were relaxing over a cigar and a glass of brandy, and watching the older members settle into comfortable chairs for their afternoon doze.

"Well, I don't think I would put it quite that way," Tom said with a grin. "It's more likely that she hasn't had a family dinner party for a while, and your presence in town reminded her of it. I'm sure that would be a more accurate interpretation."

"Trying to reduce my consequence, are you, Tom? Just don't let Elizabeth hear you doing that or she'll enlist your help on every possible occasion." He chuckled. "There's nothing like a wife for reducing a fellow to size—but then, there's nothing like a wife, or at least one like Elizabeth." His voice quite noticeably softened when he mentioned her name.

"Missing her already?" Tom's eyes were twinkling, for he well recalled David's feelings about marriage before he had met the widow who later became his wife.

"Very much. Town is just not the same without her. Isn't it time that you thought of settling down, Tom? I thought that when you saw so much of Sylvia, and then escorted her to town, you'd finally met the right one. But now I'm not so sure."

Tom bit back a sharp rejoinder for David to look to

his own affairs, but leave his alone, for they had known each other too long and too well for that.

"I thought so too," he replied on a bitter note, "but every time I think I have finally engaged her affection, she becomes quite cool, as though trying to tell me she's not interested. Although I don't yet consider myself long in the tooth, I'm not a bantling either, and have no desire to make a fool of myself by asking where I'm not wanted."

"Do you think, perhaps, that the matter of her twin is bothering her so much it's putting her off marriage?" David suggested.

"I don't know. It could be, I suppose, but the other day when I took her to the Royal College of Physicians, I borrowed a closed carriage because of the neighborhood, of course, but I must confess that it had also occurred to me how pleasant the return journey might be."

Colchester grinned, recalling just such occasions when he had been a bachelor. "And wasn't it? You must be out of practice, for I recall quite well, in Spain, when . . ." He took a deep breath and closed his eyes as though reminiscing.

"There's nothing wrong with my memory either, you old roué," Tom snapped. "On this occasion, however, we had gone no more than two streets away from the college when she became deathly ill."

"Oh, yes," David murmured, frowning. "You know, Tom, this whole thing still sounds a bit farfetched to me. The very idea of one sister feeling what the other one feels at that exact moment, when they're miles apart, is something I can't quite comprehend. I'm not saying you're wrong, or that she was just acting, but I don't understand it. There are some things I simply have to see for myself to believe, that's all.

"You never met their father before Louise's wedding, did you?" he asked, and when Tom shook his head, he continued, "A bounder if ever there was one. He'd forced Elizabeth, at the age of seventeen, before she'd even had a come-out, to marry a marquess older than he himself was at the time. Fortunately, the man died three years later—and not from what you think," he added, grinning.

"Did having a daughter who was a marchioness impress him or something?" Tom asked curiously.

"Perhaps, but the main thing it did was to temporarily fill his pockets, which, as he's a compulsive gambler, are always to let," David said in disgust. "He tried to do the same thing again when she was a widow, but by then she was strong enough to refuse outright. He even tried to get money out of me the night before we were married, but instead I told him I would take care of the twins, see they got elaborate come-outs, society weddings if they wanted them, and so on."

"Why are you telling me this, David? Do you think he would look down his nose at having a simple doctor for a son-in-law?" Tom asked dryly.

"It's exactly what he'd do if he thought you were penniless and without that title you disdain to use," his friend told him frankly.

"Now, David, can you imagine how my impoverished patients would feel if I visited them as Lord Radcliff instead of Dr. Radcliff? Most of them would be so nervous that they'd run a temperature immediately, and then how could I tell what was wrong with them?" The thought brought a smile to his face. "I'm not quite penniless, however, as you know, but I'd not pay him for his daughter, and I cannot imagine Sylvia at all liking the idea of being sold."

"Neither can I, Tom, but I wanted you to know something about him, because before long, if I'm not mistaken, he'll make a trip to London to see how Sylvia is going along—and to try his luck at the tables, of course. He may also try to bring some elderly suitors to meet her, and if he does, he'll have me to contend with, for I've already reminded him of my deal—that I would foot the bills for the twins only if they were allowed to marry men of their choice. If he interferes, I'll sue him for breaking our contract, for I made sure to put it in writing."

He rose, a grin on his face. "I'd better be going, for

my dear mama persuaded me to return in time for tea so that she can show all the young girls what they missed."

He made to leave, and then turned back. "I was about to propose something for this evening and clean forgot. One or other of the ladies will probably suggest cards afterward, and I'd like to know how well Sylvia plays piquet. Do you think you could challenge her to a game? Insist, if you have to, for it's more than likely she and Louise used to play on dull evenings in the country. If Sylvia turns out to be a first-class player, you can be sure Louise is also."

Tom shook his head. "She's told me more than once that she doesn't play that particular game, nor does Louise, because of their father's propensity to lose at the game, so I can hardly challenge her to play. I can, if you wish, suggest teaching her how to play, as you and the others will probably want to make a foursome at whist."

Colchester agreed to that, then hurried out, but Tom stayed on for a little while, thinking about Sylvia and wondering if she really thought him penniless, though he had never given her any reason to draw such a conclusion. He did recall, however, that she had been quite surprised to find that he visited his patients in a spanking new curricle.

Though she did not appear to him to be a fortune hunter, there was the possibility that she felt her papa would not permit her to marry a doctor. It would be interesting to find out, he decided.

A footman was offering sherry to Sir James and Lady Moorehead when Tom entered Lady Lavinia's drawing room unannounced. Sylvia was nowhere in sight, and Lady Lavinia was showing David a painting of Elizabeth that one of her beaux had presented to her before she married for the second time.

Tom came up quietly and heard his friend say, "It's quite lovely and I really don't care who had painted it. Would you be willing to sell it to me, my dear?"

"No, I would not," Lady Lavinia said quite sharply.

"But if you really want it and do not intend to destroy it as Elizabeth thought you might, then I will gladly make you a gift of it."

"Elizabeth was right at the time, for when we first wed I might quite easily have thrown it on a fire," he admitted, "but things are very different now and I should like to display it proudly in my study."

Lady Lavinia turned and saw Tom. "You startled me, Tom," she said reproachfully. "I had no idea you were here yet."

He took her hand and bowed in greeting. "My apologies for being a trifle late, dear lady. I don't see Sylvia. She's not feeling ill again, is she?" he inquired anxiously, but Lady Lavinia reassured him.

"She was here a minute ago and just ran back upstairs to get her fan," she said. "I believe she was disappointed when you did not arrive with Sir James and Lady Moorehead."

"I had an errand to run," Tom explained, "so I came by hackney, but I will, of course, accept their kind offer when I leave."

A few moments later, Sylvia joined them and he was happy to see the roses had returned to her cheeks and her eyes held their usual sparkle.

Seated beside him at dinner, she made the liveliest of companions as well as the loveliest.

"I must say that you look exceptionally well after your brief indisposition," he told her. "I don't think I've ever seen you look lovelier. And there are roses in your cheeks that certainly weren't there a couple of days ago."

She flushed, then felt annoyed with herself for doing so every time he paid her a compliment.

"That may be due to the fact that I spent some time in the kitchen today watching our old cook make the curry soup. It was always a specialty of hers and she swore that an Indian peddler gave the recipe to her when she was just a kitchen helper here in London," Sylvia told him. "She let me make the tansy pudding for afterward. I do hope you will like it."

Tom looked surprised. "Do you often help Cook in the kitchen?"

Her merry laugh rang out. "I wasn't helping her in the slightest. In fact, it probably took her longer to teach me than it would have done if she'd made it herself. I just wanted to try my hand at it, that's all."

"Do you think it might one day be useful to know how?" he asked gently, having the oddest feeling that she was doing it for him.

"I don't know," she said, a little embarrassed now that she'd mentioned it in the first place. "I just wanted to see if I could do it, that's all."

After the meal ended, the gentlemen stayed no more than fifteen minutes over their port before joining the ladies.

"We have decided that, if our hostess is agreeable, we'd like a friendly game of cards when you're finished with tea," Colchester announced.

Lady Lavinia beamed. "How clever of you, for I was going to make the same suggestion," she said. "Perhaps four of us could play whist, while . . ."

"While I teach Sylvia my favorite game, piquet," Tom suggested, smiling hopefully at her.

"I'm sorry, Tom, but you know that I've never played the game in my life," she told him, immediately upset at his suggestion.

"That's all right, my dear," Lady Lavinia said, "I'm sure that Tom would enjoy teaching you if it is his favorite."

Taking her aunt on one side, she whispered, "I'd really rather not, Aunt Lavinia," but to her surprise, her aunt was, for once, firm.

"If it's Tom's favorite game it would be rude to refuse, Sylvia," she said reproachfully, and Sylvia unhappily acquiesced. After all, she told herself, they were not playing for money.

Tom seated Sylvia at the smaller of the two tables, then sat across from her with the two piquet packs of thirty-two cards each set out before him, eight cards each of aces, kings, queens, knaves, tens, nines, eights and sevens, ranking in that order.

In total silence they cut for deal and Sylvia's card was highest, giving her choice of first deal.

"I'd rather you deal," she told him, and he shrugged, then selected the pack he wished to use first.

"The cards are always dealt two, or three at a time until we each have twelve," he explained, placing the remaining eight cards face-downward between them.

"Now, my dear, you must discard at least one card from your hand and take one from the top of the stack, but if you feel your hand is a poor one, you are allowed to discard up to five cards and replace the same number from the stack," he explained gently.

"What would make a good hand?" Sylvia asked, close to tears, for she could not allow herself to relax and enjoy learning something new.

"You're trying to make scoring combinations, and it is on these combinations that you hold in your hand that you first score pips, then afterward you score on the play," Tom said patiently.

He wished wholeheartedly that David had not asked him to do this, for under any other circumstances he would have told her to lay her cards on the table and shown her how to play them face-up, but then he would not have known if she could play at all on her own.

"There are three things in a hand that you can score on—the point, the sequence, and the quatorze. The point is scored by the party who has the most cards of one suit; the sequence is scored by the party who has the greatest number of consecutive cards of the same suit, but he must have at least three of them; the quatorze is four of a kind, aces through ten, and it scores fourteen points, which is why it is called a quatorze. Three of a kind, called a trio, scores three."

Sylvia looked bewildered and for a moment considered picking up the pack and throwing it at Tom, but decided against it. With a slight shrug she reached for the stack and took four cards, studied what she then had in her hand, and selected four to discard.

After Tom had done the same, taking and discarding only three, he said, "Now you state first the largest number of cards you have of one suit."

"Not the kind of cards?" she asked, and when he shook his head she said, "I have four."

Tom said, "I have five, so I score the point," and he wrote something down where he was keeping the score. "Now, the sequence. What is the greatest number of consecutive cards of the same suit that you have?"

Sylvia heaved a sigh, for it didn't make any sense to her at all. "I have five," she said, "Ace, king, queen, knave, and ten of hearts."

Tom smiled encouragingly. "You score the point this time, then. You get five for each card and ten extra, and as I cannot match it, you also score for all other sequences of two or more you are holding. Now for the quatorze."

Suddenly Sylvia put her head in her hands, letting the cards fall from her fingers onto the table.

"It's no good," she said in a voice filled with tears. "I've never wanted to learn, and I just can't."

Lady Lavinia, who was sitting nearest to them, turned her head, and Tom leaned toward her and whispered, "It's all right, I'll take her into the study for a moment, if you don't mind."

Slipping a hand under Sylvia's elbow, he guided her out of the drawing room and into the quiet of the book-lined study.

He eased her into a winged chair while he sat on the arm of it, then said soothingly, "This is not like you, my love. Tell me what is wrong, for the game is confusing at first, but not beyond your intelligence, I know."

"I've never wanted to play piquet, and both of us vowed we wouldn't learn," she muttered, hiding her face from him. "As I told you before, every time we were doing well, or seemed to be, Papa would go to London and play piquet and lose everything again."

She turned a tearstained face toward him. "If you ever came to Danville Hall, you'd find a house on the very smallest possible piece of property, with all the land around being owned by the neighboring squires.

Every time he came home with his IOU's, he'd sell another piece to pay them off. Even the drive up to the house isn't ours, but we do have the right-of-way."

"I can see why you disliked his playing the game, but I'm surprised you never played, for candies or whatever, for piquet is known to be the most interesting of all games for two people, and you and Louise must have had little entertainment when you were young," Tom said, for it was clearly the man and not the game that was at fault.

"We made a solemn oath in blood when we were quite small," she told him, smiling sadly. "We took one of the sharp knives from the kitchen upstairs with us, and we each made a cut on an arm and held them together while we swore."

His arm slid almost by accident around her shoulders, and he held her close, feeling excessively guilty for causing her unnecessary pain. His long fingers smoothed her hair where she had run her own fingers through it, and she leaned back against him, as though better to feel the warmth and comfort that seemed to flow from him.

He was gazing tenderly at her upturned face, and seriously considering placing a kiss on those delectable lips, when the door suddenly opened and Colchester walked in.

He looked from one face to the other, then said, "I'm sorry to break this up, but the two ladies were getting a bit worried. What is the matter, Sylvia?"

"I've never played piquet before because I didn't want to learn, and when Tom insisted tonight, I just became more and more upset," she tried to explain.

"I don't know what there is to get upset about in learning a simple game of cards, my girl. It isn't as though you were missish in the normal way," he scolded, "and your sister, if it really is she who is frequenting that gaming den, is obviously a most exceptional player in more ways than one."

"What do you mean by frequenting?" Sylvia asked, suddenly suspicious. "Has she been there more often than I was led to believe?"

Tom looked at David and raised his eyebrows, and when the latter nodded, he began, "We went to the gaming den where she was seen, and found out that we'd just missed her and her companion, for they had been there the night before and had left very much better off than they had entered. In fact, some of the men there were saying that the young fellow the woman had played against had been properly fleeced," he told her.

"Are you sure that the person there really was Louise?" she asked. "It could have been someone dressed to look like her."

"We spoke with a hostess named Addie, who described Louise to us, including the kind of clothing she was wearing. There was no doubt that it would have caught the eye of anyone in the place, for it sounded, at least to me, like high fashion straight from Paris," David said. "The young woman played piquet as though she'd been doing it all her life, and they're sure she was cheating but couldn't actually see her do it."

"You're wrong, both of you," Sylvia was almost shouting. "Louise never played that game all the years we were together. And she's not a cheat. Don't you dare call her one!"

She looked at Tom for support, then suddenly realized why he had put her through such an ordeal tonight.

As she turned on Tom, David slipped quietly out of the room, closing the door behind him.

"And as for you, Tom Radcliff," Sylvia snapped, looking like a rampaging virago for perhaps the first time in her life, "making me go through that farce this evening was despicable. I know now what you were trying to do. You thought I was lying and you were deliberately making me play to see if I could or not—to see if both of us were experts.

"It was an absolutely atrocious thing to do, for you could see I was getting upset about it, but you went on and on until I couldn't stand it anymore. It was all planned between the two of you, wasn't it? See if she's telling the truth, you both decided, for they've probably played cards together all their lives.

"Well, you were wrong. I've never played piquet before, and I swear I'll never try again, for you or for anyone else. I don't even want to see you . . ." As she started to say the words she didn't mean, the tears began and Tom's arms went around her, comforting and soothing her.

His fingers gently stroked her back, then pressed her face closer until it was against his chest and she could feel his heart beating rapidly.

He had heard the door close quietly, and knew they were alone and that David would make sure they stayed that way, so he slid into the chair, lifting her onto his lap and gently raising her face toward his until he could press tender, comforting lips against her forehead, her cheeks, and finally her mouth.

All the anger had deserted Sylvia the moment she felt Tom's arms come around her. A warmth she'd never known before was slowly creeping through her, and she could feel her heart begin to pound as he pressed her so close to him that she could scarcely breathe.

As his mouth traced a pattern from her chin to her lips, then settled there as if it was where it belonged, she felt a surge of longing deep inside. All the feelings for him that had been growing these last few months came rushing back in one overpowering sweep, and suddenly she was not just passively enjoying his lips, but was kissing him back with more feeling than she'd ever thought herself capable of.

Tom was delighted to feel her eager response, but realized how careful he must be in controlling his own passions. Much as he would have liked to deepen the kiss and feel her urgent response, he knew it was far too soon and might even frighten her.

With infinite finesse he slowly relaxed the pressure of his own lips upon hers and guided them down her creamy neck, pausing at the little place where her pulse beat so very fast, then trailing delicate kisses down to her throat.

His fingers stroked one perfect ear, and he murmured, "You are so lovely, my dear, that I would like to hold you like this for the rest of the evening and take away the bitter feelings that were between us a moment ago." ‑

Settling her comfortably in his arms, he placed his lips against her temple, while with strong fingers he massaged the tension away from her neck and shoulders.

"Mm," she murmured, "that feels wonderful. You must teach me how to do it to you."

"I will, my love—one day in the not-too-distant future, I hope," he said softly into her ear.

He looked down at her lovely face, seeing the newly awakened passion there, and wondered if the others would notice. It was too late now to worry about that, however, so he lowered his mouth to hers once more and marveled at her eager response.

13

Colchester was in something of a dilemma. He would never have dreamed of disturbing his best friend in the middle of a romantic interlude, but Sylvia was his sister-in-law. He had not only an obligation toward her, but also a strong affection for her and her twin sister, for he had known them and loved them when they were awkward sixteen-year-olds, and he could not stand by and let one of them be compromised, particularly by his best friend. He should never have left them alone, he realized.

Not a sound now reached his ears through the solid oak door, though he had clearly heard Sylvia's anger, even after he had closed it and stepped away. There was only one thing to do. He raised his hand and beat a loud rat-a-rat on the very center of the door, slowly counted to twenty, then opened it.

They had sprung guiltily apart at the first sound, and Sylvia had had time to run her fingers through her disordered curls, smooth her crumpled skirt, and sit upright in the chair before David entered. Tom was far more adept and was already standing behind the large mahogany desk before the door had opened more than a crack.

David raised an eyebrow. "I assume you have quarreled and made up by now, and that you, Sylvia, are capable of discussing this matter with a little less histrionics."

She flushed a bright pink and nodded her head.

"Then I believe we should return to the drawing room. The card play is over for the evening and we need to let your aunt and my mama know what we have discovered and are considering doing about it. It will take careful planning if we are to extricate your twin from this imbroglio without its becoming the *on-dit* of the year."

He held out an arm, which she took and then slipped her other hand into Tom's.

As they entered the drawing room, Lady Moorehead came forward and looked askance at her son. "David, I'm surprised at you, and you too, Tom—putting Sylvia through a most unpleasant experience in order to find out if she was telling the truth when she said she'd never played that wretched game. Even I know that the Danville daughters do not tell lies."

She did not fail to notice the pair of clasped hands, and looked more closely at Sylvia's red eyes and bee-stung lips, though she made no comment.

"Perhaps you're right, Mama," David drawled, not in the least repentant, "but it's over and done, and I now have my answer to one problem. As for the others, we would like to tell you ladies what we found out last night."

Lady Moorehead took her seat on the sofa once more and motioned for Sylvia to join her there. After a hesitant glance up at Tom, who gave her a faint nod, neither of which Lady Moorehead missed observing, Sylvia walked across the room and sat down next to David's mother.

The two men drew up chairs facing the others.

"We went to the gaming den, spoke with a hostess there by the name of Addie, and asked her if she had seen anyone answering Albertson's or Louise's description," Colchester said, pausing for effect.

Lady Lavinia leaned forward. "And had she?" she asked eagerly.

"Yes, on more than one occasion. A couple answering their general description had, regrettably, been in just the previous evening," Colchester said with a slight smile.

"David," his mother said impatiently, "you may enjoy keeping us waiting, but we certainly do not. If

you really have something to say, then say it and have
done with it."

He smiled wickedly at his mother, then went on.
"By all means, Mama, but I don't wish to raise any
false hopes, of course." Lady Moorehead glared at her
son, but he continued to take his time. "The man was
quite decidedly Albertson, and the young lady could
quite easily have been Louise, I suppose. She was
dressed in the latest rather daring French fashion, and
it was she who played against an opponent while Albertson sat and watched the game."

"Did your lady friend know when they would be
there again?" Lady Moorehead asked.

He looked at his mother with mock surprise. "What
a thing to say, Mama," he teased. "I was no friendlier
to her than Sir James was."

"Now, look here, young David," Sir James began
with a grin, "I was in enough of a predicament for
arriving home so late last night without your making
matters worse." He looked toward his wife, and the
tender smile they exchanged made a mockery of his
words.

"We asked Addie, the luscious hostess with the
henna-rinsed hair, if they might come again, and she
suggested that it would not be that night, but possibly
the next, or the one after that," he told them with a
sardonic smile.

"But you can't go there every night in case they
come," Lady Moorehead exclaimed. "They'd hear about
it and then never come again."

"We don't intend to, Mama dear," David said kindly.
"I left a man in the neighborhood, and then arranged
for Bert Eggers and his cronies to relieve him. When
they do put in an appearance, one of Bert's men will
hasten to let me know, while the others keep an eye
on the place. Once I get word, I can be there by the
time they finish the first game."

"But what do you intend to do when you get there,
David?" his mother asked rather anxiously. "If they're
not cheating, and are just spending an evening playing
cards, you can hardly do anything about it, even if it is

not the place for a lady to be. Do you suppose Timothy is there also, and sitting apart from them so that no one recognizes him?"

Tom looked up quickly. "If Timothy is there, there's really nothing at all we can do, for Louise is now her husband's property by law," he reminded them, then glanced up and saw the frown on Sylvia's face. He raised his eyebrows questioningly.

"Really, Tom, that's an awful thing to say. How can Louise be just a piece of property? She's still the same person she was before she married Timothy," Sylvia declared.

Lady Lavinia smiled a little apologetically. "Even if she is, that is not of importance, I'm afraid, my dear. Once she married him, he assumed the right, within reason, to do what he wanted with her and anything she owns. I'm afraid a woman has no rights once she's married."

"But that's nonsense," Sylvia said firmly. "If it's true, though, I'm certainly not going to marry, for I'll not make the same mistake as Louise and become the property of some gloating man to do with what he will."

She was so indignant that she did not see the hurt in Tom's eyes, but David did and was relieved. He had been quite surprised when he realized just how compromising a situation Tom had placed Sylvia in, for she had quite obviously been thoroughly kissed, but Tom's revealing eyes told him that his intentions, at least, were honorable.

Lady Moorehead smiled knowingly, for she had felt the same way once, many years ago. "My dear Sylvia, there is nothing quite like a good marriage to make a young woman positively bloom. You'll see, one day," she promised, then looked at her son. "But I have still not heard what you intend to do, David, when you find the person you believe to be Louise at that gaming den."

"Sit back and watch them at first," he said thoughtfully, "and as soon as we see anything unusual—Louise obviously upset, cheating going on—we'll just get her out of there."

"I suppose Albertson will be armed," Sir James suggested, "for he was on the night we gave him such an unhappy send-off from Colchester Castle."

David cast him a warning glance, for he did not want his mama worrying more than he could help. "I doubt it," he said, shaking his head and trying to sound casual, "for don't we all travel armed when setting out for the country?"

"Of course. I'd forgotten about that," the older man agreed.

Lady Moorehead looked at them suspiciously. "Whether he is or not, I think that you had all better be armed," she told them. "I'd feel more comfortable if you were, and I shall make a point of canceling any of my plans for the evening you go there, for I'm sure I won't sleep a wink until I know you are back safely. I shall, of course, have James leave me here with you, Lavinia, if you don't mind."

"Of course, Mildred, and then we can all be ready to help Louise in whatever way we can," Lady Lavinia agreed, not at all happy about the danger involved, but reluctant to say so and worry her friend even more. At least Tom was going also, so if anyone was injured, they would have a doctor on hand, she decided, somewhat irrationally.

Sylvia said nothing, but listened to all the plans and wondered how much pressure it had taken to persuade her twin not only to play piquet but also to cheat at it. Louise must be terribly unhappy, for she had disliked Timothy's cousin from the start, and she was not one to change her mind about a man of that sort.

It was not until they had all left, and Sylvia had said good night to Lady Lavinia, made her way up the stairs, and was being undressed by her maid, that she finally allowed herself to think about Tom. During the Season there had been several forward young men who had tried to steal kisses, and one had even been successful, but his kiss had been clumsy and inept, and had not felt at all the way Tom's had this evening.

She had wanted that glorious, exciting feeling to go on forever, and had been terribly disappointed when

David had interrupted them. Of course, she had been extremely angry with Tom beforehand, and she sincerely hoped that her upset feelings had not played any part in the thrill of his lips, for she had no wish ever to be so angry with him again.

Her maid finally left and she climbed into bed, but did not sleep right away. Tom's face kept appearing before her, and she wondered if it had been as exciting for him as it had for her. Then she shook her head. She was being foolish. Of course it had not, for hadn't Louise told her that young men did all kinds of things when they went to Eton, and he must have kissed a million girls since then.

It was a little before eleven o'clock in the morning when the doorbell sounded at number sixteen Grosvenor Street.

The two ladies were quietly relaxing in one of their favorite retreats, the small sunny sitting room decorated in soft green and yellow chintz, which adjoined the breakfast room Lady Lavinia seldom used when guests were staying with her.

She looked up from the piece of needlework in her hand and raised questioning eyebrows toward Sylvia, who had been writing a note to her mama.

"Who can possibly be calling at this hour, I wonder," she murmured. "Tom said he would not see us until this evening, when he is to take us to the Campbells' ball."

She did not have long to wait, for there was a light tap on the door and Bates entered, closing the door behind him.

"It's Sir Edward Danville, my lady," he told his mistress.

"Oh, dear," Lady Lavinia said with a frown. "And we are not yet dressed to receive visitors. Do you want to run up the back stairs and change, Sylvia, while I entertain him in the drawing room? You did show him in there, Bates, didn't you?"

"Of course, my lady," Bates said aloofly, for he had been butler here since the days when the old marquess had come to stay every Season, and he knew his position.

"Tell him I'll be along in a moment, then," Lady Lavinia said firmly, rising to follow Sylvia out of the room. "You may serve sherry in about a half-hour, and tell Cook there will probably be a guest for luncheon."

Sylvia was already out of sight by the time Lady Lavinia also went up the back stairs, for though she would not keep their guest waiting while she changed gowns, she wished to be sure that she looked her usual neat and tidy self before putting in an appearance.

Five minutes later she entered the drawing room, and Sir Edward rose to greet her.

"What a pleasant surprise, Sir Edward," she said, holding out her hand, and as he bent low over it, she added, "I had no notion that you were in town."

"Only got here last night, my lady," he said, waiting until she was seated before pulling a chair close. "Hope you'll excuse the hour, but I was anxious to see how my little girl is doing. We miss her, you know, at Danville Hall."

"I'm sure you must miss all of your daughters, sir, but I know that you want only the best for them." She smiled a little coldly. "And soon you will be a grand-papa again."

He looked startled. "You mean Louise is increasing already? She's back in London, is she?"

"Not to my knowledge, but I was referring to your eldest daughter, Elizabeth," she said a little reproachfully.

"Oh, yes. Believe my wife did say something or other about it. Thought you meant Louise, but I suppose they're still honeymooning in France," he grunted.

Lady Lavinia said nothing, for she was reluctant to tell a direct lie.

He appeared a little restless. "Where's Sylvia?" he asked. "You'd think she'd come running to see her old father, wouldn't you?"

"She's just changing her gown, Sir Edward, and will be down in a moment. If you had sent a note earlier, we would have been ready to receive you," Lady Lavinia said, trying hard to keep back any hint of reproach.

"I only arrived late last night," he said, "and decided to get up and come over here as soon as I could. What has she been doing, attending parties every night?"

"Not quite every night, sir, for this is only the Little Season, but she has certainly been enjoying herself. Your son-in-law, Colchester, is in town, and was, in fact, with us last evening. You remember his mama, Lady Moorehead? She and her husband, Sir James, were here also for dinner and cards," she said conversationally, hoping that Sylvia would not be too much longer.

Sir Edward's eye lit up. "Cards, you say? What a pity I didn't arrive a day earlier, for I'd have been happy to take one of them on at piquet." He suddenly frowned. "You said that Colchester is in town. What's he doing here? I would have thought he'd be home keeping an eye on Elizabeth, as she's breeding again."

"Perhaps you should ask him about it when you see him. He is staying with Lady Moorehead, of course." Lady Lavinia started to search her brain for something to talk to him about. "How is Lady Danville? Not too fatigued after the wedding, I hope?"

"No," he said, "no more than you'd notice, for she gets the vapors more often than a maiden lady." He suddenly remembered whom he was speaking to and flushed. "Begging your pardon, my lady, present company excepted, of course. Fact of the matter is, it was she who insisted I come and keep an eye on our last little girl. And where the devil can she have got to?— for it never took so long to change a gown when she was at home? Next thing she'll be wanting is a maid to do it for her." He shook his head in seeming disgust.

"Fortunately, she has a maid already, for Elizabeth was kind enough to provide her with one," Lady Lavinia informed him, "and I do believe I hear her now."

A moment later, Sylvia entered and dropped a curtsy to her papa, then kissed him lightly on the cheek.

"How nice to see you, Papa," she said with a smile that was not quite spontaneous. "What are you doing in London? I was just writing a letter to Mama when you arrived. How is she feeling?"

"Your mama is well enough," Sir Edward grunted. "But she's concerned about what you're doing all this time in London. You'd better not have run up any accounts here, for I've no funds to pay for a second Season for you."

Nor for the first one, Sylvia thought, but knew better than to say anything back to him.

"Elizabeth saw to my clothes before I left Colchester Castle," she said quietly, "and I don't buy anything that I cannot pay for at once. Where are you staying?"

"I'm staying at the small house not far from here where I've always stayed in London," he snapped, looking around at the delightful town house and comparing it unfavorably with his own lodgings. "And as for why I'm here, I've come to see that you get fixed up with a good husband. You've played around long enough, and it's high time you were settled and starting a family."

It was fortunate that, at that moment, Bates came in with the sherry, for Sylvia had paled visibly. This was what she had been dreading.

Sir Edward took a drink from his glass and smiled. This was what he had been needing all morning. The glasses were a bit small, but he could always help himself to a second one.

"You will join us for luncheon, won't you, Sir Edward?" Lady Lavinia asked politely. "It will be ready in about a half-hour."

"Why, thank you, my lady, I'd like that very much," he said, deciding that this spinster lady was better-mannered than he had expected. "It's been a long time since I broke bread with my daughter, and we've much to talk about."

"Are you expecting Tom to join us for luncheon, Sylvia?" Lady Lavinia asked.

"I'm not sure. He said he would try to come, but

that, if not, he would call this afternoon," Sylvia told
her a little nervously.

"Tom? Who is this that you're on a first-name basis
with, my girl? You've not written anything about him
to your mama," Sir Edward said.

Sylvia looked to her aunt for help, and Lady Lavinia
stepped into the breech. "Dr. Thomas Radcliff is the
young man who served on the Continent with Colchester.
He is the doctor who brought your two grandchildren
into the world, and is a good friend of both Elizabeth
and David," she said, feeling this would serve to di-
vert any suspicions that she had encouraged a too-
familiar relationship.

Sir Edward looked askance. "A doctor? My daughter is receiving the attentions of a doctor?" he asked,
as though he could not quite believe anything so foolish.

Once more there was an interruption as the doorbell
sounded, and a moment later Tom came into the
room, paying his respects first to his hostess and then
to Sylvia before turning to Sir Edward, whom he had
recognized at once as the twins' and Elizabeth's father.

"Sir Edward Danville, isn't it?" he said, holding out
his hand so that the older man had no option but to
grasp it in his. "Tom Radcliff, sir. You may not remember me, but I was a guest at your daughter's
wedding at Colchester Castle."

"I thought I'd seen your face somewhere before,"
Sir Edward said gruffly. "Lady Lavinia Trevelyan was
just telling me that you are my daughter Elizabeth's
doctor. She's nearing her time. Shouldn't you be up
there seeing to her?"

Sylvia was shocked at her father's rudeness. She was
about to say something when Tom caught her eye and
gave an almost imperceptible shake of his head. He
did not want her to come to his defense.

Helping himself to a glass of sherry, Tom returned
to her father's side. "To answer your question, Sir
Edward, your daughter is as healthy as a horse and
does not really need my services. I will, however, be
there long before the child is due. And what brings
you to London?"

"I'm here to see to my last daughter's interests, young man," Sir Edward said, deciding it best to make clear to this fellow exactly where he stood. "It's time she was wed, and I have some good friends here who are very anxious to meet her."

Sylvia gasped, and a few drops of her sherry spilled onto her gown. She dared not meet Tom's eyes, so she stared intently at the mark the sherry had made.

Once more, Lady Lavinia struggled to keep the conversation all that was polite. "You said you were staying not far from here, Sir Edward," she said. "Did you walk over for the exercise?"

"No, it's not that close and, in fact, it's not in as convenient a location as this." An idea suddenly occurred to him that would solve his problems admirably. "You wouldn't happen to have a spare bedroom, would you, Lady Lavinia, for I'd like to be nearer so I could see much more of my little girl," he told her.

Lady Lavinia was aghast at his audacity. "I'm afraid that would not be seemly, Sir Edward," she said coldly, "for a proper maiden lady does not have gentlemen staying in her home overnight. And I am very proper, sir."

"But I'm not what you'd call just a gentleman, my lady," Sir Edward blustered, seeing his chance of free food and lodging disappearing. "I'm family, so to speak, and with my little girl staying here too . . ."

"I'm afraid it wouldn't do, sir," Lady Lavinia said in a voice that brooked no further discussion.

It was with a feeling of relief that Sylvia heard Bates's quiet cough, and they went in to luncheon, Sir Edward jumping up immediately and leading the way, grabbing his daughter's arm so fiercely that she knew he must have left a bruise.

Tom looked at Lady Lavinia and smiled. "Permit me, my lady," he said, offering his arm.

"Thank you, Tom," she said wearily, wondering what on earth they were going to do if this well-dressed but boorish man stayed in town long.

14

Sir Edward lost no time in seeking out the gentlemen he had in mind for Sylvia. The first was a mere baron, but a childless widower in his mid-forties, who had accumulated a great deal of wealth. Sir Edward was sure that a generous settlement for himself could be agreed upon, for the man was an only son and needed a young, healthy wife to give him, preferably, a half-dozen heirs.

The fact that his eldest daughter had produced a son and a daughter within two years of her marriage, and was now breeding again, was a prime factor in his negotiations.

That very afternoon, though Lady Lavinia was not officially receiving, he arrived at the house on Grosvenor Street with Lord Greenford at about four o'clock, just as the two ladies were having their own tea and discussing Sir Edward himself.

"He is my father, Aunt Lavinia, and I have to obey him—despite the ridiculous things I said in heat the other night," Sylvia said, her eyes wide with fear. "But if I could only get word somehow to David that Papa is here, I'm sure he would do something to help."

"If I thought for a moment that he could, I would have sent him a note myself, but I've no doubt at all that Tom will talk to him, and they'll both know what to do," Lady Lavinia said, trying to reassure Sylvia.

They heard the doorbell and looked at each other warily, as the sound of a man's voice could be heard. Then Bates came into the room and closed the door behind him.

"It's Sir Edward Danville again, my lady, and with him is a Lord Greenford. Shall I tell them you are not at home?" he asked, for he was not accustomed to his mistress receiving guests at any time of day.

"No, Bates, I think I had best receive them in a few minutes." She turned to Sylvia. "You may slip through the side door to the dining room, my dear, if you wish, and as soon as you hear them greeting me, you can make your way up the stairs to your bedchamber, and stay there until they're gone."

Throwing her arms around Lady Lavinia's neck, Sylvia said, "Thank you so very much. You must be the most wonderful of adopted aunts, and I am truly grateful."

"Off with you," Lady Lavinia said gruffly. "Bates will bring them in here any minute now, and I don't want to be made to look a fool."

Without making a sound, Sylvia slipped through the side door and closed it behind her, then crossed the dining room and waited until she could hear her father and some other man greeting Lady Lavinia. Then she took the back stairs to her bedchamber.

"I'm so sorry you missed Sylvia, Sir Edward," Lady Lavinia was saying, "but you cannot expect that a young girl in London will be sitting at home every afternoon. You were, indeed, fortunate to find her home this morning."

"Where did she go?" Sir Edward asked. "For if she's in the park, we can go there ourselves and find her. If that young doctor is with her, I'll soon send him about his business."

Pointedly ignoring his last remark, Lady Lavinia said, "I'm afraid the park is not where she went. One of her many friends called for her to go shopping, and they could be on Bond Street, or Oxford Street, or even further afield, I'm afraid."

"Tell her to stay home tomorrow afternoon," Sir Edward ordered, "for I particularly want her to meet Lord Greenford."

Lady Lavinia looked at the grossly huge diamond ring on Lord Greenford's finger and at a similar-size diamond pinning his cravat. Then she stole a look at the gentleman, who had small eyes set in a large round purple-hued face, and she deeply regretted that she could not help Sylvia again tomorrow, for the very idea of the young girl having to marry someone of his ilk was intolerable. But it was her afternoon for receiving and she could not refuse to admit him.

"She will be here tomorrow, Sir Edward, for it is my day to return my friends' hospitality. We will both be at home in the afternoon, for Sylvia will, of course, be helping me with the tea urn." She smiled blandly at him but he scowled back.

"There's little point in staying here, then," he said rudely. "Would you care to join me at my club, sir, for a game of piquet?"

"My pleasure, Sir Edward," the other man replied as Lady Lavinia touched the bell.

Bates must have been waiting outside the door, for he was there in seconds.

"Good afternoon, Sir Edward, Lord Greenford. I'll expect you after three tomorrow. These gentlemen are leaving, Bates. Please show them out," she instructed with a pleasant smile, and was delighted to hear Lord Greenford say, "I'm not sure if I can come back tomorrow, Sir Edward. I'll have to send you word."

When the time came, however, Lord Greenford was not with Sir Edward, but another older gentleman was. His name was Lord Beaumont, and he was the Earl of Kingsbridge, and to Lady Lavinia he was a surprise, for though in his middle years he was not grossly overweight and red-faced, but had an excellent, unpadded figure and a kindly face when he remembered to smile.

Sylvia had been sitting before the urn, greeting Lady Lavinia's friends, pouring endless cups of tea for her guests as they arrived, and worrying as to whether she would have to marry the gross-looking man Lady Lavinia had described. When her papa arrived and brought a completely different gentleman, she was surprised. He brought him across at once to meet her.

"This is Lord Beaumont, Sylvia," her papa said,

"and he's come especially to see you this afternoon. Do you have to keep sitting at this damned urn and pouring tea?"

"It's the least I can do for Aunt Lavinia, for she feeds me and takes me places every day and is never given a penny for my keep," Sylvia told him.

"That's a fine gown you're wearing. Is it a new one?" her father asked, carefully ignoring her previous statement, though his eyes promised retribution at a later date.

"Yes, it's one of the ones Elizabeth's modiste made for me to bring to London," she said.

"That's good, for Colchester is inclined to be clutch-fisted, and the more he pays for your things, the happier I am," Sir Edward asserted. He leaned toward the man he had brought with him, who was looking around the room at the guests. "You know, Beaumont, her other two sisters married men with good old titles, but this one is a little shier than they were. Not too shy, of course, but not enough inclined to push herself, to my way of thinking."

Sylvia felt like a cow who had been taken to market and whose good features were being pointed out to a would-be buyer. She flushed a deep pink, then glanced up and noticed that Lord Beaumont was not watching her at all, but was glancing at her aunt with a most interested expression on his face.

He turned and saw Sylvia watching him, and for the first time she realized what a very nice smile he had. But he was, of course, almost as old as her papa.

"Is your aunt always as energetic as this? For almost half an hour she has been flitting from one person to another, making sure that everyone is being taken care of, and she appears to be genuinely interested in every single one of them," he said, sounding slightly bemused.

Sir Edward had started up a conversation with a young lady close by, so Sylvia felt free to say what she thought to his friend. "Lady Lavinia is not my aunt at all, but she's much better than a real one would be.

She is my eldest sister's sister-in-law, if that makes sense, but she's very dear to us, so we call her aunt."

"A charming lady," he said earnestly. "Would you both, by any chance, be at home tomorrow afternoon if I called again when it was a little less crowded? I do not think your father's presence would be necessary."

"I believe so," Sylvia told him, "but perhaps you should ask my aunt, for she may have plans for us that I am not aware of."

Lord Beaumont nodded. "I'll make a point of doing so before we leave. She is a most unusual lady. Has she never married?"

"No, my lord, she is a maiden lady, and has been a very kind and dear friend to me and my sisters," she told him. She was puzzled by his manner, for she would not be at all surprised to learn that he was more interested in her aunt than in herself.

"Do you have a family of your own, my lord?" she asked a little uncertainly.

His smile widened and his eyes softened at Sylvia's question. "I most certainly do, my dear. I have two sons of whom I am inordinately proud. The elder is at Cambridge and the younger still at Eton, and they are both doing exceptionally well, both at games and at their studies. Then I have an exceptionally pretty thirteen-year-old daughter who lives at home and is cared for and educated by a governess."

Wouldn't it have been wonderful, Sylvia thought, if her own papa had ever felt like that about them?

"And your wife." Sylvia hesitated, not knowing quite how to ask. "Did your wife pass away recently?"

His eyes clouded over and it was a minute before he answered. "My wife died two years ago, after a lengthy illness, and my little girl is badly in need of a mother's care," he said quietly.

"I'm so sorry I asked, my lord. I didn't mean to pry into your affairs," Sylvia said earnestly.

He smiled gently. "On the contrary, you had a right to ask, for your father did bring me here to meet you. I see your aunt is free for a moment. I think it is time I took my leave of her now, and I'll ask her at the same time if I may call tomorrow." He raised her hand almost to his lips. "It was a pleasure to meet you, my dear."

He rose and crossed the room to where Lady Lavinia was saying something to a servant, and Sylvia watched him speak to her aunt and take her hand in much the same way. Then, as he left the room, her father jumped up and followed him without bothering to say his farewells to either her or his hostess.

Sylvia shrugged slightly and shook her head, for her papa had always behaved this way. He could be the most charming and well-mannered gentleman, but when he had his mind set on something, he forgot everything else, and had often ignored her mama for days without really meaning to.

When all the guests had left, Sylvia and her aunt sat down for a moment while the servants cleared away the remains of the tea.

"I must apologize for my papa," Sylvia said. "It was most rude of him to leave without so much as thanking you, but I'm afraid he is like that. He must have feared that Lord Beaumont would leave without him."

"I think Lord Beaumont intended to," Lady Lavinia said with a laugh. "He was not the kind of man that I expected your papa to bring with him, for I found him quite charming."

"He was," Sylvia agreed, "as a father or uncle, but not as a husband for me. He has two sons and a thirteen-year-old daughter, and he's very proud of all of them."

"Then he's not looking for an heir. How strange that he is one of your father's would-be suitors," Lady Lavinia remarked. "I would hardly have thought him the type to seek a very young bride."

"He's looking for a mother for his young daughter, he told me, and it's possible that Papa did not tell him how old I am," Sylvia suggested, deciding it was more prudent not to say that he had been curious about Lady Lavinia.

*   *   *

When Tom arrived to escort them that evening to the Eveshams' dinner and card party, he told them that there was still no news from Colchester's men who were keeping an eye on the gaming den.

"I have been quite busy at the hospital, but David sent word only this afternoon that Albertson seems to be lying low for a few days. They know where to find us this evening, however, if he should so much as put his nose in the door of that gaming den," he assured them.

"What would you do if he went there alone?" Sylvia asked, curious as to what their plans were.

"Nab him, of course, and make him tell us where Louise and Timothy are," Tom assured them.

Sylvia's eyes lit up. "How would you do—?" she started to say, but Lady Lavinia placed a hand on her arm to stop her. "I think that, as ladies, we'd rather not know the details," she said firmly, but her eyes were twinkling. "Does David know that Sir Edward is in town, Tom?"

"I haven't actually seen him, for I've been so busy, but he sent messages to keep me abreast of things. Has Sir Edward been bothering you again?" he asked, frowning.

"Yesterday he brought the most awful-looking man to meet Sylvia," Lady Lavinia told him sadly, "a wealthy baron he introduced as Lord Greenford, who must have been fifty if he was a day."

"Aunt Lavinia let me escape through the side door," Sylvia explained, ignoring her aunt's frown, "and Papa would have brought him back for tea today except that Lord Greenford had another appointment. Instead, he brought a Lord Beaumont, who was really rather nice."

"Except that he was old enough to be your father, I'll be bound," Tom said grimly. He looked extremely worried, for he was feeling quite remorseful about those stolen kisses. He had realized some weeks ago that he had grown to love Sylvia, and had considered going to Danville Hall and asking Sir Edward's permission to marry her, but wanted first to be quite sure that this was what she wanted.

The kiss had told him that she was by no means cold toward him, but now he wondered if he might have waited too long. If she thought this Lord Beaumont was rather nice, then it was time for him to find out once and for all if she felt about him the same way he did about her.

The opportunity came after dinner, when Lady Lavinia had joined a group playing whist, and he was taking Sylvia to the drawing room, where the guests not playing cards were to engage in a game of charades. There was no one in the hallway, and the open door to the small anteroom showed that it was empty.

Taking a firm grip on her arm, he steered her into the room and closed the door quietly behind them.

As he seated her on a small sofa, Sylvia was puzzled but not afraid, for she knew that Tom would do nothing to hurt her. And if he intended to kiss her again, as he had before, she would not be at all averse to it.

"Someone will miss us and come looking," she said in a hushed voice as he sat down beside her.

"No they won't, for each group will think we're with the others," he said gently, reaching for her hand. "With your father intent on marrying you off to some wealthy old man, I just had to find out if you feel the same way I do. Oh, dear, I'm doing this all wrong, for I should be kneeling on the floor, I suppose."

Sylvia chuckled, realizing what he intended. "Do be careful, for I don't think those breeches were meant for kneeling," she warned, trying hard to control her laughter.

"You have a point there," he agreed with a grin as he patted her hand. "Can we assume I am on my knees on the floor, clutching your hand and asking for it in marriage?"

Once the words were out, even in seeming jest, Sylvia felt a rush of feelings pass through her that she had never before experienced. She suddenly wanted to marry him more than anything else in the world and, looking into his now-serious face, she whispered, "Yes, please, Tom."

"Are you sure," he asked gently, "for I know I am

rushing you without ever having talked of my feelings, but I have come to love you dearly over these last few months, and cannot allow you to marry someone else unless you have no love for me."

"I love you, Tom," she said softly, "and if only you can find some way to make Papa agree to it, I'll be proud to marry you and take care of you for the rest of our lives. But you do realize that my papa is a snob and will never agree to my marrying a commoner. Do you think, perhaps, that we should elope?"

Tom started to laugh; then, seeing Sylvia's hurt look, he framed her face between his hands and placed a soft kiss on her lips, then told her, "I am the one who is supposed to take care of you, wigeon. And though I don't think there's anything wrong with being a commoner, I'm afraid that I'm no longer one, for I now hold the courtesy title of lord, though I prefer not to use it."

She looked at him in amazement. "Why not?" she asked, for she had never heard of anyone having a rank and not using it.

"Because I'd rather use the title I have earned, that of doctor, and I feel that many of my poorer patients would be intimidated if they had to call me Lord Thomas Radcliff. You see, I am now the third son of the Marquess of Bradington," he explained, "my father having come into the title just a year ago on the death of my grandfather.

"And though I would not normally speak of financial matters to a lady, I'd much rather you hear them from me than from your father. I receive little recompense from my patients, for the poor seldom have money to spare and often pay me in the things they can afford, part of a pig when it's been slaughtered, or a ham they have cured, or even fresh eggs or a chicken.

"As for the wealthy, for the most part they dislike paying bills on principle, and do so only if they are compelled to. But I have a private income from my grandmama's side of the family, which is more than enough for us to live very comfortably," he assured her. "You won't need to make any tansy pudding for me in our kitchen, my love, for we will have a full staff to take care of our needs."

"How did you know why I wanted to learn to cook?" she asked.

"It wasn't difficult to guess, once you told me you'd take care of me, my love," he murmured, taking her into his arms again.

He held her close and drew her face toward him, lightly touching the tip of her nose with his lips, but Sylvia wanted more than that. She raised her head a fraction until her mouth was against his, then felt his strong arms pull her close as he lengthened and strengthened the kiss. He parted her lips with a gentle tongue and then she felt an unbelievable sensation of her body merging with his, while her heart raced and her ears rang with the most incredible music.

She felt suddenly abandoned when his mouth left hers, and he held her cheek to his until she came down to earth again from the sensuous heights to which she had climbed.

"I just had a thought," he whispered. "If you would really like to use the title once we are married, we will do so, but you know, surely, that all my patients already call you 'the doctor's lady'?"

"Tom, I have a favor to ask," Sylvia said, biting her lip as she tried to think how to phrase it. "Could we not tell anyone for now, until all this problem with Louise has been settled? When we announce it, I want to feel carefree and happy, and I couldn't if she was still in trouble," Sylvia explained.

"Whatever you want to do is all right," Tom agreed gladly. "I'll not speak to your father, then, until this other matter is settled, but don't accept any invitations from his elderly friends, for I would not like that at all," he warned her.

"I won't, for I believe the last one he brought is more interested in Aunt Lavinia than in me," she said, smiling mischievously.

"And you tried to pretend you found him rather nice, didn't you? Were you trying to make me jealous?" Tom asked, a dangerous gleam in his eyes.

"Perhaps a little," Sylvia confessed, looking at him impishly. "Did I succeed?"

"You certainly did. I'm not sure I would have said anything to you just yet if you had not said Lord Beaumont was rather nice," he told her, chuckling.

He moved a little away from her, and she frowned until he explained why he had done so. "You'd best not join the others looking so obviously just kissed, as you did the other night, for these are not family, and I'm afraid it may cause some awkward questions. And if I continue to sit close to you, I will not be able to help myself."

She gave him a rueful smile. "I hadn't thought of that, but you are right, of course."

They sat for a long moment, just looking at each other; then Tom said, "I'm sure you won't want to live in the small house that I presently use as both home and surgery. We'll have to look around the area and find something more suitable."

"Yes, I suppose we will," she agreed. "Elizabeth and David probably know what is available, but if there's nothing you like, we could live quite modestly until you have something built to your liking."

15

"I have a very important question to ask you both," Lady Lavinia said quietly, settling back against the squabs as the carriage started back to Grosvenor Street. "I know you were not present when partners for whist were being selected, and when you were nowhere to be seen, I assumed that Sylvia had decided she would rather not play. However, when I left the game room for a few minutes, I looked into the drawing room, hoping to see you enjoying yourselves at charades. Yet neither of you was there. Would one or both of you care to tell me where you were?"

She looked at Sylvia, who was glad of the dimness inside the carriage, for her cheeks were burning. Then she looked at Tom, who gazed back at her with a slightly guilty look.

"I'm afraid, Lady Lavinia, that we were in a small salon off the hall, alone, with the door closed," he told her quietly. "And we had just made each other the promise to say nothing, for the time being, of what we were doing there," he added. "I must take all the blame, of course, for I led a quite reluctant young lady inside, and it was I who closed the door."

"I'm too fond of you, Tom, to refuse you admittance to my home without an explanation," Lady Lavinia said, "but if Sylvia's reputation is at stake, I will be forced to do so."

"Please don't spoil everything, Aunt Lavinia," Sylvia's tearful voice begged from the corner. "Tell her, Tom, please."

"I was proposing marriage to Sylvia, which I preferred to do in private, and I'm happy to say that she accepted me," Tom said, "but we decided to say nothing for now because Sylvia wants to wait until the problems of her twin are settled, so she can be completely happy when she becomes engaged."

"You do not intend to ask her father's permission in the usual way?" Lady Lavinia asked dryly.

"Not until he runs out of wealthy old men, for, on principle, I would not buy my bride. I find the idea quite revolting unless there are special circumstances to warrant such a thing," Tom said curtly.

"And how long do you think you can stand by and watch Sir Edward bring suitors to Sylvia who ogle her and make pointed remarks?" Lady Lavinia asked.

"I don't know, my lady, but I had thought that you would have preferred my suit to that of such gentlemen. As you obviously do not, I regret my foolishness in informing you of our plans," he said stiffly.

"I assume that something else occurred in that room after you made your proposal, Tom?" Lady Lavinia suggested very quietly.

"I kissed Sylvia, of course, but nothing else happened," Tom snapped, now becoming angry at being put through an interrogation of this sort as though he were a schoolboy.

The carriage drew up outside the house and Tom jumped out to hand down first Lady Lavinia and then Sylvia, squeezing her hand as he did so and whispering, "Don't worry, my love, it will all come out right."

Then he bowed to Lady Lavinia, who was standing at the foot of the steps, and said, "Good night, my lady."

"Are you not coming in for a few minutes, Tom? I think we have still some things that need to be discussed," she said quietly.

Tom moved closer so that his words would not be heard by the waiting coachman. "I see no purpose in coming in to be further cross-examined like some philanderer. I love your niece, wish to marry her, and am in a position to support her better than she is accustomed to. I do not appreciate your attitude, my lady."

Lady Lavinia placed a hand on his arm and said

earnestly, "It is my duty to protect her, Tom, and you know it. If you wish me to remain on your side in this, you really should come in for a few minutes where we can talk in private."

"Very well," he said, and held out an arm to each to assist both ladies up the steps.

Once they entered the drawing room, Lady Lavinia closed the doors and indicated the decanters on the sideboard. "Help yourself, Tom, and then join us by the fire."

After pouring himself a stiff brandy, he went to join them, leaning against one corner of the mantelpiece over the fireplace rather than taking a seat.

"Now, you both want to be married, and Sylvia is very much under the age at which she can marry without parental consent. You're not planning a trip to Gretna Green, are you?" Lady Lavinia asked blandly.

"Not unless we have to," Tom informed her. "I'm hoping David has some ideas, for I know he is the one responsible for keeping Sir Edward away from town this long."

"He agreed to pay everything for our come-outs and our weddings as long as Papa did not try to arrange marriages for us," Sylvia told them.

"How do you know?" Tom asked. "Did David tell you?"

Sylvia shook her head. "It was Elizabeth who told us. It was arranged at the time she got married. Papa told David that he had been arranging a marriage for Elizabeth that would have helped him financially, but David refused point-blank to pay him anything. He did, however, say that he would take care of Louise and me provided Papa did not try to plan any more convenient marriages." She thought for a moment. "It has to be still true, Tom, for Papa wanted me to come home after the wedding. Then David wrote to him about my coming to London, and there was nothing more said."

"I'll speak to David first thing in the morning. Your father is a monster and should not be allowed to do such things. I assume the money disappears at the tables?" Tom asked.

Sylvia nodded. "Mostly at piquet," she said.

"Then, if that's decided, I'll take my leave. I assume I have been forgiven for my indiscretion, my lady?" he asked Lady Lavinia softly.

"As long as there is not a repeat of your performance of tonight, but you know, I am sure, that I will be watching you both from now on, and you will not get as much time alone as in the past," she warned.

He bent and kissed her cheek. "We will both try to behave with the utmost discretion," he assured her, and proved himself by simply taking Sylvia's hand and kissing it, though his eyes spoke so expressively that her heart leapt for joy.

After he had left, Lady Lavinia took Sylvia in her arms and hugged her. "He is a wonderful young man, and so right for you, my dear. Everything will work out once Colchester is apprised of the situation."

The following morning, a little before eleven o'clock, Sir Edward Danville paid them a visit.

Lady Lavinia told Bates to show him into the drawing room, and as soon as she entered, he stopped his pacing back and forth.

"What emergency brings you here at this hour, Sir Edward?" she asked. "Is Lady Danville all right?"

"Where's Sylvia?" he asked. "I came to make sure that she's going to be here this afternoon. Lord Greenford is available now and I'm bringing him here at three o'clock. He can take her for a drive or something."

Lady Lavinia would have liked to tell him that this was her house and that she said who would be admitted and at what time, but she was afraid that if she did, he would take Sylvia away.

Instead, she contented herself with saying simply, "I'm sorry, Sir Edward, but Lord Beaumont will be here today at three o'clock also, and I hardly think that Sylvia can entertain both gentlemen at the same time."

"He arranged that before he left?" Sir Edward asked, making it clear that he had not been apprised of Lord Beaumont's plans. "Now, that's a pretty kettle of fish! Why on earth didn't he say he liked my little girl?"

"What do you want to do about it, Sir Edward?" Lady Lavinia asked sweetly. "Which man has the most money?"

"Beaumont, of course," Danville snorted. "He's got money to burn, and I can't afford to offend him. I'd better tell Lord Greenford that Sylvia's not feeling well and we'll have to come another day."

They had neither of them heard the doorbell, and looked up with surprise to see Colchester standing in the doorway, with Tom just behind him.

"I was just about to leave," Sir Edward said, somewhat flustered, "for I have to cancel something I arranged for this afternoon."

"I am sure it can wait until you and I have a word in the study," Colchester said coldly, then added, "If you wouldn't mind, Lavinia."

Lady Lavinia not only did not mind; she was delighted that he had arrived at just the right time. "Of course, David," she murmured, but was somewhat surprised when Tom went with the other two men.

"Where is everybody, Aunt Lavinia?" Sylvia asked as she came hurrying into the room. "Bates said that Papa was here, and then I'm sure I heard David's voice."

"They're in the study—your papa, David, and Tom," Lady Lavinia told her. "I'm beginning to feel that my house is a meeting place for all and sundry. Can you believe that your papa wanted to bring that awful Lord Greenford here this afternoon?"

"You did tell David, didn't you?" Sylvia asked. "For I know he'll stop him. I couldn't marry someone like that, even if I were not already promised to Tom."

"I had no opportunity to tell David anything," Lady Lavinia said caustically, "for he seems to have come here for the sole purpose of meeting with your papa. But in any event, Lord Greenford won't be coming, for I told Sir Edward that Lord Beaumont would be here at that time."

Sylvia threw her arms around her aunt, causing that lady to squirm until Sylvia asked with a low chuckle, "Did you also tell him that Lord Beaumont showed considerable interest in you?"

There was the sound of the study door banging, and hurried footsteps down the hall. Then Sir Edward's voice snapped, "My coat and hat, Bates, and be quick about it."

The two ladies listened, looking at each other with raised eyebrows. "He's leaving without saying good-bye, Aunt Lavinia," Sylvia whispered. "He must be very angry indeed."

The outer door slammed at the same time that the study door opened again and David and Tom came into the drawing room.

"Allow me to be the first to wish you every happiness, my dear," David said to Sylvia, taking her into his arms and giving her a brotherly kiss on the cheek. "You couldn't have picked a better man."

"Papa agreed to it?" Sylvia asked, not yet believing that everything was all right.

"Of course he did. How could he refuse such an excellent fellow?" David asked, winking at Tom. "And now I suppose you will have to take your betrothed to meet Lord and Lady Radcliff?"

"I believe so, but first I'll send her a note, for Mama gets a little flustered when anyone comes to see her unexpectedly, even one of her sons," Tom said with a shrug. "What I would like to do, however, is take my betrothed for a ride in the park this afternoon, so that we can discuss our wedding plans in private. We don't want an official announcement, however, until this matter of Louise and Albertson is cleared up."

"You'll take my carriage, of course," Lady Lavinia said. "I'll order it for two o'clock, which should give you time to have luncheon with us first, and you also, David, unless you're expected elsewhere."

She did not see David have a quiet word with Bates,

but just before they were ready to go in to lunch, the butler appeared with a bottle of the finest French champagne, iced and ready.

It was a lively party that sat down to luncheon, for Sylvia was bubbling with excitement without the assistance of the champagne, and Lady Lavinia was almost as gay, for a happy marriage was what she had hoped would result from this visit, and despite last night, when she could not recall ever being so angry, she was very fond of Tom.

"To Sylvia and Tom," David said when the glasses were all filled. "May they be as happy as Elizabeth and I are, and as prolific."

Lady Lavinia, a little shocked by the toast but happy nonetheless, raised her glass and drank; then Tom toasted his beloved, and they were all pleased to drink to Sylvia.

Not to be outdone, Sylvia proposed a toast to her dearest doctor, and then they all partook of some of the quite delicious luncheon before the champagne went to their heads.

"You have heard nothing of Louise and Albertson or the gaming den, David?" Sylvia asked as they sipped their after-luncheon coffee.

"No, though Bert Eggers, my old army batman, has spent a great deal of his time there since our visit. He has a couple of trustworthy fellows with him, and sends one to report each day, so we're bound to hear something eventually," he assured her.

"What if they have decided to pick another gaming den and will not return to that one?" Sylvia asked.

"It's most unlikely," David said, "for gamblers are usually very superstitious, and I'll guarantee that Albertson wouldn't dare stop going to a place where they've won a considerable sum at least three times in a row."

Sylvia just wished the luncheon would come to an end, for she wanted to be alone with Tom, and from the way he kept looking at her, he was waiting eagerly for the same thing.

She suddenly remembered something. "Aunt Lavinia,

isn't Lord Beaumont coming this afternoon at three o'clock?"

Lady Lavinia looked surprised. "So he is, and I had forgotten all about him," she said. "Well, I'll just have to explain what has happened, and I doubt he'll stay long."

"You could tell Bates to say that we had to go out unexpectedly," Sylvia suggested, but Lady Lavinia would have none of it.

"He was invited," Lady Lavinia said, "so I'll not do that, but will pay him the courtesy of receiving him and giving him a truthful explanation. He appeared to be a very nice gentleman, and I'm sure he'll understand. Why don't you two run along now and enjoy your ride, and when you come back, I shall expect you to tell me all your plans."

"I'll take my leave also, Lavinia," David said, "for I've much still to do in town, and once this matter is taken care of, I'll have to get back home as soon as possible, for Elizabeth must be missing me as much as I miss her."

Lady Lavinia smiled understandingly, and a few minutes later they went their separate ways.

"Would you mind if we had a small, quiet wedding up at Colchester Castle, Tom?" Sylvia asked when they were riding along Park Lane. "I don't want to wait until spring or summer, but, if it's not being forward, I'd like to get married just as soon as we can."

Tom was both surprised and pleased. "Of course you're not being forward. This is a decision for the two of us to make, not just one, and the less fuss and palaver, the better I shall like it. I could get a special license if you like, so that we could marry anytime we wished."

Sylvia nodded. "I think that would be best, and we could have just close friends and family there. I have a quite simple white gown that has never been worn, so I could save it for the occasion."

"We're agreed, then, my love," Tom said. "I'll get a special license, and just as soon as this business with

Louise is straightened out, we'll go back to Colchester Castle and tie the knot.''

He reached over and squeezed her hand, and the glance they exchanged was one of those private ones for lovers only.

When they were once more moving through the park, Sylvia frowned and asked, "This Bert Eggers that David has set to watching the gambling place—is he reliable?''

"The best," Tom assured her, "for he went with us through all the battles and you couldn't have a more careful, loyal soldier.''

"But what will he do if he sees Louise and Albertson go into the gaming den?''

"He'll send one of his men to wherever David has told him he'll be going that night, for gaming dens don't come alive until well after midnight; then he will take up watch, inside the place, until we arrive.''

"Won't it be a long time before you get there, for surely it is in an unpleasant part of London?'' she suggested, hoping he might give her the actual address.

"It's closer than you would imagine, for it's not far from the Royal College of Physicians, where you went with me. The place has the usual kind of odd name— it's called Ned's Den, and it's also off Newgate Street, at the end of Warwick Lane.'' Tom was amused at the interest Sylvia was showing in their plans, but shocked when he heard her next question.

"Can I go with you? Louise will need me if she is in as much trouble as you think she is, and I can bring her home," she suggested, then saw the look of horror on Tom's face.

"You can no more be seen in a place like that than Louise can," he snapped. "It's dangerous, to say the least, and we will have enough to do getting your sister out of there without having to worry about you also. I never heard of such a ridiculous suggestion.''

He saw the disappointment on her face and realized he had been a little harsh. Reaching for her hand, he said gently, "I can completely understand your wanting to help, for she is your closest family, but you would hinder rather than help on something of this sort. The arrangement is that when we get word, unless it's in the middle of the night, Lady Moorehead will join you and Lady Lavinia and wait until we return."

Sylvia smiled a little hesitantly, for she did not want him to exact a promise from her, or it would only make everything worse later. She had no intention of staying home and waiting with Lady Lavinia and Lady Moorehead, no matter what he said, but she would have to rely on her instincts, hoping that Louise's feelings would let her know when next she went gambling, as they had before.

"Didn't you say you were sending a note to Lady Radcliff?" she asked, changing to a safer subject. "Are you sure she's in town?"

"Yes, I did send a note, although I don't know if the family is in town still," he said with a warm smile, relieved that she had dropped the subject of her sister. "I see them no more than once a week when I'm here and they're at the town house, and much less frequently when I'm out of town. You see, I do not care for the social scene as much as they do. When they're at the country estate, which is about twenty miles south of London, they are constantly entertaining guests."

"But you volunteered and seemed quite happy to escort Aunt Lavinia and me to almost every function we've attended," Sylvia protested, surprised at his admission.

"I knew my mind before we left for London," he told her gently. "I wanted to see as much as I possibly could of you here, and it was the only way I could think of to do so."

Sylvia flushed and looked down. "I hadn't thought of that, but I'm very glad you did," she said, and added a little self-consciously, "You see, I knew I was falling in love with you before we left, but I tried not to, for I really thought you were a poor doctor, and was sure Papa would not let us marry."

Tom nodded. "I realize that now, but at the time I

had no idea you thought me penniless. I suppose I expected you to have checked me out with Elizabeth before you even accepted my first invitation."

"They receive all kinds of people at the castle, both rich and poor," she protested, "and I would never have thought to ask her about anyone's financial position."

"Perhaps not, but had any of the ones who were not suitable asked you to take a drive with him, she would have put a stop to it immediately, I'm sure," he told her, then added, "It might actually be a good thing if the *ton* allowed themselves to marry cits and the like, for this intermarriage between an elite few could prove dangerous in the years ahead."

"Do you mean because of the riots and restlessness, there might be an uprising, as there was in France?" Sylvia asked, curious but not worried.

"No, and I can't imagine that happening here, for the English people are a completely different temperament than the French. What I meant was that the study of science is revealing that so much inbreeding— marriages between first cousins over and over again— can cause serious illnesses and even madness to occur more frequently."

Sylvia was extremely interested, though she knew that Lady Lavinia would consider this a most improper conversation.

"You mean, like King George's illness?" she asked.

"Yes, that's exactly what I mean, but it's difficult to prove and it would be even more difficult to persuade anyone to do anything about it—including you and me, my love," he told her, looking at her so lovingly that Sylvia again felt that unaccustomed warmth deep inside—the very pleasant, happy feeling she was becoming used to.

"And now I believe we should return and see if Lady Lavinia succeeded in chasing away the last of your elderly suitors," he told her, turning the carriage around.

"You know, he was rather nice, Tom, and he had heirs, so that he did not need to marry someone very young. You don't suppose that he came back just to see Aunt Lavinia and not me, do you, for he did ask a lot of questions about her."

Tom grinned. "Wouldn't that be an interesting turnabout?" he said. "I've heard of a Lord Beaumont who is immensely wealthy, but do not recall anything unpleasant said about him."

"Perhaps we'd better not get back too soon," Sylvia said mischievously. "They may want to be alone to get to know each other better."

"I do not particularly relish another interview of the sort we had with her last night," Tom said seriously. "If she thinks we deliberately got lost in the park, who knows what she might say?"

"It was only to protect my reputation, Tom," Sylvia said, "for you don't know how difficult it must have been for someone like Aunt Lavinia to watch Louise and me when we were here before. Young men were calling at all hours, and constantly underfoot. She's extremely conscientious, you know."

"I suppose she is," Tom agreed, "but I could not help resenting it when she charged us with an impropriety last night, for we had really done nothing that could be interpreted as wrong. We behaved with far less discretion the other night in her home."

"Do you think that she did not realize that, Tom?" Sylvia asked. "Both she and Lady Moorehead knew exactly what we'd been doing, I'm sure, and that is why she's going to watch us so carefully from now on."

"Perhaps, but if she and Lord Beaumont start to see more of each other, you may be sure that I'll question her just as thoroughly as she did me, and enjoy every minute of it," he vowed.

16

~~~

"Of course I did not turn Lord Beaumont away without offering him at least a cup of tea," Lady Lavinia said to her curious niece. "I found him to be a most charming gentleman, and not at all like one expects of your papa's usual acquaintances."

"Not at all like Lord Greenford, to be sure," Sylvia said with a laugh, for she was enjoying seeing her aunt's pink cheeks and indignant expression as she teased her. "I thought he was very nice, as a matter of fact, and I didn't mind at all the questions he kept asking me about my Aunt Lavinia."

"He asked you questions about me?" Lady Lavinia asked in some surprise. "But you did not tell me so last evening."

"I didn't think there was any need, for I felt sure you would send him about his business now that Tom and I are to be married," she said, trying to sound very innocent. Then she chuckled. "As you didn't, I think I was right in believing his interests were fixed elsewhere than on me."

"Now, don't you go making a scandal broth out of a simple cup of tea offered to a gentleman who had come to see you and found you not at home. I should have insisted that you and Tom remain here and help entertain your guest, young lady," Lady Lavinia said sharply.

Sylvia put her arms around her aunt and gave her a hug. "It would probably have been the correct thing to do, but then, I would not have been able to tease you about it, would I, dearest of adopted aunts? Let me tell you what Tom and I have decided," she said eagerly.

She was in the middle of explaining their plans when she started to feel odd. Not a sharp pain anywhere this time, but just a general feeling of foreboding, and she was suddenly quite sure that Louise was being made to go to the gaming hell again tonight. It couldn't have happened on a better evening, for, with nothing that they absolutely must attend, they had decided to stay home tonight and catch up on their sleep in preparation for a grand ball the following evening.

Careful not to let her aunt realize that anything unusual was occurring, she continued to describe the plans they had made for a simple wedding at Colchester Castle, but as soon as she could, she excused herself and went to her bedchamber to rest until dinner.

Once there, she opened the bottom drawer of her dressing table and found the box of paints and powders, masks, and false noses that she and Louise had procured during the Season. On wet afternoons they had disguised themselves as all kinds of creatures and playacted as a realistic practice for the charades so popular at parties.

There was also an old gray cotton gown, clean but much worn and stained, that one of the maids had given them to protect their own gowns when applying the different paints, and a gray wig that Louise had found in the attic.

She put her old black boots at the bottom of the armoire in readiness, and made sure her hooded black cape was there, for it would cover her disguise from the hackney driver. Then she lay down on her bed and, surprisingly, fell asleep and was awakened by Lady Lavinia, who was wondering where she had got to.

"It's a good thing we are staying home this evening," Lady Lavinia remarked as they went together down the stairs. "You must be more tired than I thought. Why don't you retire immediately after dinner and tell Maude not to disturb you until morning?" she suggested. "A good night's sleep will do you good."

"Perhaps I will," Sylvia said, trying not to show her glee. Everything was working out just as she wanted. "We do have that ball tomorrow evening, and I'd like to look rested for it."

By ten o'clock the house was quiet, and Sylvia decided she could safely start to apply her disguise. A half-hour later, no one would have recognized the old slattern as anything but what she appeared to be. She had found no difficulty in tearing the gray gown in a couple of places, and her black hair was completely hidden under the dirty-looking, untidy gray wig. A small pillow was fastened firmly in place under the gray dress to give her the appearance of having a humped back.

Throwing the black cloak around her shoulders and fastening it firmly, she pulled the hood up until it almost covered her face; then she quietly opened her bedroom door. The lights in the corridor had been dimmed, which meant that Bates had closed up the house for the night and retired to the servants' quarters.

With her boots in her hand, she stealthily crept down the stairs, pausing every few steps to listen, but there was not a sound save for the ticking of the grandfather clock in the hall. The door to the breakfast room made a slight squeak as she turned the knob, and she slipped quickly inside and waited, but it had not been loud enough for anyone to hear.

Then she swiftly crossed the room to the French windows, slid back the bolts, and, unlocking the door with the key that was always in the keyhole, stepped quietly out into the dark night.

There were lights still in the servants' quarters and the kitchen, and she knew they would serve to conceal her as she trod the grass border beside the footpath that led directly to the back gate and into the mews, where their carriage was kept and the horses stabled. She regretted that she could not use them tonight, for her journey would have been much more comfortable had she been able to do so. The hackney rank in Brook Street was quite close, however, and she made her way directly there and went boldly up to the first carriage in line.

"I want you to put me down on Newgate Street at Warwick Lane," she told the waiting driver, muttering the words and making sure that her face was covered by her cloak as she stepped up into the carriage.

For a moment she thought he was going to argue with her, for few women hired hackneys at this hour of the night to go anywhere, never mind to such an area, but he must have thought better of it, for he stepped up on top and they set off at a trot.

The streets were quiet, and it took no more than a half-hour to get to her destination, but by the time she had stepped down and paid the driver what she thought was probably an outrageous sum, she felt herself becoming extremely nervous.

She started to walk down Warwick Lane, keeping to the shadows, for even at this late hour there were a number of people in the streets. Then she turned a corner and saw a carriage dropping off a couple of gentlemen, and she knew she was there.

Now to get into the place without being noticed. She could not, of course, walk straight in, for they would probably throw out a woman of her disguised appearance. What she needed was a back entrance, but she did not want to get into the wrong place, so she walked along the wall to the corner of the building, carefully counting her paces. Then she walked to the next corner and turned to walk along the back of the building the same number of paces as before.

There was an entrance, dark and gloomy-looking, but the sounds of coarse laughter could clearly be heard, so she carefully opened the door, slipped inside, and found herself at the foot of some stairs that led to an empty, smelly corridor. Now her cloak was a handicap, for it looked too good for the part she was playing, so she discarded it, dropping it in a dark corner.

Moving as quietly as she could, she reached the entrance to a large room, poorly lit save for the chandeliers above the gaming tables. As her eyes adjusted to the lighting, she saw the three men she had expected, sitting around a table, and with them was a flashy henna-haired woman. Addie, she decided, and the small man must be Eggers. David said something, and Addie got up and went through a door just behind their table.

Instinctively, Sylvia turned to look in the direction they were staring, and she saw Albertson and another, older man at a table in the center of the room. Although she was sitting half turned away from her, there was no question but that the woman with them was her twin, Louise.

She was dressed in a most revealing gown of scarlet trimmed with silver sequins, and there was a slit down the back bodice of the dress, through which Albertson's huge hand was possessively inserted. Louise looked miserably unhappy as she concentrated on the game, and suddenly Sylvia saw her wince, and realized that the loathsome brute had pinched her back in some sort of a signal.

As Sylvia rose from her hiding place, Eggers got up and approached the table, glass in hand, then stumbled awkwardly, spilling the contents of his glass over Louise's gown.

"My profound apologies, madam," Eggers started to say in a slurred voice while he attempted to place himself between Albertson and Louise. But Albertson was having none of it, moving swiftly to Louise's other side. Looking every bit the part of a slatternly old woman, Sylvia appeared as if from nowhere, and to his surprise, she grasped Louise's hand and pulled her to her feet.

Murmuring, "Come along with me, dearie, and I'll have ye dry in a minute," she pushed her toward the doorway, placing herself between Louise and Albertson and leaving Eggers free to take care of him.

Sylvia heard the murmur of voices behind her, but had no time to turn around and see what was happening, for they were nearing the doorway. Then the three watchers—David, Tom, and Sir James—rushed

forward and steered the two women through the door
where the henna-haired woman had gone.

It was a private room with a door leading directly
into the outside corridor, and as soon as they were
inside, Tom and David came forward, intending to
take Louise and give the old woman something for her
unwitting help. But Louise was crying and clinging to
the old hag for dear life.

"Where is Timothy, Louise?" Sylvia asked her twin
as she pulled off her wig, while the two men stared in
disbelief.

"He's in a house on Cow Lane, number five, and
he's tied up in a room on the second floor. Please
don't let Albertson get to him first or he'll kill him,"
Louise whispered.

Sir James had been watching from the doorway as
the scene in the main room unfolded. "Albertson will
be lucky to get out of here alive," he told them, "for
the denizens must have realized what he's been doing
and are out for blood."

"Can Eggers handle it?" David asked.

"At the moment, no one can, for they're after him,
and Eggers and his men are with them, keeping an eye
on the situation, I believe," Sir James replied.

"Then why don't you take Louise and Sylvia back to
Lady Lavinia's house, and Tom and I will go around
to Cow Lane and rescue Timothy," David suggested.
"We'll bring him there also, for I think that is where
we'll be less likely to run into someone we know."

Sir James gasped. "I'd no idea that Sylvia was in
this with us," he started to say.

"She wasn't," David said, "and I'll be interested to
know later how she knew the time and place this was
coming off."

Silent now, Sylvia gathered her cape from where she
had dropped it in the corridor and placed it around
Louise's shoulders. Then she allowed herself to be led
out the back way and around to where the carriage
waited.

Meanwhile, David and an extremely tight-lipped
Tom, who had not spoken a single word to Sylvia,

went to find the place in Cow Lane where Louise and Timothy had been staying.

Sylvia was now shaking almost as much as Louise, for she had glanced at Tom when they were in that squalid little room, and he had gazed back at her with eyes as cold as steel.

"Is Lady Moorehead with Aunt Lavinia?" Sylvia asked Sir James.

"No," he said, "for she was fast asleep when the message came, and I hadn't the heart to waken her. I left a note by her bed, however, in case she should wake up and worry."

They turned the corner into Grosvenor Street, and when Sylvia saw that there were no lights in number sixteen, she looked across at Sir James and told him, "Aunt Lavinia is probably still fast asleep, and believes that I am also. You can either waken the whole house, for the staff will not yet be up, or we can go in by the breakfast-room French doors, which I left open. It will mean going around to the mews, for the breakfast room is in the back of the house."

"You can find that entrance better than I can, Sylvia, so I suggest we drop you in the mews. Then you can go in the way you came out, and open the front door for Louise and me. But be sure to leave all the doors and gates the way you found them before you went out, or the servants will think there has been a burglary," Sir James told her.

Ten minutes later, they entered Sylvia's bedchamber, where the fire was still glowing. Louise sat in front of it, shivering, while Sylvia went to waken Lady Lavinia and explain the events of the evening, for it was now three o'clock in the morning.

"Tom and David will be bringing Timothy back here soon, I hope," Sylvia told her aunt, "and it would perhaps be best if they took my bedchamber, and I could spend the rest of the night on your chaise, if you wouldn't mind."

"Very well, my dear," said a remarkably calm Lady Lavinia. "I'll just come and thank Sir James for all his trouble, and let him go home to Mildred if he wishes;

then we'll wait for Timothy to get here, and spirit him straight up to your bedchamber. It would be easier to prevent a scandal if no one, not even any of my servants, knows they were ever in London."

Sir James was only too happy to go home and leave Louise in the ladies' capable hands. While Lady Lavinia was trying to comfort her still-weeping twin, Sylvia heard the carriage and sped down the stairs to let the men in before they rang the bell.

It seemed that Timothy could scarcely walk, for he had been bound tightly for a considerable length of time, so David carried him up the stairs while Sylvia led the way, and Tom followed behind.

Once in the room with the door closed and locked, David laid the young man on the bed and pulled the screen around, procuring more candles so that Tom could properly check on his condition.

The three ladies sat around the fire, which they had banked, and Louise tried to explain, as best she could, what had happened.

"We were very happy at first in Paris," she said softly, "for it was so beautiful, but then Albertson arrived. He must have had everything planned before we were married. He kidnapped Timothy, and I did everything he demanded of me, for I truly believed, and still do believe, that he meant to kill Timothy in the end so that he would ultimately inherit when Timothy's papa dies. Of course, it would have looked like an accident and I would have died with him, I'm sure, for I knew too much.

"He was desperately in need of money, and took everything we had with us, then started this scheme of cheating, first in Paris, and then in London."

"Albertson didn't do anything to you, did he?" Sylvia asked.

"Not what you have in mind," Louise said, "for I think he took those pleasures elsewhere. But he did beat me on several occasions when I refused to go with him to cheat people until I saw for myself that Timothy was still all right. You won't believe it, I am sure, but I reached a point where I didn't care whom I

cheated and robbed as long as I could keep Timothy
alive.''

Sylvia leaned forward, her hand outstretched. "Were
you hurt here . . . and here . . . and once on the back
of your head?" she asked her twin.

"How did you . . .?" Louise began, then asked,
unbelieving, "You mean you felt it at the time?"

"Probably not the way you did," Sylvia said softly,
"but that's how I knew you were in trouble."

Tom and David came from behind the screen.

"He's in better shape than I had at first thought,"
Tom told Louise. "The bonds were not quite tight
enough to cut off the circulation, but being in the
same position for such a long time has made him weak
and he'll have to start walking with a stick at first, just
for short distances, until the muscles strengthen. You
needn't look so worried, my dear, for with the proper
care he'll soon be back to normal again."

"We heard what happened," David told Louise,
"and Tom would like to examine you now, to be sure
nothing was broken. Lady Lavinia will go with you
behind the screen while I talk to Sylvia."

They went over to the bed, while Sylvia waited for
the scolding she knew to expect from David. "I'm very
angry with you for interfering with our plans, for you
could have ruined everything and got yourself or Louise killed. But I know that you are so close to her that
you couldn't help yourself," he told her quietly so the
others would not hear. "What I would like to know is
how you found out that they were there tonight, for
Tom was with me when we got word."

"You could say I felt it in my bones, David. After
Tom and I got back from our drive, I was talking with
Aunt Lavinia and suddenly I felt whatever it was that
Louise was feeling. I knew she was being made to go
there tonight, and I just had to be there too, to help
her," she whispered. "Can you make Tom understand?"

David shook his head. "Not at the moment, for he
feels you deliberately put him in an impossible position with me. It didn't occur to him, when he told you
what we meant to do, that you were using him in

order to make yourself a part of our plan. You were, weren't you?"

"I suppose I was, David, but I didn't think of it that way. All I thought of was helping Louise," Sylvia said, trying to keep the tears in her eyes from spilling over.

He bent over and kissed her cheek. "Leave it alone for a while, and if he doesn't see sense within a week or so, I may do a little interfering myself." He grinned. "Of course, that outfit you were wearing may just have made him see how you might look forty years from now, and put him off somewhat."

Sylvia laughed a little shakily, then turned to her Aunt Lavinia, who had rejoined them at the fire.

"Apart from a few bruises, Louise is fine, my dear, and she's getting into bed now for a few hours' sleep. Before they leave London, David wants to be sure that Albertson is safely under lock and key, and Timothy a little stronger, so they will stay here another day. How trustworthy is your maid?"

"She's part of David's staff and her whole family works for him, so she'll not dare do anything to jeopardize their jobs, if we put it that way," Sylvia assured her aunt.

"Very well. She can look after them as well as you, and now you'd better come and stretch out on my chaise. We'll keep this door locked so that Maude doesn't wander in and scream the place down a few hours from now. I'll just see Tom and David out."

The two men walked to the door, where Sylvia and her aunt waited, and David bent down and kissed Sylvia's cheek. "Try not to get into any more mischief," he said with a grin.

Then she looked up at Tom appealingly, but he just looked back at her and shook his head slightly. "I'll talk to you tomorrow," he said, then followed David along the corridor and down the stairs.

Either the chaise was lumpy or Sylvia was oversensitive, but she tossed and turned upon it for the remainder of the night, and by seven o'clock gave up trying to get any rest.

She slipped on her robe and went out into the

corridor, where she found Maude trying to open her bedroom door.

Explaining that she was the only servant in the house to know, which made the girl feel very important, she told her that a married couple were using her room and that she was to take care of their needs as well as Sylvia's own today. They would not be needing anything yet, but Sylvia needed a cup of tea, and asked the girl to get her one as quickly as possible.

"You may bring one for me, Maude, at the same time," Lady Lavinia called from inside her room, and Sylvia went back to commiserate with her aunt for her lack of sleep also.

"Now, young lady, would you like to tell me what part you played in last night's little adventure?" Lady Lavinia asked.

It did not take long for Sylvia to confess to her own scheme, and how she had taken advantage of her aunt's suggestion for an early night to get into a disguise and sneak out of the house in the dead of night.

"You are quite incredible, Sylvia," Lady Lavinia said, "but I really cannot blame Tom for being extremely angry with you. It was very wrong to use someone you love in that way, even though it was in order to help someone else you love."

"I really didn't think about it that way, Aunt Lavinia," she said. "It seemed to me that when I knew it was going to happen that night, I was meant to be there or else I wouldn't have known. And now I don't know what I can do to make amends to Tom."

"All I can tell you is to give him time. If he still loves you in spite of your deception, then he will come back to you, but if he finds that he no longer feels the same way about you, you will just have to accept it and let him go," the older lady said sadly.

She bent and kissed Sylvia's cheek. "Try to rest a little now, my dear, if you can. I would imagine that the gentlemen will be here for breakfast quite early, so I don't intend to try to go back to sleep, but I will rest a little also."

17

While Louise and Timothy spent a delightful day relaxing in Sylvia's bedchamber, the other occupants of number sixteen Grosvenor Street had a very busy day.

In anticipation of this, Lady Lavinia and Sylvia rose and dressed earlier than they really wished after such a sleepless night, and were just starting breakfast at eight o'clock when Colchester was announced.

"Come in, David, and close the door behind you. There's enough food on the sideboard for an army, so please help yourself," Lady Lavinia told him.

"Perhaps I will," David said, glancing at the ham, kippers, scrambled eggs, and toast, "for I am rather hungry. I have been so busy that I didn't really notice before now."

He helped himself to a large plate of food, then took a seat halfway between the two ladies.

"First and foremost, there's a possibility that Albertson drowned, but we're not certain yet. I met with Eggers and his accomplices not more than an hour ago, and he told me what happened after we left last night, or rather, early this morning," he said, then paused to take a little sustenance, while Lady Lavinia and Sylvia exchanged alarmed glances.

"The reason the owners of the gaming den cooperated with us was that they suspected something was going on, and though it frequently does in that type of place, I'm sure, they're probably used to getting a portion of the winnings," he told them, "but Albertson was unwilling to part with any of the proceeds.

"There were apparently some of the men there last night who had lost money to him, and when we spirited Louise away, they realized what he must have been doing. They attacked him in the place and chased him out and all the way down to the Thames. By the time Eggers and his men caught up with them, he was pretty badly beaten and the crowd then picked him up and heaved him into the river."

"He could still be alive, then," Sylvia said with obvious regret.

David grinned. "I had no idea you were so blood-thirsty, my dear, but I tend to feel the same way also. Anyway, I'm sure he will be in no condition to follow Timothy and Louise, so I'll take them with me to Colchester Castle this evening, and from there they will go on to Timothy's parents' home for a few days. How are they feeling now that they are safe?"

"Very romantic," Lady Lavinia said with a warm smile, "and being confined to a bedroom does not seem at all an imposition to them."

"I should think not, but that's good news. She really must love him if she would put up with so much abuse just to keep him alive, though at first I had not considered it a love match." He looked over at Sylvia. "Speaking of which, Tom went ahead with his plan to get a special license, but unfortunately he will not be here to see you today, for he had received a note from his mother, at their country estate, that she is not feeling well, so he has, of course, gone to see what he can do for her."

Sylvia knew that her face revealed her acute disappointment, for she could not conceal it. She had been looking forward to seeing him today and had hoped all would be well. Now she would have to wait and ponder the fact that if he had had time to tell David, he could instead have let her know himself.

After taking another helping of food, causing Sylvia to wonder how he could possibly eat so much food when her own appetite had completely disappeared, David finally left, and the next person to call was his mother, Lady Moorehead.

"I just wanted to say how glad I am that this problem is finally at an end," she said, "but as for you, young lady, I hope you've learned your lesson and will never interfere in such a dangerous enterprise again. Had Albertson been armed, you could have been killed, and David and James with you."

Or Tom, Sylvia thought, but knew she could hardly expect Lady Moorehead to be as concerned about Tom as she was about her son and her husband. It was wisest to say nothing, so she just gave her a weak smile that could have passed for an apology.

Lady Moorehead did not stay long, for she had a number of other calls to make, trying to be sure, as before, that no rumors of last night's events were circulating.

Then, in the afternoon, though no one was expected to tea, Lord Beaumont arrived, bending so low over Lady Lavinia's hand that Sylvia was sure she had been right. He was courting her aunt. "I understand that your papa has returned to Danville Hall now that you are affianced," he said to Sylvia, looking questioningly at her left hand, bare of any ring.

Aware of the deficiency, Sylvia looked angrily back at him; then her aunt attempted to fill the breach. "Dr. Radcliff had to visit his family early this morning, so there has been no time to formalize the arrangements," she told him.

"He is a lucky man," Lord Beaumont said, more gently than before. "Are you planning an early wedding?"

"Yes, my lord, we are. There is no reason to wait, for we both prefer to have a quiet one," she said.

"Most sensible of you, and you will live in the country?" he asked.

"Quite close to where my older sister lives, sir, near Colchester Castle," she said a little irritably, for she disliked being questioned.

"So your Aunt Lavinia will soon be all alone in London," he remarked softly, turning to Lady Lavinia with eyebrows raised.

"I am quite accustomed, by now, to being alone, Lord Beaumont. Though London is cold and damp in the winter, it makes me appreciate the warm glow of a log fire blazing in a hearth. And there is a strange peacefulness in seeing all the trees in the parks and the squares, bare of leaves, but beautiful in their form, particularly when they wear a mantle of snow," she told him softly.

"I have never before realized how much you love London, Aunt Lavinia," Sylvia said.

"I always have, and I enjoy it all the more for the many years when I was forced to remain all year round in the country, keeping house for my brother and his children," her aunt told her.

Sylvia turned to say something to Lord Beaumont, but remained silent when she saw the way he was looking at her aunt. He was like a man spellbound—or in love. A pain seemed to stab deep into her heart as she thought of Tom, and wished that he would look at her again in just that way.

"I seem to have forgotten my embroidery. Will you excuse me for a moment while I run upstairs and get it?" she asked first her aunt, and then turned to Lord Beaumont, who smiled and nodded.

It did not, of course, take her a full half-hour to find her needlework box and take out her embroidery and threads, but when she returned she was not at all surprised that neither of them seemed to notice she had been gone so long.

Tonight was, of course, the grand ball that she had been looking forward to, for Tom had promised to escort them, and she had secretly hoped that their betrothal would have been made official by that evening. She had saved one of her new gowns just for this occasion, but now she decided there was no use in wasting it and she might just as well wear her old blue one, bought for and worn several times last Season.

After Lord Beaumont left, saying he would see them at the ball, Lady Lavinia suggested they might both go upstairs and rest for a while. "If you don't, my dear, you'll be so tired that you'll not enjoy yourself as much," she said. "The bed in the guest room has now been aired, and a fire lit."

"I wish that I didn't have to attend the ball," Sylvia said, "but I'll not let you down, Aunt Lavinia, for I know that you're looking forward to it."

"Oh, my dear, you'll enjoy it when you get there and see all your friends," Lady Lavinia assured her. "It's the uncertainty that is worrying you, isn't it, for you did not have time to make up your differences."

Sylvia nodded. "I know it has been only a day, but if he should come back tomorrow or the next day and has not yet forgiven me, I'll not stay here any longer. I'll return home and let Papa do his worst."

Lady Lavinia's arms were around her niece, and she held her close for several minutes, saying soothingly, "You mustn't make such decisions now, my love, but wait and see how you both feel in a day or two. Tom's a good man and I know everything is going to work out all right for you both."

Sylvia raised her head and smiled sadly at her. "You are an optimist, but I'm glad you are my very best adopted aunt. I'll rest for a while in the guest room, where my clothes for tonight have already been hung, and will see you at eight o'clock."

She turned and left the room, her feet making little sound as she ran lightly up the stairs and along the corridor.

Three hours later, much rested and dressed in her old blue gown, Sylvia ran down the stairs to the drawing room, where her aunt was waiting.

"Have you said good-bye to your sister and her husband?" Lady Lavinia asked. "They will be leaving for Colchester Castle in about an hour."

Sylvia smiled. "Yes, I stopped in a few minutes ago and, for the first time, I feel that they will have a very happy marriage. This trouble seems to have brought them closer together." She grinned. "I hate to see them go, but it will be nice to have my own room back. I'd swear it took me twice as long to dress because everything I wanted was still in my own room, and Maude kept running backward and forward until she made me quite dizzy."

Lady Lavinia made no comment on the old blue gown that Sylvia was wearing, for she fully understood how the girl was feeling, and only wished she could help her in some way.

Lady Howard welcomed them as old friends when they arrived, and Sylvia went to join some of her acquaintances while Lady Lavinia stayed talking for a moment with some of her own contemporaries. Within a few minutes a half-dozen dances had been promised to young men she knew quite well. A waltz was about to start, and Sylvia turned away, slipping behind a large potted plant, for the last time she had waltzed had been with Tom, and she didn't want to dance it with anyone else.

Suddenly a familiar voice sounded close by. "This is my dance, I believe," Tom said, smiling warmly and raising a rakish eyebrow. He held out his arms and she went thankfully into them, and together they swirled around the room.

Sylvia was unaware that her eyes shone with tears of happiness until Tom said softly, "There wasn't time to send word that I was back in town, so I stopped by your aunt's house, but missed you by not more than two minutes. I hope no one else has told you yet how beautiful you look tonight, my love, or I may challenge him to a duel."

She shook her head, for once quite speechless, and listened while he explained that he had left very early that morning, deciding to do so on his way home from her aunt's house, which was why he had asked David to give her the message instead of bringing it himself.

"My mama's indisposition did not sound very serious and fortunately it was not. I wanted to be back for this ball if I possibly could," he told her, "for I knew you were looking forward to it. Your gown is quite exquisite. Is it a new one?"

Sylvia shook her head. "No, it's been worn several times, but I just hadn't the heart to wear my new one, for I thought you would not be here to see it."

"Did it matter so much, my love?" he asked, smiling so lovingly into her eyes that her heart began to beat faster than the music.

She nodded. "You were angry with me when you left early this morning, and I didn't think you would even try to get back in time."

"Foolishly angry, for when I thought it over, I realized that had it been my brother or sister, I would have wanted to help also," he said, caressing her palm with his thumb as he held her arm high.

"I put you in an embarrassing situation with David, for I wheedled the whereabouts of the gaming hell out of you, and found out some of your intentions," she said remorsefully.

"You did, but it was my own fault for telling you those things when I knew you wanted to be there yourself." He smiled that warm smile that always made her feel as though she was melting inside. "If you'll forgive me for being such a crosspatch last night, I'll forgive you for everything else that you did, and we can start off afresh with a clean slate." His mouth was close to her ear, and as she felt the warmth of his breath, she wanted to burst with excitement.

The music stopped, and she was surprised when, instead of taking her to her aunt, he took her back behind the potted plant where he had found her. Reaching into his pocket, he produced a small box, opened it, and showed her a lovely sapphire-and-diamond ring.

"It's a family heirloom. If it doesn't fit, a jeweler can alter it," he said, taking it out of the box and slipping it onto the third finger of the hand she held out.

"A perfect fit," she breathed, "and it's the most beautiful ring I've ever seen."

"It matches your eyes, but tonight they outshine it, my love. Do you think your aunt would get upset again if I were to find a small anteroom where I could kiss you?" he asked.

Sylvia shook her head. "No, for she'd be glad to see us together again."

Hand in hand they stole down a corridor until they found just the right room; then, keeping his back to the door in case anyone should try to come in, he looked down at the happy face she raised to his, and let his lips barely touch hers.

Gradually the kiss deepened, until she thought she would melt right into him. Her body was on fire, her breasts ached for him, and she was completely unaware at first that she was kissing him back with a passion she'd never known she possessed.

Finally he pulled away. "We must go back into the ballroom, or someone will come looking for us, and I don't want you to look too disheveled, though you're allowed to look dreamy on the night you become betrothed, I'm sure."

Her legs didn't want to move at first, but he slipped her hand beneath his arm and they gradually gained some momentum until they reached the ballroom; then she stopped again of her own accord, for her aunt was at the entrance, looking worried.

"You had me concerned, Sylvia, but I'm glad to see it was Tom you were with," she said, keeping her voice low so that no one around could hear. "You'll have to stop doing this kind of thing, or you'll get a bad reputation."

"Not for long," Tom said, "for we'll be leaving town in a few days to get married."

Sylvia held out her hand and Lady Lavinia gasped when she saw the ring. "What a gorgeous sapphire, and how it becomes you, my dear," she said. "You must let Lady Howard make the announcement, for it has not yet appeared in the *Times*."

Tom was watching Sylvia's face, which seemed to glow with happiness, and when she turned and asked him, "Do you want to announce it tonight?" he readily agreed, for this was the perfect occasion to do so.

From now onward it would mean that he would be able to dance as many dances with her as he wished, though this might quite easily be the last ball they would attend in a while, for after their marriage in a few days' time, he did not expect that they would be returning to London for several months.

It was the dance before supper, and Lady Howard was in her element, for when the twins had taken London by storm last Season, many bets had been placed as to which twin would marry first, and whom they might take as husbands. When her father had come to town recently with pockets to let as usual, the betting odds had been five to one that he would find Sylvia a wealthy old man to wed. There would be some disappointed losers when she announced this turn of events.

Before the orchestra started to play, someone tapped on one of her priceless cut-crystal glasses and she shuddered in fear that it might break. It did its job, however, and the ballroom fell silent as Lady Howard told them she had an announcement to make.

"I am delighted to tell you that Miss Sylvia Danville, youngest daughter of Sir Edward and Lady Danville, has accepted a proposal of marriage from Lord Thomas Radcliff, better known as Dr. Radcliff, younger son of the Marquess and Marchioness of Bradington. I understand the wedding will take place quite soon at the home of the bride's sister and her husband, the Earl and Countess of Colchester."

Tom led Sylvia forward, and after the applause died down the orchestra struck up a waltz. The expressions on their faces as he took her into his arms to begin the dance caused a tear to form in the eye of many a dowager, but no jealous glances from any of the young ladies present, for Sylvia had always been popular with her contemporaries.

"After that, I'd best take you to meet my family tomorrow," Tom whispered in her ear, "or Mama will be upset that an announcement was made before she met you."

"I never thought of that," Sylvia said, "when Lady Howard was so eager to make it known to her guests. But your mama and papa do know about me, don't they?"

"Of course, my love, and before even meeting you they gave their wholehearted approval, for I think they were worried I might not wed. With my brothers still childless, the succession is at stake, and this was of grave concern to them, but not to me, as you know." Tom smiled down at her lovingly. "We will have children because we want them, not for any succession, won't we, darling?"

Sylvia smiled and nodded but said nothing, for it was a subject dear to her heart that she wished to discuss with him in private—probably on their way to see his parents—not in the center of an empty ballroom with a crowd of people looking on.

After their second time around, the floor filled with smiling dancers who stopped to wish them happy and admire her beautiful ring.

They returned to the ballroom after supper, and Tom had to reluctantly step aside, for Sylvia had promised to dance with a half-dozen young men she knew, who had signed her card when she first arrived. To pass the time, he strolled into the card room, where games of whist and piquet were being enjoyed, and he came out only when the music stopped, so that he could at least talk to Sylvia between dances.

But search as he might, he could not see any sign of his betrothed. She could have gone to the ladies' retiring room, but would not have done so without telling Lady Lavinia, so he went over to where she sat talking to friends, and stood a little away from her until he caught her eye.

She rose immediately, a small questioning frown on her face.

"Sylvia had promised the next few dances to friends, but I haven't seen her here since the music stopped. Did she by any chance go to repair her gown or something?" he asked.

"She would have told me if she was going to do so, for she would have needed help," she said, quite puzzled, for the only person she'd ever disappeared with was Tom. "Did you look over there behind those plants?"

"Yes," he said abruptly. "I'm going to take a look in the gardens and see if I can see anything of her."

But a half-hour later there was still no sign of Sylvia, and after checking every single room adjacent to the ballroom, and receiving a number of angry glares from their occupants, Tom took his hostess aside.

"Do you think I might see your guest list, my lady?" he asked. "I was wondering if a certain gentleman of my acquaintance is here, and in this crush it's difficult to be sure."

"Of course you may see it, Tom. I know you must be restless, watching your betrothed dancing with other men, but you'll get used to it eventually." She went over to a small ornate gold desk, reached into a drawer, and withdrew a long list of people.

"Thank you, Lady Howard. I must congratulate you on your efficiency," he told her, quickly glancing down the list until he came to one that was only too familiar. Suppressing a groan, he asked, "Do you know if Sir Roger Albertson arrived?"

"Oh, yes, I do recall, for he came in late, when you and Sylvia were dancing alone, and I told him that you were celebrating your betrothal. He did not look at all well, and he did not stay long, for I was near the door when he left after supper, and he apologized for having to leave so soon—'It is a shame to grab a delicious morsel and run,' was the strange way he put it," Lady Howard said with a slight shrug.

For a moment Tom saw nothing but a red blur before his eyes, and he knew now what was meant by a blind rage. If he had had Albertson here at this moment, he knew that he would have killed him with his bare hands.

"Is everything all right, Tom?" Lady Howard asked, and immediately he was back to normal, the mask of the civilized human being back in place.

He managed a smile. "Perfectly all right, my lady," he said. "My mind was wandering for a minute, that's all."

"We all do that sometimes, don't we?" she said with a bright smile. "You've much to think about, with a wedding coming up so soon. Again, let me wish you both every happiness in the world."

"Thank you, my lady, you're very kind," he murmured automatically, and turned away.

18

Tom did not recall what he had said to Lady Howard, but knew it must have been something appropriate, for she had continued to smile like the excellent hostess she was. After he left her, he walked blindly past the dancers, nodding automatically to well-wishers, but pausing to speak to no one until he reached the card room, where Sir James Moorehead and Lady Moorehead were engaged in a game of whist.

Glancing up and seeing Tom's grim face, Sir James hurriedly excused himself and went to see what was wrong. It took but a moment to explain; then Sir James said, "I'm sorrier than I can say, Tom, for he undoubtedly knew that Lady Howard is well-known for her excellent memory and wanted to make you sweat until his blackmail note arrives."

"Is that what you think it is?" Tom asked.

"Has to be—and revenge also, of course," Sir James said. "The man dared not show his face in here for long, so he probably waited behind those plants until she finished a dance."

"And she may have come looking for me and walked unwittingly into his arms, for we had been talking in that very spot a short while before." Tom groaned, then thought of something else.

"Lady Howard said he was alone when she saw him leave," he pointed out. "I hate to even think of it, but he must have either left her with an accomplice or left her unconscious in the garden—just so that he could deliver that message."

"We'll have to tell the ladies and leave at once, for we cannot stay here any longer without Sylvia, or it will be obvious something has happened." Sir James beckoned to Lady Mildred, who rose and came over right away, while Tom went to talk to Lady Lavinia again.

"Something dreadful has happened," Sir James told his wife. "The blackguard we hoped had drowned in the Thames surfaced here tonight and we believe he kidnapped Sylvia."

Lady Moorehead's face went as white as death. "Oh, no," she said, "that poor girl. We must leave at once before anyone realizes that something is amiss."

They met in the hall. Tom had found Lady Lavinia, and with her Lord Beaumont, who also wanted to be of service. The ladies said their good-byes to their hostess, who thought nothing of their early departure, for it was common for guests to go to more than one party in an evening. While they were doing so, the men had their carriages brought around. It was agreed that they would all go to Grosvenor Street right away.

"We'll need Eggers and his men to help us, for the more men we have, the easier it will be to watch and follow when the ransom note is delivered," Tom said grimly, "but we'll let him think that I'm the only one he has to deal with."

"I know where to put my hands on Eggers, and I'll send someone tonight to get him," Sir James said. "The question is, where can Albertson have taken her?"

"Somewhere close, I would think," Lord Beaumont said, "for he'll want to get his money as quickly as possible and get out of the country while he can. Have you notified her parents?"

"No," Tom said, "and I don't intend to, for her father wouldn't even try to help, and the fewer who know what has happened, the better chance we have of getting her back a—" He did not complete his sentence, for he could not bring himself to say the word "alive."

Once they reached the house on Grosvenor Street, and the carriages were driven around into the mews, the five people gathered in the drawing room, for there would be no sleep this night.

"If you have pen and paper, Lady Lavinia, Sir James will send for Eggers right away. He is in touch with many of the underworld of this city and may be able to find out where Albertson has been these last few days," Tom told them.

"There is no doubt that he wants money," he continued, "so someone, probably Lady Lavinia or me, will receive a ransom note in the very near future, I would say. Eggers' men will be able to watch this house and also my rooms, and follow anyone suspicious-looking who comes to either place."

"I am being most selfish," Lady Moorehead said, "but I wish my son was here, and yet I don't want him to leave Elizabeth when she is so close to her time."

Sir James shook his head. "This time we'll have to manage without him, my dear, for he will still be on his way north, and by the time a messenger got to him and he came back, it would probably be too late for him to be of help." He looked at Tom as he rose from the desk. "This is ready, Tom. I'll go through to the stables and have one of my men take it right away. With a bit of luck, Eggers may be there and come right back with him."

Bates knocked and entered unobtrusively, placing a pot of coffee, cups, and saucers on the sideboard.

Lady Lavinia looked at Tom's anxious face and realized that should anything happen to Sylvia, he would never be the same again. And the fact that he would probably hunt Albertson down would be of little good. She went over to the coffee tray and poured, taking a cup to each person, for she had told Bates they would serve themselves.

"How could such a man be on the guest list of someone like Lady Howard?" Tom asked impatiently.

"He is a member of society, though admittedly on the fringes, and with single men in short supply, it is usual to ask even such as he to a ball of that proportion. He probably accepted weeks ago, as we did," Lady Moorehead said soothingly.

Almost half an hour had gone by since they reached the house. They all talked, but more for talking's sake than anything else, for they were just saying meaningless things, Tom realized, while they waited either for Eggers to get here or for that villain to send his ransom note.

The twins had been able to communicate without words at times, and now he wished he had that facility and could let his love know that they would move heaven and earth to find her and bring her back here safely.

He turned his head away from the others, to blink back the tears that had suddenly filled his eyes at the thought of her lying, probably bound and gagged, in some cellar, as Timothy had been. But Timothy hadn't been in a cellar, he recalled, and wondered why he thought Sylvia might be.

They all jumped when the doorbell sounded, then fixed their eyes on the closed drawing-room door as Bates knocked and came in.

"There's a Mr. Eggers to see you, my lady," he said.

"Ask him to come in at once, Bates, and bring some more coffee, please," Lady Lavinia said, her voice shaking a little.

It did not take long for the story to be told, and for the little batman to hang his head in shame. "I knew I should've made sure of 'im, sir. An extra bang on 'is 'ead before they shoved 'im in t' river would've done it. Now 'e's back making more mischief."

He refused the coffee, saying his men were outside awaiting his orders, and he would assign two of them to each place—this house, Tom's rooms, and the Mooreheads' residence. He left behind a happier group of people, for now they could do something instead of just sit around and talk about it.

But it was a little after nine in the morning before anything happened, and by then the Mooreheads and Lord Beaumont had returned to their respective homes, and Tom had gone reluctantly to his rooms in case he was the one Albertson would approach.

The note was sent, however, to the Mooreheads', and addressed to the Earl of Colchester, to be forwarded.

"Lord Beaumont was mistaken. Albertson must feel himself very safe, and that he has lots of time, if he intended to wait for this to go to Colchester Castle," Sir James said, carefully examining the envelope that had just been delivered.

"In the normal way, it would have been sent to David without a second thought, for we often get notes for him here. Open it and see what it says, James." Lady Moorehead was near the exhaustion point.

Bring ten thousand pounds to Hyde Park Corner at eight o'clock on Monday. Wrap it in Monday's *Times* and leave it under the first bench on the right. If it's not there, she goes in the Thames.

There was a knock on the door, and one of Eggers' men came in. "My partner's followed the bloke as brought that note, sir. If it's the one we were expecting, I'm supposed to take it to Eggers."

"By all means," Sir James said, "as soon as I make a copy."

He wrote down the exact words on a piece of paper and gave the original to the man, then watched him leave the house and set off at a trot for Eggers' lodgings.

"We may be in luck, for I don't think Albertson thought we would even look at it. He would expect us to assume it was a bill and send it on," Sir James said to his wife, "so he won't be expecting a visit from us."

Sylvia regained consciousness to find herself in total darkness, but she had not been tied up, so Albertson must not have thought it necessary. She shivered, for she was wearing only her ball gown and she was lying on cold stone slabs. She must be in a cellar, she decided.

It was difficult to think with her head pounding so, but she did recall going behind a group of tall potted plants at one end of the ballroom to look for Tom.

She had started to scream when Albertson grabbed her, and he had thrust a piece of fabric into her mouth to stop her, almost causing her to choke. She remembered hearing the sound of her gown ripping as he dragged her out and through the garden, but nothing after that, so he must have knocked her out with something heavy, by the feel of her aching head. But at least she was no longer gagged.

There was a smell of wine, and of cheese also, so the cellar was probably still in use. She only hoped that she was not sharing it with rats or mice, but so far she had not heard a sound. Cautiously she reached out a hand and came into contact with a stone step, then felt higher and touched another one.

It must be night still, she decided, for even a cellar was not entirely dark during the day. There were gratings and windows in her aunt's cellar, and also in the one at home, as she recalled. Then she touched her left hand and realized that her betrothal ring was missing. Albertson must have taken it, she decided, and she could not hold back her tears, for she had felt so proud when Tom placed it on her finger.

She must have slept for a while, for the next time she opened her eyes there was a faint light coming from some gratings, making it possible for her to see the outlines of wine racks and some wooden kegs. She inched herself into a position where she could not immediately be seen by anyone coming down the steps, and then waited, quite confident that Tom would find her somehow.

But when she heard a key turn in a lock somewhere above her, some of that confidence faded. Footsteps were coming slowly down the steps, but who was it, for surely Albertson would use a lantern down here? There was the sound of a flint being struck and a candle suddenly glowed in the darkness, and she breathed a sigh of relief.

"Eggers," she called softly, "I'm over here, beside the steps."

He swung around and came toward her. "Are you hurt, miss?" he asked in a whisper.

"No, I don't think so. Is there a way out of here?" She hated it that her voice sounded so weak, for she was trying hard to be brave.

"Not for him, there isn't."

She recognized the gravelly voice before the words made sense to her, and they were followed only a second later by gunfire and then a dull thud as Eggers fell to the ground and the candle went out.

Albertson started down the steps, but it was too dark and he turned back to get a lantern, which proved his undoing, for Tom had caught up with him. A blow from the pistol Tom carried sent him flying down the steps, to land in a heap on the hard stone floor.

"Are you down there, Sylvia?" Tom called, and she managed a faint "Yes."

Then, fearing that he might try to come down those stone steps in the darkness, she called more loudly, "You'll need a light, Tom, for I believe Eggers has been shot and Albertson is lying at the bottom of the steps."

It had been bad enough for Sylvia already, but the darkness had concealed much of the horror. When Tom came down into the cellar carrying a lantern, however, it was like a terrible nightmare, for its light first revealed Albertson, who had broken his neck in the fall, and then Eggers, David's faithful batman, who had taken a bullet in the head and was quite dead.

Though Sylvia insisted she could walk, Tom half-carried her up the treacherous steps and into the house, where Sir James and Lord Beaumont waited, and it was a good thing that they were not far from Grosvenor Street, for Sylvia was temporarily in a state of shock.

This time she made no protest when Tom carried her into the Grosvenor Street house and took her straight up the stairs to her bedchamber. He allowed only Lady Lavinia near while he gently undressed her and examined her for bruises and lacerations, of which there were quite a few, for she had not received gentle handling while unconscious in Albertson's charge.

He prescribed and administered a sedative, and refused to leave her side until she fell into a deep sleep. Only then did he go downstairs to the others. Lady Lavinia would let no one watch by the bedside but herself.

Sir James handed him a glass of brandy, and he drank it down in one swallow, then turned to face an anxious Lady Moorehead.

"Is she going to be all right, Tom?" she asked.

"I believe so," he said quietly. "There are no broken bones, but she is quite bruised, and will feel those tomorrow, I'm sure. I am concerned about her mental state, and would have prevented her seeing what she did, had I known what was down there."

"She'll get over that, Tom," Lady Moorehead said firmly. "I don't know where they got it from, but the Danville daughters are much stronger-minded than either of their parents. But the sooner you get her to Colchester Castle, the better she will be. Must you take her to meet your family before the wedding?"

He shook his head. "My parents can meet her at the wedding if they wish," he said, "and I am sure they will understand. I'd like to get her out of London as soon as she's fit to travel."

Tom spent the night there, and the next morning he got a welcome surprise, for Sylvia was a little shaky but otherwise almost back to normal, and anxious to leave London as soon as possible.

"I have a feeling that Elizabeth's baby is coming early, Tom," she told him, "and I think we ought to get there as soon as we can."

"Another of your 'feelings,' my love?" he asked, smiling tenderly.

"I know you find them hard to believe, darling, but you must admit that they have been of help these last few months," she argued.

He threw up his hands. "I'm a believer. Why do you think I knew to go to the cellar when the others started to look upstairs for you?" he asked, grinning. Then he became serious. "If you need more time to get over this before entering into marriage, I'll give you as much as it takes. You only have to say the word."

Sylvia looked unhappy. "Are you changing your mind, Tom?" she asked. "I'll not hold you to it if you have any doubts."

"You silly wigeon," he said. "I have no doubts whatever. I've never felt this way before, as though I want to make life perfect for you, take away all your hurts both big and small and bear them myself. I know it won't always be possible, but I intend to try, and to keep on trying for the rest of my life."

He took her left hand in his, then, reaching into his pocket, took out the sapphire-and-diamond betrothal ring and slipped it back onto her finger.

"Lord Beaumont had a hunch and found it in a pawnbroker's shop not far from Albertson's lodgings," Tom told her. "He'd borrowed a considerable sum on it, but most of that was still on his person."

They left for Colchester Castle the next day, with only a few of Sylvia's clothes, for Lady Lavinia was going to pack the rest and bring them with her in a couple of days when she and the Mooreheads came for the wedding.

The only time they were alone, however, was when they had dinner in the inn that night, for Maude rode in the carriage with her mistress, and Tom rode most of the way on horseback.

"We should have stopped earlier, my love," Tom said, seeing the dark rings under Sylvia's eyes, "but you can sleep longer in the morning, for we won't have far to go. We'll be there long before dark."

"We'll be there before luncheon if we start out at dawn," Sylvia said. "I'll go to bed just as soon as I've finished dinner, and then you can ask the innkeeper to send a light breakfast to my room at six o'clock, for I want to get as early a start as possible."

Tom looked disappointed. "I had hoped to have a leisurely dinner this evening, for we've had no time together since we left London," he told her. "There's really no need for such haste."

"We'll have all the years ahead to be together,"

Sylvia said earnestly, "but right now I feel that Elizabeth needs you more than I do."

She looked so determined that he decided it best to humor her. Elizabeth was extremely healthy, and her child was not expected for two months yet, but Sylvia's happiness was of the utmost importance right now, and if it was what she wanted, then they would start out tomorrow the minute the sun came up.

They reached Colchester Castle a little before one o'clock, for Sylvia had refused to stop for luncheon, saying she would rather eat late at the castle than early in some unknown inn.

As the carriage pulled up in front of the castle, the great door was flung open and the usually dignified Shackleton came hurrying down the steps and over to where Tom was dismounting.

"Thank the good Lord that you got the message, Doctor," he said, his usually impassive face showing extreme agitation. "Her ladyship's in the master suite and needing you something badly."

Tom turned to help Sylvia out of the carriage, but she had heard Shackleton and had scrambled down in a most unladylike fashion.

"I know it's your sister, Sylvia, but I want your promise that you'll wait downstairs until I call you," he said sternly as they reached the front door.

He was holding her firmly by the arm, so the only thing Sylvia could do was to give him the promise he asked for and let him go to her sister.

She smiled weakly at Shackleton, who led her into the dining room, while Tom took the stairs two at a time.

"You'll be needing some luncheon, I'm sure, Miss Danville," he said, his dignity restored now that help had arrived. "I'll ask Cook to send something to you at once, for Mrs. Fowler is busy with her ladyship."

"Is it the baby?" Sylvia asked impatiently. "Did she fall or something?"

"I really couldn't say, but I'm sure everything will be all right now that Dr. Radcliff's here," he said confidently.

An hour later, having eaten only a little of the excellent luncheon set before her, Sylvia wanted to kick herself for having given Tom that promise. Then the door opened and David came in looking decidedly unkempt, but with a happy glow about him.

"For goodness' sake, tell me, David," Sylvia begged. "What is it this time, and how is my sister?"

"It is a pair of boys, my dear, tiny but complete to the last toe, and my darling Elizabeth is exhausted but very happy," David told her, sinking into a chair and stretching his legs out.

"I asked Tom what had delayed you, but he has not had time yet to tell me. You do look a little peaked, come to think of it. Were you not well?" he asked curiously.

She said the first thing that came into her head. "Eggers is dead, David. Albertson shot him in the head." Then Colchester took her in his arms, and she buried her head against his shoulder and wept, letting out all the tension that had been needing to come out since the frightening episode took place.

At that moment Tom walked in, having done all that was necessary for Elizabeth. He looked at Sylvia, still sobbing in David's arms, and said, "That's good. I thought she was recovering from the shock a little too quickly. She'll be much better after this. What did she tell you?" he asked his friend, drawing his betrothed into his own arms and cradling her gently.

"That Albertson killed Eggers," David said, his soft tone belying his feelings. "Does the blackguard still live?"

Tom shook his head. "This time there's no question about it," he said grimly, then added, "I'll tell you everything later, but for now I'd like to get this young lady to her bedchamber. Do you know if a room has been prepared?"

"I'm sorry, Tom. My curiosity can wait, but Sylvia cannot. She needs rest, and her old room is all ready for her." Colchester rose a little unsteadily. "I'll show you the way and then join you in the dining room for luncheon, for I've not eaten or slept in more than twenty-four hours."

Once in her bedchamber, Sylvia insisted that Tom go back with David and that they both get something to eat at once. "Maude is here to look after me, and I promise I'll rest for a while," she told him.

Taking her at her word, he went back with David and they had a glass of sherry before sitting down to a large luncheon. As if by agreement, they ate in silence at first, until the edge of their appetite was gone; then Tom told David of everything that had happened since he left the city.

"He grabbed her out of a ball?" David said in astonishment. "He must have been desperate to do that."

"Not really. He'd planned it well and was quite confident he could pull it off, or he would never have left that message with Lady Howard," Tom said. "Sylvia was probably lying unconscious in some dark spot in the garden, near the back gate, and all he had to do was drive around, pick her up, and throw her into his carriage."

"And Eggers was killed instantly, you think?" David asked sadly.

"There's no question about it," Tom told him. "He was holding a lighted candle, so it was easy for Albertson to take aim and put the bullet where he wanted to. I didn't know it until I heard the shot, but I was not far behind him, with a loaded gun also, and when he started to come back up the steps, I instinctively hit him with it rather than firing. And you know the rest."

"Where were Sir James and Beaumont all this time?" David asked.

Tom grinned. "You won't believe this," he said, "but when we entered the house, we thought it was empty except for Eggers and possibly Sylvia. Because we had found Timothy in an upstairs room, the other two wanted to look there first, but some instinct told me that she was down in the cellar. And, of course, that's where she was."

"Don't you start with the hunches as well," David warned. "We've quite enough with Sylvia's. When I saw you come into our bedchamber, I thought you'd finally gotten my message, but I realize now that you couldn't possibly have done so, for you had already started out when I sent it. That was Sylvia also, I believe."

Tom nodded. "She insisted that Elizabeth needed me, and so we left the inn at dawn and she refused point-blank to stop for luncheon. She was right, of course, for Elizabeth could not have gone on like that much longer."

"I know. I'm a very lucky man, and I'm going up now to see how my wife's doing. I promise not to waken her if she's asleep." He gave Tom a friendly pat on the shoulder as he walked past him, and, tired as he was, there was a spring in his step as he left to visit his wife and the newborns.

19

David, Sylvia, and Tom sat down to dinner, their minds filled with feelings of joy and a little sorrow also.

"I looked in on Elizabeth, Tom, but found her fast asleep," Sylvia said, "and then I went into the nursery to see the babies. They are the most beautiful infants I have ever seen, but so very tiny."

"I'm glad they were no bigger, or it would have been even more difficult for Elizabeth," he said quietly, but there was a look of satisfaction on his face. "I'll never again argue against your hunches."

"Elizabeth was in labor last night," David said, then asked curiously, "Did you know she was, Sylvia?"

She shook her head. "I didn't know anything except that we must get here as quickly as possible. We left the inn at dawn, you know, and came right through without stopping."

"Thank goodness you did, is all I can say, for the first baby was the wrong way round and completely stuck, and Elizabeth was getting weaker and weaker," David told her, completely disregarding the fact that such a subject was not usually discussed with single females.

Sylvia was, however, most interested. "What did you do?" she asked Tom.

"It is difficult to explain to someone unfamiliar with childbirth," Tom said, with not a moment's hesitation, for he knew she really wanted to know. "Elizabeth was getting weak, but I was able to give her something to ease the pain so that I could manipulate the baby without hurting her too much. It's fortunate that it was not her first birthing, or it would have been much worse. As soon as I got the first one out, somewhat to my surprise, out came the second one, though I knew there was a possibility of twins, of course."

"After we're married, you'll have to teach me about these things so that I can assist you when necessary," Sylvia told him. "I don't intend to be a helpless ninnyhammer where such matters are concerned."

Tom looked across at David and shrugged helplessly.

"Didn't anyone teach you that ladies of the *ton* do not learn any of these things?" David asked. "You're supposed to be all fluttering eyelashes and helplessness. That's what comes of taking her out to visit your patients, Tom, my boy."

When the gentlemen were served their brandy and cigars, Sylvia excused herself and went upstairs to see if her sister was awake yet.

She found Elizabeth sitting up and contentedly nursing one of the baby boys. "Come in, Sylvia," she called. "I understand I have you to thank for getting Tom here so quickly."

"I was anxious to get here, that's all," Sylvia muttered, for she did not want everyone to think she was some kind of a freak. "Should you be sitting up so soon?"

"Of course I should, my love, but I'm afraid you're going to have to be hostess here for the next few days. I understand that you've decided on a small wedding, but I'm sure we'll still have quite a few guests arriving."

"Only Sir James and Lady Moorehead and Aunt Lavinia, as far as I know. I've not asked anyone else," Sylvia told her, "and they should be here in a couple of days. Aunt Lavinia is bringing the rest of my clothes, for we were in a hurry to get here."

"You were?" Elizabeth said. "Once Louise and Timothy left, I would have thought that you could take your time, but I did hear that you did something very sneaky in rescuing Louise."

"Some other things happened after they left with David, but he'll tell you all about it if you ask him," she murmured, then remembered. "Tom did say that his mama and papa might come, for they've not yet met me. I don't suppose that our mama and papa will do so, though, for Papa left in a bit of a hurry after David talked with him."

"Yes, he told me so," Elizabeth said with a laugh. "But don't be too sure. Papa may decide he wants to meet his new son-in-law's parents."

Sylvia grimaced, then said brightly, "What I'm waiting for is to hold that little one when he's filled his tummy enough."

Just then a maid came in with the other little one, and Sylvia got her wish. She smiled down at the little bundle in her arms, enjoying the baby smell of him, and when he started to cry, the maid quickly showed her how to hold him to help get the wind up.

"I think I would like a round half-dozen, just like this one," she told her sister.

"You'll probably have them, then," Elizabeth said, amused at the way Sylvia had immediately taken to the child. "But I think we've talked enough for now. I'm getting a little tired, love, so I'll see you in the morning. If any guests should arrive early, there's plenty of room. Twenty guest rooms are always kept aired, and another thirty can be readied at half a day's notice. Mrs. Fowler will come to you for approval, but she's very capable of doing everything herself."

After giving the infant back to the maid, Sylvia kissed her sister's cheek and then left her to rest. She decided not to have tea downstairs, for the two men did not need her company, for this evening at least, so she went to the chamber that had been prepared for her, and told Maude that she would have her tea there.

The castle was immense, but it was somehow very comforting to be back here among the people she loved, and who loved her. She had deliberately put out of her mind the hours she had spent in that dark cellar, and the horror of the last few minutes there until Tom had brought her out of it. Now it seemed unreal, like a nightmare that went away when daylight came.

What was real was that in a few days she and Tom would be married, and would spend the rest of their lives together. And despite his surprise when she had said she wanted to know how to help him in his work, she knew that he would teach her and allow her to become a helpmate as well as a wife.

It had been a long day, and on this thought she fell asleep, not waking until Maude came in with her hot chocolate.

When she went down to breakfast, to her delight, Tom was there alone, waiting for her.

"I thought you might like to come with me, for I'm going to talk to the vicar this morning, my love," he said, "and tell him we're having a small wedding, just family, in four days' time. That should give your Aunt Lavinia and the Mooreheads time to get here, and your parents also if they wish to come. My mother and father should arrive sometime tomorrow, I believe, and that will probably be all the guests we'll have."

"That sounds plenty to me," Sylvia said, lifting her cheek for his kiss as he seated her, "though I do wish Louise could be there. Perhaps some of your patients will come, and the church will not seem so empty."

Snow had been falling softly all night, and in the morning there was a thick white carpet underfoot, deadening the sound of horses' hooves as the carriages drew up to the old church. Unseen hands had swept the snow away and laid down the long red carpet so that the bride and her family need not get their feet wet.

Inside, the church had been beautifully decorated with the last chrysanthemums of the season, gathered by loving hands before the snows could take away their splendor, for the villagers wanted their church to look its finest.

It would be a small wedding compared to the last one, and there would be only a handful of the elegantly dressed ladies and gentlemen of the *ton*. But the villagers had all turned out in their Sunday best, coming in by the side door so as not to put a single mark on that lovely red carpet. They had left the three front rows empty for the family, and were now seated in the back, filling it to capacity, waiting to see their doctor wed the younger sister of the Countess of Colchester, the pretty young girl so many of them called "the doctor's lady."

Sylvia walked down the aisle on David's arm, for her parents had not arrived, and the heavy snows to the north had probably delayed Louise. But she could not believe it when she saw how many people had come to see the wedding. Lady Lavinia was there, soon to be married herself to the gentleman at her side, Lord Beaumont; and Tom's mama and papa were sitting in the front, a charming couple who seemed to have taken to her immediately; then there were Sir James and Lady Moorehead, of course.

She thought at first that it was Elizabeth standing near the altar in a pale blue gown, but it couldn't be, for she'd left her sister in bed, nursing her babies. Then she saw that it was her twin, Louise, smiling at her and holding out her hand for her bouquet, and she had to sniff to hold back the tears of happiness.

Tom's eyes were warm and loving as he turned to look at her before coming to stand on her right so that the ceremony could commence.

"Dearly beloved, we are assembled here in the presence of God, to join this man and this woman in holy marriage . . ." the vicar intoned, and Sylvia's thoughts went back to that cold stone cellar floor, to Eggers lighting his candle, and to Tom coming to her rescue.

David had taken her right hand, and the vicar had given it to Tom now, who squeezed it gently as he made his promises, and then the gold band was on her finger.

"Whom therefore God hath joined together, let no man put asunder," the vicar proclaimed, and then she was hugging Louise and the family was milling around them in the vestry.

It was all like a dream until she found herself in

Tom's arms, and then it was a dream no more. She would remember the horror again from time to time, but Tom would always be there, holding her as he was now, kissing her, and driving away life's sorrows.